Ian Watson was bor~~~
English at Balliol Co~~~
fiction stories were s~~~
lecturer in Japan. In~~~
short story, was publ~~~
since then his stories have appeared in various magazines
and anthologies. They have also been published in book
form in two previous collections, *The Very Slow Time
Machine* and *Sunstroke*.

Ian Watson's first novel, *The Embedding*, was published in 1973 and received enormous critical acclaim.
His second novel, *The Jonah Kit*, became a British
Science Fiction Award winner as well as confirming his
position in the front rank of contemporary writers. He
has been features editor of the journal *Foundation* since
1975 and a full-time writer since 1976. His most recent
novels are *Chekhov's Journey* (1983), *Converts* (1984),
The Book of the River (1984) and *Queenmagic, Kingmagic*
(1986).

By the same author

The Embedding
The Jonah Kit
The Martian Inca
Alien Embassy
Miracle Visitors
The Very Slow Time Machine
God's World
Under Heaven's Bridge (with Michael Bishop)
Deathhunter
Sunstroke
Chekhov's Journey
Converts
The Book of the River
The Book of the Stars
The Book of Being
Queenmagic, Kingmagic

IAN WATSON

Slow Birds

and other stories

GRAFTON BOOKS

A Division of the Collins Publishing Group

LONDON GLASGOW
TORONTO SYDNEY AUCKLAND

Grafton Books
A Division of the Collins Publishing Group
8 Grafton Street, London W1X 3LA

Published by Grafton Books 1987

First published in Great Britain by
Victor Gollancz Ltd 1985

ISBN 0-586-07143-1

ACKNOWLEDGEMENTS
'Slow Birds' first appeared in *The Magazine of Fantasy & Science
Fiction*, 1983. 'The Width of the World' first appeared in *Universe
13* edited by Terry Carr, 1983. 'White Socks' first appeared in *The
Magazine of Fantasy & Science Fiction*, 1985. 'Ghost Lecurer' first
appeared in *Isaac Asimov's Science Fiction Magazine*, 1984.
'Mistress of Cold' first appeared in *Ambit*, 1984. 'In the Mirror of
the Earth' first appeared in *Lands of Never* edited by Maxim
Jakubowski, 1983. 'Cruising' first appeared in *Isaac Asimov's
Science Fiction Magazine*, 1983. 'Universe on the Turn' first
appeared in *Last Wave*, 1984. 'The Flesh of her Hair' first appeared
in *The Magazine of Fantasy & Science Fiction*, 1984. 'The Mystic
Marriage of Salome' first appeared in *Pictures at an Exhibition*
edited by Ian Watson, 1981. 'The Bloomsday Revolution' first
appeared in *Light Years and Dark* edited by Michael Bishop, 1984.

Printed and bound in Great Britain by
Collins, Glasgow

Set in Times

Contents

Introduction: In the Hothouse   7
Slow Birds   9
The Width of the World   44
White Socks   61
Ghost Lecturer   92
Mistress of Cold   112
In the Mirror of the Earth   125
Cruising   142
Universe on the Turn   150
The Flesh of her Hair   168
The Mystic Marriage of Salome   188
The Bloomsday Revolution   203

Introduction: *In the Hothouse*

The stories gathered in this collection all first saw the light of day in magazines or anthologies; and it occurs to me that there's as much pleasure in seeing a short story – the work of a week – in print, as in receiving newly minted copies of a full-length novel which may have been the labour of a year.

Novels are monsters which escape from the author to make their own independent way in the world. (How many novelists can actually read right through their own books? As a fresh and, hmm, *novel* experience?) Or, to put it another way, novels are full-grown trees – even forests – transplanted suddenly into the wild. But with short stories the situation is different, for me at least. Short stories stay at home in the mental garden; or rather, in the hothouse. For me these are the orchids, the bonsai of a writer's creativity. (Or perhaps the sundews, pitcher plants, and Venus fly traps – seductive nightmares to the creatures trapped in them?)

Short stories still need to be looked after. Periodically they need to be collected, re-exhibited; whereupon they still do not become, collectively, a Monster – monstrous though some of their individual shapes may be.

If a novelist designs whole landscapes, too large for him or her to tread from north to south, the door to the short story planthouse remains wide open still.

Years ago I used to grow cacti and succulents avidly; and in fact my first paid publications, at age thirteen and fourteen, were columns about succulents in gardening magazines. (Given the resources, I would have grown orchids, too, and bonsai.) But then I stopped.

Yet actually, putting these stories together, I realize that I never stopped at all, but began instead to breed my own species – not by genetic, but by verbal engineering.

So here are some of my bonsai, fly traps, crowns of thorns, and queens of the night. Such are the sorts of plants I would have grown.

'Slow Birds' is, of course, about Cruise missiles – fantastically transplanted. 'Cruising' is more obviously about Cruise missiles; while it isn't too hard to guess which Prime Minister is the 'Mistress of Cold'. Fantastic fiction often has its roots firmly planted in the fears and madness of the present day; and to a gardener of words, the new Cold War and threatened nuclear winter (or the thermonuclear heat-wave) are abominable. We might destroy not just ourselves, and any civilization, but possibly the only garden of life in the whole galaxy.

Other stories are more obvious exotics; whilst in a few the ordinary world is invaded by strangeness.

To me, it is strangeness which brings a story alive; which makes it real and believable. For our own situation is very strange indeed. Here we are, treading a time-line between birth and death, not knowing why time flows onward. Here we are in a universe whose existence remains a huge enigma; observing it with a consciousness which we don't understand. Our flesh is composed of exotic particles which may just be energetic aspects of nothing. Our apparently long, rich history is really just an eye-blink. Our unknowable future is one in which humans would surely evolve into beings quite alien to us now.

Our future . . . if we can survive the Armageddon preachers and the nuclear war lords.

Slow Birds

It was Mayday, and the skate-sailing festival that year was being held at Tuckerton.

By late morning, after the umpires had been out on the glass plain setting red flags around the circuit, cumulus clouds began to fill a previously blue sky, promising ideal conditions for the afternoon's sport. No rain; so that the glass wouldn't be an inch deep in water as last year at Atherton. No dazzling glare to blind the spectators, as the year before that at Buckby. And a breeze verging on brisk without ever becoming fierce: perfect to speed the competitors' sails along without lifting people off their feet and tumbling them, as four years previously at Edgewood when a couple of broken ankles and numerous bruises had been sustained.

After the contest there would be a pig roast; or rather the succulent fruits thereof, for the pig had been turning slowly on its spit these past thirty-six hours. And there would be kegs of Old Codger Ale to be cracked. But right now Jason Babbidge's mind was mainly occupied with checking out his glass-skates and his fine crocus-yellow hand-sail.

As high as a tall man, and of best old silk, only patched in a couple of places, the sail's fore-spar of flexible ash was bent into a bow belly by a strong hemp cord. Jason plucked this thoughtfully like a harpist, testing the tension. Already a fair number of racers were out on the glass, showing off their paces to applause. Tuckerton folk mostly, they were – acting as if they owned the glass hereabouts and knew it more intimately than any visitors could. Not that it was in any way different from the same glass over Atherton way.

Jason's younger brother Daniel whistled appreciatively as a Tuckerton man carrying purple silk executed perfect circles at speed, his sail shivering as he tacked.

'Just look at him, Jay!'

'What, Bob Marchant? He took a pratfall last year. Where's the use in working up a sweat before the whistle blows?'

By now a couple of sisters from Buckby were out too with matching black sails, skating figure-eights around each other, risking collision by a hair's breadth.

'Go on, Jay,' urged young Daniel. 'Show 'em.'

Contestants from the other villages were starting to flood on to the glass as well, but Jason noticed how Max Tarnover was standing not so far away, merely observing these antics with a wise smile. Master Tarnover of Tuckerton, last year's victor at Atherton despite the drenching spray . . . Taking his cue from this, and going one better, Jason ignored events on the glass and surveyed the crowds instead.

He noticed Uncle John Babbidge chatting intently to an Edgewood man over where the silver band was playing; which was hardly the quietest place to talk, so perhaps they were doing business. Meanwhile on the green beyond the band the children of five villages buzzed like flies from hoop-la to skittles to bran tub, to apples in buckets of water. And those grown-ups who weren't intent on the band or the practice runs or on something else, such as gossip, besieged the craft and produce stalls. There must be going on for a thousand people at the festival, and the village beyond looked deserted. Rugs and benches and half-barrels had even been set out near the edge of the glass for the old folk of Tuckerton.

As the band lowered their instruments for a breather

after finishing *The Floral Dance*, a bleat of panic cut across the chatter of many voices. A farmer had just vaulted into a tiny sheep-pen where a lamb almost as large as its shorn, protesting dam was ducking beneath her to suckle and hide. Laughing, the farmer hauled it out and hoisted it by its neck and back legs to guess its weight, and maybe win a prize.

And now Jason's mother was threading her way through the crowd, chewing the remnants of a pasty.

'Best of luck, son!' She grinned.

'I've told you, Mum,' protested Jason. 'It's bad luck to say "Good luck".'

'Oh, luck yourself! What's luck, anyway?' She prodded her Adam's apple as if to press the last piece of meat and potatoes on its way down, though really she was indicating that her throat was bare of any charm or amulet.

'I suppose I'd better make a move.' Kicking off his sandals, Jason sat to lace up his skates. With a helping hand from Daniel he rose and stood knock-kneed, blades cutting into the turf while the boy hoisted the sail across his shoulders. Jason gripped the leather straps on the bow-string and the spine-spar.

'Okay.' He waggled the sail this way and that. 'Let go, then. I won't blow away.'

But just as he was about to proceed down on to the glass, out upon the glass less than a hundred yards away a slow bird appeared.

It materialized directly in front of one of the Buckby sisters. Unable to veer, she had no choice but to throw herself backwards. Crying out in frustration, and perhaps hurt by her fall, she skidded underneath the slow bird, sledging supine upon her now snapped and crumpled sail . . .

* * *

They were called slow birds because they flew through the air – at the stately pace of three feet per minute.

They looked a little like birds, too, though only a little. Their tubular metal bodies were rounded at the head and tapering to a finned point at the tail, with two stubby wings midway. Yet these wings could hardly have anything to do with suspending their bulk in the air; the girth of a bird was that of a horse, and its length twice that of a man lying full length. Perhaps those wings controlled orientation or trim.

In colour they were a silvery grey; though this was only the colour of their outer skin, made of a soft metal like lead. Quarter of an inch beneath this coating their inner skins were black and stiff as steel. The noses of the birds were all scored with at least a few scrape marks due to encounters with obstacles down the years; slow birds always kept the same height above ground – underbelly level with a man's shoulders – and they would bank to avoid substantial buildings or mature trees, but any frailer obstructions they would push on through. Hence the individual patterns of scratches. However, a far easier way of telling them apart was by the graffiti carved on so many of their flanks: initials entwined in hearts, dates, place names, fragments of messages. These amply confirmed how very many slow birds there must be in all – something of which people could not otherwise have been totally convinced. For no one could keep track of a single slow bird. After each one had appeared – over hill, down dale, in the middle of a pasture or half way along a village street – it would fly onward slowly for any length of time between an hour and a day, covering any distance between a few score yards and a full mile. And vanish again. To reappear somewhere else unpredictably: far away or close by, maybe long afterwards or maybe soon.

Usually a bird would vanish, to reappear again.

Not always, though. Half a dozen times a year, within the confines of this particular island country, a slow bird would reach its journey's end.

It would destroy itself, and all the terrain around it for a radius of two and a half miles, fusing the landscape instantly into a sheet of glass. A flat, circular sheet of glass. A polarized, limited zone of annihilation. Scant yards beyond its rim a person might escape unharmed, only being deafened and dazzled temporarily.

Hitherto no slow bird had been known to explode so as to overlap an earlier sheet of glass. Consequently many towns and villages clung close to the borders of what had already been destroyed, and news of a fresh glass plain would cause farms and settlements to spring up there. Even so, the bulk of people still kept fatalistically to the old historic towns. They assumed that a slow bird wouldn't explode in their midst during their own lifetimes. And if it did, what would they know of it? Unless the glass happened merely to bisect a town – in which case, once the weeping and mourning was over, the remaining citizenry could relax and feel secure.

True, in the long term the whole country from coast to coast and from north to south would be a solid sheet of glass. Or perhaps it would merely be a chequerboard, of circles touching circles; a glass mosaic. With what in between? Patches of desert dust, if the climate dried up due to reflections from the glass. Or floodwater, swampland. But that day was still far distant: a hundred years away, two hundred, three. So people didn't worry too much. They had been used to this all their lives long, and their parents before them. Perhaps one day the slow birds would stop coming. And going. And exploding. Just as they had first started, once. Certainly the situation was no different, by all accounts, anywhere else in the world. Only the seas were clear of slow birds. So maybe

the human race would have to take to rafts one day.
Though by then, with what would they build them?
Meanwhile, people got by; and most had long ago given
up asking why. For there was no answer.

The girl's sister helped her rise. No bones broken, it
seemed. Only an injury to dignity; and to her sail.

The other skaters had all coasted to a halt and were
staring resentfully at the bird in their midst. Its belly and
sides were almost bare of graffiti; seeing this, a number
of youths hastened on to the glass, clutching penknives,
rusty nails and such. But an umpire waved them back
angrily.

'Shoo! Be off with you!' His gaze seemed to alight on
Jason, and for a fatuous moment Jason imagined that it
was himself to whom the umpire was about to appeal;
but the man called, 'Master Tarnover!' instead, and Max
Tarnover duck-waddled past then glided out over the
glass, to confer.

Presently the umpire cupped his hands. 'We're delaying
the start for half an hour,' he bellowed. 'Fair's fair: young
lady ought to have a chance to fix her sail, seeing as it
wasn't her fault.'

Jason noted a small crinkle of amusement on Tarnover's face; for now either the other competitors would
have to carry on prancing around tiring themselves with
extra practice which none of them needed, or else troop
off the glass for a recess and lose some psychological
edge. In fact almost everyone opted for a break and some
refreshments.

'Luck indeed!' snorted Mrs Babbidge, as Max Tarnover
clumped back their way.

Tarnover paused by Jason, 'Frankly I'd say her sail's a
wreck,' he confided. 'But what can you do? The Buckby
lot would have been bitching on otherwise. "Oh, she

could have won. If she'd had ten minutes to fix it."
Bloody hunk of metal in the way.' Tarnover ran a lordly
eye over Jason's sail. 'What price skill, then?'

Daniel Babbidge regarded Tarnover with a mixture of
hero worship and hostile partisanship on his brother's
behalf. Jason himself only nodded and said, 'Fair enough.'
He wasn't certain whether Tarnover was acting gener-
ously – or with patronizing arrogance. Or did this word in
his ear mean that Tarnover actually saw Jason as a valid
rival for the silver punch-bowl this year round?

Obviously young Daniel did not regard Jason's
response as adequate. He piped up: 'So where do *you*
think the birds go, Master Tarnover, when they aren't
here?'

A good question: quite unanswerable, but Max Tarnover would probably feel obliged to offer an answer if only
to maintain his pose of wordly wisdom. Jason warmed to
his brother, while Mrs Babbidge, catching on, cuffed the
boy softly.

'Now don't you go wasting Master Tarnover's time.
Happen he hasn't given it a moment's thought, all his
born days.'

'Oh, but I have,' Tarnover said.

'Well?' the boy insisted.

'Well . . . maybe they don't go anywhere at all.'

Mrs Babbidge chuckled, and Tarnover flushed.

'What I mean is, maybe they just stop being in one
place then suddenly they're in the next place.'

'If only you could skate like that!' Jason laughed. 'Bit
slow, though . . . Everyone would still pass you by at the
last moment.'

'They must go somewhere,' young Dan said doggedly.
'Maybe it's somewhere we can't see. Another sort of
place, with other people. Maybe it's them that builds the
birds.'

'Look, freckleface, the birds don't come from Russ, or 'Merica, or anywhere else. So where's this other place?'

'Maybe it's right here, only we can't see it.'

'And maybe pigs have wings.' Tarnover looked about to march towards the cider and perry stall; but Mrs Babbidge interposed herself smartly.

'Oh, as to that, I'm sure our sow Betsey couldn't fly, wings or no wings. Just hanging in the air like that, and so heavy.'

'Weighed a bird recently, have you?'

'They look heavy, Master Tarnover.'

Tarnover couldn't quite push his way past Mrs Babbidge, not with his sail impeding him. He contented himself with staring past her, and muttering, 'If we've nothing sensible to say about them, in my opinion it's better to shut up.'

'But it isn't better,' protested Daniel. 'They're blowing the world up. Bit by bit. As though they're at war with us.'

Jason felt humorously inventive. 'Maybe that's it. Maybe these other people of Dan's are at war with us – only they forgot to mention it. And when they've glassed us all, they'll move in for the holidays. And skate happily for ever more.'

'Damn long war, if that's so,' growled Tarnover. 'Been going on over a century now.'

'Maybe that's why the birds fly so slowly,' said Daniel. 'What if a year to us is like an hour to those people? That's why the birds don't fall. They don't have time to.'

Tarnover's expression was almost savage. 'And what if the birds come only to punish us for our sins? What if they're simply a miraculous proof – '

' – that the Lord cares about us? And one day he'll forgive us? Oh goodness,' and Mrs Babbidge beamed, 'surely you aren't one of *them*? A bright lad like you.

Me, I don't even put candles in the window or tie knots in the bedsheets anymore to keep the birds away.' She ruffled her younger son's mop of red hair. 'Everyone dies sooner or later, Dan. You'll get used to it, when you're properly grown up. When it's time to die, it's time to die.'

Tarnover looked furiously put out; though young Daniel also seemed distressed in a different way.

'And when you're thirsty, it's time for a drink!' Spying an opening, and his opportunity, Tarnover sidled quickly around Mrs Babbidge and strode off. She chuckled as she watched him go.

'That's put a kink in his sail!'

Forty-one other contestants, besides Jason and Tarnover, gathered between the starting flags. Though not the girl who had fallen; despite all best efforts she was out of the race, and sat morosely watching.

Then the Tuckerton umpire blew his whistle, and they were off.

The course was in the shape of a long bloomer loaf. First, it curved gently along the edge of the glass for three quarters of a mile, then bent sharply around in a half circle on to the straight, returning towards Tuckerton. At the end of the straight, another sharp half circle brought it back to the starting – and finishing – line. Three circuits in all were to be skate-sailed before the victory whistle blew. Much more than this, and the lag between leaders and stragglers could lead to confusion.

By the first turn Jason was ahead of the rest of the field, and all his practice since last year was paying off. His skates raced over the glass. The breeze thrust him convincingly. As he rounded the end of the loaf, swinging his sail to a new pitch, he noted Max Tarnover hanging back in fourth place. Determined to increase his lead,

Jason leaned so close to the flag on the entry to the straight that he almost tipped it. Compensating, he came poorly on to the straight, losing a few yards. By the time Jason swept over the finishing line for the first time, to the cheers from Atherton villagers, Tarnover was in third position; though he was making no very strenuous effort to overhaul. Jason realized that Tarnover was simply letting him act as pacemaker.

But a skate-sailing race wasn't the same as a foot-race, where a pacemaker was generally bound to drop back eventually. Jason pressed on. Yet by the second crossing of the line Tarnover was ten yards behind, moving without apparent effort as though he and his sail and the wind and the glass were one. Noting Jason's glance, Tarnover grinned and put on a small burst of speed to push the front-runner to even greater efforts. And as he entered on the final circuit Jason also noted the progress of the slow bird, off to his left, now midway between the long curve and the straight, heading in the general direction of Edgewood. Even the laggards ought to clear the final straight before the thing got in their way, he calculated.

This brief distraction was a mistake: Tarnover was even closer behind him now, his sail pitched at an angle which must have made his wrists ache. Already he was drifting aside to overhaul Jason. And at this moment Jason grasped how he could win: by letting Tarnover think that he was pushing Jason beyond his capacity – so that Tarnover would be fooled into over-exerting himself too soon.

'Can't catch me!' Jason called into the wind, guessing that Tarnover would misread this as braggadocio and assume that Jason wasn't really thinking ahead. At the same time Jason slackened his own pace slightly, hoping that his rival would fail to notice, since this was at odds with his own boast. Pretending to look panicked, he let

Tarnover overtake – and saw how Tarnover continued to grip his sail strenuously even though he was actually moving a little slower than before. Without realizing it, Tarnover had his angle wrong; he was using unnecessary wrist action.

Tarnover was in the lead now. Immediately all psychological pressure lifted from Jason. With ease and grace he stayed a few yards behind, just where he could benefit from the 'eye' of air in Tarnover's wake. And thus he remained till half way down the final straight, feeling like a kestrel hanging in the sky with a mere twitch of its wings before swooping.

He held back; held back. Then suddenly changing the cant of his sail he did swoop – into the lead again.

It was a mistake. It had been a mistake all along. For as Jason sailed past, Tarnover actually laughed. Jerking his brown and orange silk to an easier, more efficient pitch, Tarnover began to pump his legs, skating like a demon. Already he was ahead again. By five yards. By ten. And entering the final curve.

As Jason tried to catch up in the brief time remaining, he knew how he had been fooled; though the knowledge came too late. So cleverly had Tarnover fixed Jason's mind on the stance of the sails, by holding his own in such a way – a way, too, which deliberately created that convenient eye of air – that Jason had quite neglected the contribution of his legs and skates, taking this for granted, failing to monitor it from moment to moment. It only took moments to recover and begin pumping his own legs too, but those few moments were fatal. Jason crossed the finishing line one yard behind last year's victor; who was this year's victor too.

As he slid to a halt, bitter with chagrin, Jason was well aware that it was up to him to be gracious in defeat rather than let Tarnover seize that advantage, too.

He called out, loud enough for everyone to hear: 'Magnificent, Max! Splendid skating! You really caught me on the hop there.'

Tarnover smiled for the benefit of all onlookers.

'What a noisy family you Babbidges are,' he said softly; and skated off to be presented with the silver punchbowl again.

Much later that afternoon, replete with roast pork and awash with Old Codger Ale, Jason was waving an empty beer mug about as he talked to Bob Marchant in the midst of a noisy crowd. Bob, who had fallen so spectacularly the year before. Maybe that was why he had skated diffidently today and been one of the laggards.

The sky was heavily overcast, and daylight too was failing. Soon the homeward trek would have to start.

One of Jason's drinking and skating partners from Atherton, Sam Partridge, thrust his way through.

'Jay! That brother of yours; he's out on the glass. He's scrambled up on the back of the bird. He's riding it.'

'*What?*'

Jason sobered rapidly, and followed Partridge with Bob Marchant tagging along behind.

Sure enough, a couple of hundred yards away in the gloaming Daniel was perched astride the slow bird. His red hair was unmistakable. By now a lot of other people were beginning to take notice and point him out. There were some ragged cheers, and a few angry protests.

Jason clutched Partridge's arm. 'Somebody must have helped him up. Who was it?'

'Haven't the foggiest. That boy needs a good walloping.'

'Daniel *Babbidge*!' Mrs Babbidge was calling nearby. She too had seen. Cautiously she advanced on to the glass, wary of losing her balance.

Jason and company were soon at her side. 'It's all right, Mum,' he assured her. 'I'll fetch the little . . . perisher.'

Courteously Bob Marchant offered his arm and escorted Mrs Babbidge back on to rough ground again. Jason and Partridge stepped flat-foot out across the vitrified surface accompanied by at least a dozen curious spectators.

'Did anyone spot who helped him up?' Jason demanded of them. No one admitted it.

When the group was a good twenty yards from the bird, everyone but Jason halted. Pressing on alone, Jason pitched his voice so that only the boy would hear.

'Slide off,' he ordered grimly. 'I'll catch you. Right monkey you've made of your mother and me.'

'No,' whispered Daniel. He clung tight, hands splayed like suckers, knees pressed to the flanks of the bird as though he was a jockey. 'I'm going to see where it goes.'

'Goes? Hell I'm not going to waste time arguing. Get down!' Jason gripped an ankle and tugged, but this action only served to pull him up against the bird. Beside Dan's foot a heart with the entwined initials 'ZB' and 'EF' was carved. Turning away, Jason shouted, 'Give me a hand, you lot! Come on someone, bunk me up!'

Nobody volunteered, not even Partridge.

'It won't bite you! There's no harm in touching it. Any kid knows that.' Angrily he flat-footed back towards them. 'Damn it all, Sam.'

So now Partridge did shuffle forward, and a couple of other men too. But then they halted, gaping. Their expression puzzled Jason momentarily – till Sam Partridge gestured; till Jason swung around.

The air behind was empty.

The slow bird had departed suddenly. Taking its rider with it.

* * *

Half an hour later only the visitors from Atherton and their hosts remained on Tuckerton green. The Buckby, Edgewood, and Hopperton contingents had set off for home. Uncle John was still consoling a snivelling Mrs Babbidge. Most faces in the surrounding crowd looked sympathetic, though there was a certain air of resentment, too, among some Tuckerton folk that a boy's prank had cast this black shadow over their Mayday festival.

Jason glared wildly around the onlookers. 'Did nobody see who helped my brother up?' he cried. 'Couldn't very well have got up himself, could he? Where's Max Tarnover? Where is he?'

'You aren't accusing Master Tarnover, by any chance?' growled a beefy farmer with a large wart on his cheek. 'Sour grapes, Master Babbidge! Sour grapes is what that sounds like, and we don't like the taste of those here.'

'Where is he, dammit?'

Uncle John laid a hand on his nephew's arm. 'Jason, lad. Hush. This isn't helping your Mum.'

But then the crowd parted, and Tarnover sauntered through, still holding the silver punch-bowl he had won.

'Well, Master Babbidge?' he enquired. 'I hear you want a word with me.'

'Did you see who helped my brother on to that bird? Well, did you?'

'I didn't see,' replied Tarnover coolly.

It had been the wrong question, as Jason at once realized. For if Tarnover had done the deed himself, how could he possibly have watched himself do it?

'Then did you – '

'Hey up,' objected the same farmer. 'You've asked him, and you've had his answer.'

'And I imagine your brother has had his answer, too,' said Tarnover. 'I hope he's well satisfied with it. Naturally I offer my heartfelt sympathies to Mrs Babbidge. If indeed the boy *has* come to any harm. Can't be sure of that, though, can we?'

''Course we can't!''

Jason tensed, and Uncle John tightened his grip on him. '*No*, lad. There's no use.'

It was a sad and quiet long walk homeward that evening for the three remaining Babbidges, though a fair few Atherton folk behind sang blithely and tipsily, nonetheless. Occasionally Jason looked around for Sam Partridge, but Sam Partridge seemed to be successfully avoiding them.

The next day, May the Second, Mrs Babbidge rallied and declared it to be a 'sorting out' day; which meant a day for handling all Daniel's clothes and storybooks and old toys lovingly before setting them to one side out of sight. Jason himself she packed off to his job at the sawmill, with a flea in his ear for hanging around her like a whipped hound.

And as Jason worked at trimming planks that day the same shamed, angry, frustrated thoughts skated round and round a single circuit in his head:

'*In my book he's a murderer . . . You don't give a baby a knife to play with. He was cool as a cucumber afterwards. Not shocked, no. Smug . . .*'

Yet what could be done about it? The bird might have hung around for hours more. Except that it hadn't . . .

Set out on a quest to find Daniel? But how? And where? Birds dodged around. Here, there and everywhere. No rhyme or reason to it. So what a useless quest that would be!

A quest to prove that Dan was alive. And if he were alive, then Tarnover hadn't killed him.

'*In my book he's a murderer . . .*' Jason's thoughts

churned on impotently. It was like skating with both feet tied together.

Three days later a slow bird was sighted out Edgewood way. Jim Mitchum, the Edgewood thatcher, actually sought Jason out at the sawmill to bring him the news. He'd be coming over to do a job, anyway.

No doubt his visit was an act of kindness, but it filled Jason with guilt quite as much as it boosted his morale. For now he was compelled to go and see for himself, when obviously there was nothing whatever to discover. Downing tools, he hurried home to collect his skates and sail, and sped over the glass to Edgewood.

The bird was still there; but it was a different bird. There was no carved heart with the love-tangled initials 'ZB' and 'EF'.

And four days after that, mention came from Buckby of a bird spotted a few miles west of the village on the main road to Harborough. This time Jason borrowed a horse and rode. But the mention had come late; the bird had flown on a day earlier. Still, he felt obliged to search the area of the sighting for a fallen body or some other sign.

And the week after that a bird appeared only a mile from Atherton itself; this one vanished even as Jason arrived on the scene . . .

Then one night Jason went down to the Wheatsheaf. It was several weeks, in fact, since he had last been in the alehouse; now he meant to get drunk, at the long bar under the horse brasses.

Sam Partridge, Ned Darrow and Frank Yardley were there boozing; and an hour or so later Ned Darrow was offering beery advice.

'Look, Jay, where's the use in your dashing off every time someone spots a ruddy bird? Keep that up and you'll make a ruddy fool of yourself. And what if a bird pops up in Tuckerton? Bound to happen sooner or later. Going to rush off there too, are you, with your tongue hanging out?'

'All this time you're taking off work,' said Frank Yardley. 'You'll end up losing the job. Get on living is my advice.'

'Don't know about that,' said Sam Partridge unexpectedly. 'Does seem to me as a man ought to get his own back. Supposing Tarnover did do the dirty on the Babbidges – '

'What's there to suppose about it?' Jason broke in angrily.

'Easy on, Jay. I was going to say as Babbidges are Atherton people. So he did the dirty on us all, right?'

'Thanks to some people being a bit slow in their help.'

Sam flushed. 'Now don't you start attacking everyone right and left. No one's perfect. Just remember who your real friends are, that's all.'

'Oh, I'll remember, never fear.'

Frank inclined an empty glass from side to side. 'Right. Whose round is it?'

One thing led to another, and Jason had a thick head the next morning.

In the evening Ned banged on the Babbidge door.

'Bird on the glass, Sam says to tell you,' he announced. 'How about going for a spin to see it?'

'I seem to recall last night you said I was wasting my time.'

'Ay, running around all over the country. But this is just for a spin. Nice evening, like. Mind, if you don't want to bother . . . Then we can all have a few jars in the Wheatsheaf afterwards.'

The lads must really have missed him over the past few weeks. Quickly Jason collected his skates and sail.

'But what about your supper?' asked his mother. 'Sheep's head broth.'

'Oh, it'll keep, won't it? I might as well have a pasty or two in the Wheatsheaf.'

'Happen it's better you get out and enjoy yourself,' she said. 'I'm quite content. I've got things to mend.'

Twenty minutes later Jason, Sam, and Ned were skimming over the glass two miles out. The sky was crimson with banks of stratus, and a river of gold ran clear along the horizon; foul weather tomorrow, but a glory this evening. The glassy expanse flowed with red and gold reflections: a lake of blood, fire, and molten metal. They did not at first spot the other solitary sail skater, nor he them, till they were quite close to the slow bird.

Sam noticed first. 'Who's that, then?'

The other sail was brown and orange. Jason recognized it easily. 'It's Tarnover!'

'Now's your chance to find out, then,' said Ned.

'Do you mean that?'

Ned grinned. 'Why not? Could be fun. Let's take him.'

Pumping their legs, the three sail-skaters sped apart to outflank Tarnover – who spied them and began to turn. All too sharply, though. Or else he may have run into a slick of water on the glass. To Jason's joy Max Tarnover, champion of the five villages, skidded.

They caught him. This done, it didn't take the strength of an ox to stop a skater from going anywhere else, however much he kicked and struggled. But Jason hit Tarnover on the jaw, knocking him senseless.

'What the hell you do that for?' asked Sam, easing Tarnover's fall on the glass.

'How else do we get him up on the bird?'

Sam stared at Jason, then nodded slowly.

It hardly proved the easiest operation to hoist a limp and
heavy body on to a slowly moving object whilst standing
on a slippery surface; but after removing their skates they
succeeded. Before too long Tarnover lay sprawled atop,
legs dangling. Quickly with his pocket knife Jason cut the
hemp cord from Tarnover's sail and bound his ankles
together, running the tether tightly underneath the bird.

Presently Tarnover awoke, and struggled groggily
erect. He groaned, rocked sideways, recovered his
balance.

'Babbidge . . . Partridge, Ned Darrow . . .? What the
hell are you up to?'

Jason planted hands on hips. 'Oh, we're just playing a
little prank, same as you did on my brother Dan. Who's
missing now; maybe forever, thanks to you.'

'I never – '

'Admit it, then we might cut you down.'

'And happen we mightn't,' said Ned. 'Not till the
Wheatsheaf closes. But look on the bright side: happen
we might.'

Tarnover's legs twitched as he tested the bonds. He
winced. 'I honestly meant your brother no harm.'

Sam smirked. 'Nor do we mean you any. Ain't our
fault if a bird decides to fly off. Anyway, only been here
an hour or so. Could easily be here all night. Right,
lads?'

'Right,' said Ned. 'And I'm thirsty. Race you? Last
one buys?'

'He's admitted he did it,' said Jason. 'You heard him.'

'Look, I'm honestly very sorry if – '

'Shut up,' said Sam. 'You can stew for a while, seeing
as how you've made the Babbidges stew. You can think

about how sorry you really are.' Partridge hoisted his sail.

It was not exactly how Jason had envisioned his revenge. This seemed like an anti-climax. Yet, to Tarnover no doubt it was serious enough. The champion was sweating slightly . . . Jason hoisted his sail, too. Presently the men skated away . . . to halt by unspoken agreement a quarter of a mile away. They stared back at Tarnover's little silhouette upon his metal steed.

'Now if it was me,' observed Sam. 'I'd shuffle myself along till I fell off the front . . . Rub you a bit raw, but that's how to do it.'

'No need to come back, really,' said Ned. 'Hey, what's he trying?'

The silhouette had ducked. Perhaps Tarnover had panicked and wasn't thinking clearly, but it *looked* as if he was trying to lean over far enough to unfasten the knot beneath, or free one of his ankles. Suddenly the distant figure inverted itself. It swung right round the bird, and Tarnover's head and chest were hanging upside down, his arms flapping. Or perhaps Tarnover had hoped the cord would snap under his full weight; but snap it did not. And once he was stuck in that position there was no way he could recover himself upright again, or do anything about inching along to the front of the bird.

Ned whistled. 'He's messed himself right up now, and no mistake. He's ruddy crucified himself.'

Jason hesitated before saying it: 'Maybe we ought to go back? I mean, a man can die hanging upside down too long . . . Can't he?' Suddenly the whole episode seemed unclean, unsatisfactory.

'Go back?' Sam Partridge fairly snarled at him. 'You were the big mouth last night. And whose idea was it to tie him on the bird? You wanted him taught a lesson, and he's being taught one. We're only trying to oblige you, Jay.'

'Yes, I appreciate that.'

'You made enough fuss about it. He isn't going to wilt like a bunch of flowers in the time it takes us to swallow a couple of pints.'

And so they skated on, back to the Wheatsheaf in Atherton.

At ten thirty, somewhat the worse for wear, the three men spilled out of the alehouse into Sheaf Street. A quarter moon was dodging from rift to rift in the cloudy sky, shedding little light.

'I'm for bed,' said Sam. 'Let the sod wriggle his way off.'

'And who cares if he don't?' said Ned. 'That way, nobody'll know. Who wants an enemy for life? Do you, Jay? This way you can get on with things. Happen Tarnover'll bring your brother back from wherever it is.' Shouldering his sail and swinging his skates, Ned wandered off up Sheaf Street.

'But,' said Jason. He felt as though he had blundered into a midden. There was a reek of sordidness about what had taken place. The memory of Tarnover hanging upside-down had tarnished him.

'But what?' said Sam.

Jason made a show of yawning. 'Nothing. See you.' And he set off homeward.

But as soon as he was out of sight of Sam he slipped down through Butcher's Row in the direction of the glass, alone.

It was dark out there with no stars and only an occasional hint of moonlight, yet the breeze was steady and there was nothing to trip over on the glass. The bird wouldn't have moved more than a hundred yards. Jason made good speed.

The slow bird was still there. But Tarnover wasn't with it; its belly was barren of any hanged man.

As Jason skated to a halt, to look closer, figures arose in the darkness from where they had been lying flat upon the glass, covered by their sails. Six figures. Eight. Nine. All had lurked within two or three hundred yards of the bird, though not too close – nor any in the direction of Atherton. They had left a wide corridor open; which now they closed.

As the Tuckerton men moved in on him, Jason stood still, knowing that he had no chance.

Max Tarnover skated up, accompanied by that same beefy farmer with the wart.

'I did come back for you,' began Jason.

The farmer spoke, but not to Jason. 'Did he now? That's big of him. Could have saved his time, what with Tim Earnshaw happening along – when Master Tarnover was gone a long time. So what's to be done with him, eh?'

'Tit for tat, I'd say,' said another voice.

'Let him go and look for his kid brother,' offered a third. 'Instead of sending other folk on his errands. What a nerve.'

Tarnover himself said nothing; he just stood in the night silently.

So, presently, Jason was raised on to the back of the bird and his feet were tied tightly under it. But his wrists were bound together too, and for good measure the cord was linked through his belt.

Within a few minutes all the skaters had sped away towards Tuckerton.

Jason sat. Remembering Sam's words he tried to inch

forward, but with both hands fastened to his waist this proved impossible; he couldn't gain purchase. Besides, he was scared of losing his balance as Tarnover had.

He sat and thought of his mother. Maybe she would grow alarmed when he didn't come home. Maybe she would go out and rouse Uncle John . . . And maybe she had gone to bed already.

But maybe she would wake in the night and glance into his room and send for help. With fierce concentration he tried to project thoughts and images of himself at her, two miles away.

An hour wore on, then two; or so he supposed from the moving of the moon-crescent. He wished he could slump forward and sleep. That might be best; then he wouldn't know anything. He still felt drunk enough to pass out, even with his face pressed against metal. But he might easily slide to one side or the other in his sleep.

How could his mother survive a double loss? It seemed as though a curse had descended on the Babbidge family. but of course that curse had a human name; and the name was Max Tarnover. So for a while Jason damned him, and imagined retribution by all the villagers of Atherton. A bloody feud. Cottages burnt. Perhaps a rape. Deaths even. No Mayday festival ever again.

But would Sam and Ned speak up? And would Atherton folk be sufficiently incensed, sufficiently willing to destroy the harmony of the five villages in a world where other things were so unsure? Particularly as some less than sympathetic souls might say that Jason, Sam, and Ned had started it all.

Jason was involved in imagining a future feud between Atherton and Tuckerton that he almost forgot he was astride a slow bird. There was no sense of motion, no feeling of going anywhere. When he recollected where he was, it actually came as a shock.

He was riding a bird.

But for how long?

It had been around, what, six hours now? A bird could stay for a whole day. In which case he had another eighteen hours left to be rescued in. Or if it only stayed for half a day, that would take him through to morning. Just.

He found himself wondering what was underneath the metal skin of the bird. Something which could turn five miles of landscape into a sheet of glass, certainly. But other things too. Things that let it ignore gravity. Things that let it dodge in and out of existence. A brain of some kind, even?

'Can you hear me, bird?' he asked it. Maybe no one had ever spoken to a slow bird before.

The slow bird did not answer.

Maybe it couldn't, but maybe it could hear him, even so. Maybe it could obey orders.

'Don't disappear with me on your back,' he told it. 'Stay here. Keep on flying just like this.'

But since it was doing just that already, he had no idea whether it was obeying him or not.

'Land, bird. Settle down on to the glass. Lie still.'

It did not. He felt stupid. He knew nothing at all about the bird. Nobody did. Yet somewhere, someone knew. Unless the slow birds did indeed come from God, as miracles, to punish. To make men God-fearing. But why should a God want to be feared? Unless God was insane, in which case the birds might well come from Him.

They were something irrational, something from elsewhere, something which couldn't be understood by their victims any more than an ant colony understood the gardener's boot, exposing the white eggs to the sun and the sparrows.

Maybe something had entered the seas from elsewhere

the previous century, something that didn't like land dwellers. Any of them. People or sheep, birds or worms or plants . . . It didn't seem likely. Salt water would rust steel. But for the first time in his life Jason thought about it intently.

'Bird, what are you. Why are you here?'

Why, he thought, is anything here? Why is there a world and sky and stars? Why shouldn't there simply be nothing for ever and ever?

Perhaps that was the nature of death: nothing for ever and ever. And one's life was like a slow bird. Appearing then vanishing, with nothing before and nothing after.

An immeasurable period of time later, dawn began to streak the sky behind him, washing it from black to grey. The greyness advanced slowly overhead as thick clouds filtered the light of the rising but hidden sun. Soon there was enough illumination to see clear all around. It must be five o'clock. Or six. But the grey glass remained blankly empty.

Who am I? wondered Jason, calm and still. Why am I conscious of a world? Why do people have minds, and think thoughts? For the first time in his life he felt that he was really thinking – and thinking had no outcome. It led nowhere.

He was, he realized, preparing himself to die. Just as all the land would die, piece by piece, fused into glass. Then no one would think thoughts any more, so that it wouldn't matter if a certain Jason Babbidge had ceased thinking at half past six one morning in May. After all, the same thing happened every night when you went to sleep, didn't it? You stopped thinking. Perhaps everything would be purer and cleaner afterwards. Less untidy, less fretful: a pure ball of glass. In fact, not fretful at all, even if all the stars in the sky crashed into each other, even if the earth was swallowed by the sun. Silence, forever: once there was no one about to hear.

Maybe this was the message of the slow birds. Yet people only carved their initials upon them. And hearts. And the names of places which had been vitrified in a flash; or else which were going to be.

I'm becoming a philosopher, thought Jason in wonder.

He must have shifted into some hyperconscious state of mind: full of lucid clarity, though without immediate awareness of his surroundings. For he was not fully aware that help had arrived until the cord binding his ankles was cut and his right foot thrust up abruptly, toppling him off the other side of the bird into waiting arms.

Sam Partridge, Ned Darrow, Frank Yardley, and Uncle John, and Brian Sefton from the sawmill – who ducked under the bird brandishing a knife, and cut the other cord to free his wrists.

They retreated quickly from the bird, pulling Jason with them. He resisted feebly. He stretched an arm towards the bird.

'It's all right, lad,' Uncle John soothed him.

'No, I want to *go*,' he protested.

'Eh?'

At that moment the slow bird, having hung around long enough, vanished; and Jason stared at where it had been, speechless.

In the end his friends and uncle had to lead him away from that featureless spot on the glass, as though he was an idiot. Someone touched by imbecility.

But Jason did not long remain speechless.

Presently he began to teach. Or preach. One or the other. And people listened; at first in Atherton, then in other places too.

He had learned wisdom from the slow bird, people

said of him. He had communed with the bird during the night's vigil on the glass.

His doctrine of nothingness and silence spread, taking root in fertile soil, where there was soil remaining rather than glass – which was in most places, still. A paradox, perhaps; how eloquently he spoke – about being silent! But in so doing he seemed to make the silence of the glass lakes sing; and to this people listened with a new ear.

Jason travelled throughout the whole island. And this was another paradox, for what he taught was a kind of passivity, a blissful waiting for a death that was more than merely personal, a death which was also the death of the sun and stars and of all existence, a cosmic death which transfigured individual mortality. And sometimes he even sat on the back of a bird that happened by, to speak to a crowd – as though chancing fate or daring, begging, the bird to take him away. But he never sat for more than an hour, then he would scramble down, trembling but quietly radiant. So besides being known as 'The Silent Prophet,' he was also known as 'The Man who rides the Slow Birds.'

On balance, it could have been said that he worked great psychological good for the communities that survived; and his words even spread overseas. His mother died proud of him – so he thought – though there was always an element of wistful reserve in her attitude . . .

Many years later, when Jason Babbidge was approaching sixty, and still no bird had ever borne him away, he settled back in Atherton in his old home – to which pilgrims of silence would come, bringing prosperity to the village and particularly to the Wheatsheaf, managed now by the daughter of the previous landlord.

And every Mayday the skate-sailing festival was still

held, but now always on the glass at Atherton. No longer was it a race and a competition; since in the end the race of life could not be won. Instead it had become a pageant, a glass ballet, a re-enactment of the event of many years ago – a passion play performed by the four remaining villages. Tuckerton and all its folk had been glassed ten years before by a bird which destroyed itself so that the circle of annihilation exactly touched that edge of the glass where Tuckerton had stood till then.

One morning, the day before the festival, a knock sounded on Jason's door. His housekeeper, Martha Prestidge, was out shopping in the village; so Jason answered.

A boy stood there. With red hair, and freckles.

For a moment Jason did not recognize the boy. But then he saw that it was Daniel. Daniel, unchanged. Or maybe grown up a little. Maybe a year older.

'Dan . . .?'

The boy surveyed Jason bemusedly, his balding crown, his sagging girth, his now spindly legs, and the heavy stick with a stylized bird's head on which he leaned, gripping it with a liver spotted hand.

'Jay,' he said after a moment, 'I've come back.'

'Back? but . . .'

'I know what the birds are now! They *are* weapons. Missiles. Tens and hundreds of thousands of them. There's a war going on. But it's like a game as well: a board game run by machines. Machines that think. It's only been going on for a few days in their time. The missiles shunt to and fro through time to get to their destination. But they can't shunt in the time of that world, because of cause and effect. So here's where they do their shunting. In our world. The other possibility-world.'

'This is nonsense. I won't listen.'

'But you must, Jay! It can be stopped for us before it's

too late. I know how. Both sides can interfere with each other's missiles and explode them out of sight – that's here – if they can find them fast enough. But the war over there's completely out of control. There's a winning pattern to it, but this only matters to the machines any longer, and they're buried away underground. They build the birds at a huge rate with material from the Earth's crust, and launch them into other-time automatically.'

'Stop it, Dan.'

'I fell off the bird over there – but I fell into a lake, so I wasn't killed, only hurt. There are still some pockets of land left, around the Bases. They patched me up, the people there. They're finished, in another few hours of their time – though it's dozens of years to us. I brought them great hope, because it meant that all life isn't finished. Just theirs. Life can go on. What we have to do is build a machine that will stop their machines finding the slow birds over here. By making interference in the air. There are waves. Like waves of light, but you can't see them.'

'You're raving.'

'Then the birds will shunt here. But harmlessly. Without glassing us. And in a hundred years' time, or a few hundred, they'll even stop coming at all, because the winning pattern will be all worked out by then. One of the war machines will give up, because it lost the game. Oh I know it ought to be able to give up right now! But there's an element of the irrational programmed into the machines' brains too; so they don't give up too soon. When they do, everyone will be long dead there on land – and some surviving people think the war machines will start glassing the ocean floor as a final strategy before they're through. But we can build an air-wave-maker. They've locked the knowledge in my brain. It'll take us a few years to mine the right metals and tool up and provide a power source . . .' Young Daniel ran out of breath briefly. He gasped. 'They had a prototype slow bird. They sat me on it and sent me into other-time again. They managed to guide it. It emerged just ten miles from here. So I walked home.'

'Prototype? Air-waves? Power source? What are these?'

'I can tell you.'

'Those are just words. Fanciful babble. Oh for this babble of the world to still itself!'

'Just give me time, and I'll . . .'

'Time? You desire time? The mad ticking of men's minds instead of the great pure void of eternal silence? You reject acceptance? You want us to swarm forever aimlessly, deafening ourselves with our noisy chatter?'

'Look . . . I suppose you've had a long, tough life, Jay. Maybe I shouldn't have come here first.'

'Oh, but you should indeed, my impetuous fool of a brother. And I do not believe my life has been ill-spent.'

Daniel tapped his forehead. 'It's all in here. but I'd better get it down on paper. Make copies and spread it around – just in case Atherton gets glassed. Then somebody else will know how to build the transmitter. And life can go on. Over there they think maybe the human race is the only life in the whole universe. So we have a duty to go on existing. Only, the others have destroyed themselves arguing about which way to exist. But we've still got time enough. We can build ships to sail through space to the stars. I know a bit about that too. I tell you, my visit brought them real joy in their last hours, to know this was all still possible after all.'

'Oh, Dan.' And Jason groaned. Patriarch-like, he raised his staff and brought it crashing down on Daniel's skull.

He had imagined that he mightn't really notice the blood amidst Daniel's bright red hair. But he did.

The boy's body slumped in the doorway. With an effort Jason dragged it inside, then with an even greater effort up the oak stairs to the attic where Martha Prestidge hardly ever went. The corpse might begin to smell after a while, but it could be wrapped up in old blankets and such.

However, the return of his housekeeper down below distracted Jason. Leaving the body on the floor he hastened out, turning the key in the lock and pocketing it.

It had become the custom to invite selected guests back to the Babbidge house following the Mayday festivities; so Martha Prestidge would be busy all the rest of the day cleaning and cooking and setting the house to rights. As was the way of the housekeepers, she hinted that Jason would get under her feet; so off he walked down to the glass and out on to its perfect flatness to stand and meditate. Villagers and visitors, spying the lone figure out there nodded gladly. Their prophet was at peace, presiding over their lives. And over their deaths.

The skate-sailing masque, the passion play, was enacted as brightly and gracefully as ever the next day.

It was May the Third before Jason could bring himself to go up to the attic again, carrying sacking and cord. He unlocked the door.

But apart from a dark stain of dried blood the floorboards were bare. There was only the usual jumble stacked around the walls. The room was empty of any corpse. And the window was open.

So he hadn't killed Daniel after all. The boy had recovered from the blow. Wild emotions stirred in Jason, disturbing his usual composure. He stared out of the window as though he might discover the boy lying below on the cobbles. But of Daniel there was no sign. He searched around Atherton, like a haunted man, asking no questions but looking everywhere piercingly. Finding no clue, he ordered a horse and cart to take him to Edgewood. From there he travelled all around the glass, through Buckby and Hopperton; and now he asked wherever he went, 'Have you seen a boy with red hair?' The villagers told each other that Jason Babbidge had had another vision.

As well he might have, for within the year from far away news began to spread of a new teacher, with a new message. This new teacher was only a youth, but he had also ridden a slow bird – much farther than the Silent Prophet had ever ridden one.

However, it seemed that this young teacher was somewhat flawed, since he couldn't remember all the details of his message, of what he had been told to say. Sometimes he would beat his head with his fists in frustration, till it seemed that blood would flow. Yet perversely this touch of theatre appealed to some restless, troublesome streak in his audiences. They believed him because they saw his anguish, and it mirrored their own suppressed anxieties.

Jason Babbidge spoke zealously to oppose the rebellious new ideas, exhausting himself. All the philosophical beauty he had brought into the dying world seemed to hang in the balance; and reluctantly he called for a 'crusade' against the new teacher, to defend his own dream of Submission.

Two years later, he might well have wished to call his words back, for their consequence was that people were tramping across the countryside in between the zones of annihilation armed with pitchforks and billhooks, cleavers and sickles. Villages were burnt; many hundreds were massacred; and there were rapes – all of which seemed to recall an earlier nightmare of Jason's from before the time of his revelation.

In the third year of this seemingly endless skirmish between the Pacifists and the Survivalists Jason died, feeling bitter beneath his cloak of serenity; and by way of burial his body was roped to a slow bird. Loyal mourners accompanied the bird in silent procession until it vanished hours later. A short while after that, quite suddenly at the Battle of Ashton Glass, it was all over, with victory for the Survivalists led by their young red-haired champion, who it was noted bore a striking resemblance to old Jason Babbidge, so that it almost seemed as though two basic principles of existence had been at contest in the world: two aspects of the selfsame being, two faces of one man.

Fifty years after that, by which time a full third of the land was glass and the climate was worsening, the Survival College in Ashton at last invented the promised machine; and from then on slow birds continued to appear and fly and disappear as before, but now none of them exploded.

And a hundred years after that all the slow birds vanished from the Earth. Somewhere, a war was over, logically and finally.

But by then, from an Earth four-fifths of whose land surface was desert or swamp – in between necklaces of barren shining glass – the first starship would arise into orbit.

It would be called *Slow Bird*. For it would fly to the stars, slowly. Slowly in human terms; two generations it would take. But that was comparatively fast.

A second starship would follow it; called *Daniel*.

Though after that massive and exhausting effort, there would be no more starships. The remaining human race would settle down to cultivate what remained of their garden in amongst the dunes and floods and acres of glass. Whether either starship would find a new home as habitable even as the partly glassed Earth, would be merely an article of faith.

On his deathbed, eighty years of age, in Ashton College lay Daniel who had never admitted to a family name.

The room was almost indecently overcrowded, though well if warmly ventilated by a wind whipping over Ashton Glass, and bright-lit by the silvery blaze reflecting from that vitrified expanse.

The dying old man on the bed beneath a single silken sheet was like a bird himself now: shrivelled with thin bones, a beak of a nose, beady eyes and a rooster's comb of red hair on his head.

He raised a frail hand as if to summon those closest, even closer. Actually it was to touch the old wound in his skull which had begun to ache fiercely of late as though it was about to burst open or cave in, unlocking the door of memory – notwithstanding that no one now needed the key hidden there, since his Collegians had discovered it independently, given the knowledge that it existed.

Faces leaned over him: confident, dedicated faces.

'They've stopped exploding, then?' he asked, forgetfully.

'Yes, yes, years ago!' they assured him.

'And the stars – ?'

'We'll build the ships. We'll discover how.'

His hand sank back on to the sheet. 'Call one of them – '

'Yes?'

'*Daniel*. Will you?'

They promised him this.

'That way . . . my spirit . . .'

'Yes?'

'. . . will fly . . .'

'Yes?'

'. . . into the silence of space.'

This slightly puzzled the witnesses of his death: for they could not know that Daniel's last thought was that, when the day of the launching came, he and his brother might at last be reconciled.

The Width of the World

There were four of us in Dave Bartram's office at Geo-Graphics that afternoon: Dave himself, puffing his pipe, Sally-Ann from design, Maggie from marketing, and myself from the computer graphics side.

After hours of gentle gloomy rain, the sun had finally come out over Launchester. The steeply pitched slate roofs of the town outside were shimmering blue and green as though slicked with oil, while the stone of the cathedral glowed almost golden.

And I was scrapping with Maggie, as usual.

This time it was over the idea I'd had that we ought to expand the Mappamundi to include optional programmes for maps of imaginary worlds – Tolkien's Middle Earth, Donaldson's the Land, that sort of thing. I wasn't exactly winning the argument, but I had certainly managed to rile Maggie.

'For heaven's sake, we're just about to launch the Mappamundi! The thing's a surefire best seller as it is – for the whole educational market, *and* for the mums and dads. And that's because it's an *accurate* record of what the world was like in the past. Your idea would turn it into' – she searched for a suitable term of abuse – 'into a video game!'

'I'm betting that we could expand the appeal enormously.'

'No takers, Alan. Mappamundi's a serious project.'

A brief reprieve, by buzzer. Dave flicked his intercom, and we heard Dorothy sing out from Reception:

'Mr MacNamara called from Heathrow, sir. He said

not to bother you in conference, but his flight was late from New York. So he won't be at your house till about seven.' Dan MacNamara was our American marketing agent for Mappamundi; this visit mattered to us.

'Right,' said Dave. 'Call Mrs B, will you? Dinner at eight, to be on the safe side.'

In a sense, of course, Maggie was quite right. For Mappamundi – as the brochure boasted – was the ultimate teaching aid: a home computer package displaying on your own TV screen the changing map of the world from the Paleozoic through to modern times. You could zoom in on any million-square-kilometre section; that's roughly the size of France. You could overlay appropriate animated graphics which were just as good as movie footage: of dinosaurs grazing or fighting, of primitive hominids bashing flints together, of the *Niña, Pinta,* and *Santa Maria* sailing to discover America, of Napoleon marching on Moscow . . .

'Apparently a lot of other planes were late, sir.'

'Tut tut.'

I myself had been hooked on geography, as a boy, by something much more vulgar: an adventure magazine, long defunct, called *Wide World*. I still had a stack of these at home, and every once in a while I hauled them out for a nostalgic chuckle. What lurid covers! And what tall tales inside! Seventy-foot-long anacondas outracing galloping horses; six weeks alone on a raft in the shark-infested South Seas . . .

By the time I grew up, alas, the job of geography was somewhat different. It didn't involve drawing pirate charts with X marking where the sea chest lay buried.

Dave was champing impatiently at his pipe, and it seemed to have gone out.

'Well, Alan?'

'Look, if we include a stylus and digitizing tablet, and

modify the software slightly, we can even let people design their own maps – of their own imaginary worlds . . .'

'No,' said Maggie flatly.

'But, Dave, don't you think we should keep a trick up our sleeves?'

Our chairman read the auspices in the hot dottle of his pipe bowl.

'Hmm, hmm, hmm,' he said.

'I'm willing to work up a presentation in my spare time.' Oh, yes, Sarah should *love* that . . . I'd been eating and breathing Mappamundi for the best part of two years now . . .

'Spare time?' said Maggie archly. 'I trust you weren't thinking of taking a holiday right now?'

'Whatever for? They don't schedule flights to El Dorado.'

'What a weird remark.'

'There be no dragons on our maps.'

'And a good thing too!'

'We'd better wind this up,' said Dave, consulting his watch. 'Listen, Alan, your idea *might* have merits. Nothing ventured, eh? So why don't you go ahead and work up something for us to get our teeth into?'

Maggie grinned at me, conceding tactical defeat. But she would make sure, by next time, that she had her teeth sharpened.

It's a twelve-mile drive home over the moors to Ferrier Malvis. The Volvo always got me back there in just under twenty minutes, and I'd long since stopped paying much conscious heed to the business of steering, or to the sheep grazing amidst heather and bracken.

But this time, just as I was zipping along smartly past a certain ruined dry-stone barn, an alarm bell went off in my head. Because I had left GeoGraphics exactly as usual . . . and I ought to have been home already.

A glance at my watch confirmed this; twenty minutes had passed.

'The world's been stretched,' I thought ridiculously. 'It's been inflated, like a balloon. The surface looks the same, but there's farther to go.'

It didn't seem very likely.

I arrived at Ferrier Malvis fifteen minutes late, and Sarah's green Renault wasn't parked outside the house. She must be late home too, from the craft shop in Forby.

En route to the kitchen, I flipped on a Vivaldi cassette. I poured some chilled wine from the fridge, then opened my briefcase on the pine table, to work in the golden light of the westering sun.

Maybe I was heading for a nervous breakdown? Could the weird stretching of the journey home be a warning sign from my psyche – a shot across the bows?

Presently a car door thumped outside.

'Kitchen, love!'

Silver Sarah looked distraught, as though she had been combing her blond hair with her fingers.

'Hullo, Silver.'

'Haven't you been listening to the radio, Alan?'

'No, I was listening to *The Four Seasons*. Should I have been?

She darted back towards the lounge, presumably to kill the Vivaldi, but checked herself.

'Faster to tell you, my mappaholic husband! The latest planes from the States are landing up to three hours overdue at Heathrow.'

'So?'

'One of them just barely got down at Shannon, out of fuel. A jumbo from Brazil has ditched off Lisbon. It's the same all over. It took me *far* too long to drive home.'

'Oh, my God, I thought it was just me. Hell, I don't know what I thought it was!'

'Those planes aren't leaking, you know. They're using their fuel. They're still travelling at the same speed.'

'And yet there's farther to go – '

'Miles and miles farther.'

'I'll get you a drink, love.'

'Scotch. Neat.'

As I went through to the lounge for the Famous Grouse, *The Four Seasons* was just over. The tape ran on for a moment. Then click, and silence. Silver Sarah followed me.

'So how do you explain it?' She sounded accusatory – as if I had programmed untold square kilometres of blank space into the Mappamundi and these had suddenly sprung into being in the real world.

I poured a few fingers of the noble bird for both of us.

'Something must be happening to space,' I said lamely.

'Space?'

'I mean the nature of space. The universe is expanding, isn't it? So space is expanding too. And now the space between places is getting bigger into the bargain. It takes longer to get from A to B.' I laughed.

Four hours later – after several more fingers of the bird, a scratch meal and much TV-viewing – we knew that space was just the same today as it had been yesterday. The moon hadn't moved one inch farther away from Earth. Satellite data confirmed that the earth's circumference was exactly the same as usual.

Nevertheless, radar and laser fixes from orbit upon jets sent up specially showed that these aircraft certainly weren't covering the distances as measured by airspeed and fuel consumption. There was much talk that night –

to little effect – of lasers and the speed of light and trigonometry, and how photons are massless particles . . .

When we went to bed eventually, all airports around the world were closed, and all flights grounded. Apparently the 'distance effect' was still on the increase.

Next morning, when the alarm clock grabbed me out of the middle of some silly dream, the radio was repeating the same bulletin – with minor updates – every fifteen minutes.

The distance effect seemed to have stabilized overnight. Imagine a graph with a curve on it, rising gently at first, then ever more steeply. Distances of up to fifty miles were now doubled. A journey of a hundred miles was in the region of five hundred. And the distance between London and New York, say – measured by radio-wave delays – was something of the order of a hundred thousand miles. It might be as far as a million miles from England to Australia, unless the distance effect followed a bell curve, though no one was certain. The American government, in consultation with the Russians, intended to test-fire an ICBM with an instrument package in place of its warhead from Nevada across the Pacific towards Guam . . .

'Wouldn't they just?' exclaimed Silver. 'All they can think about is whether they can still fight a nuclear war! Just try flying a B-1 bomber to Russia now – '

'Or a Backfire bomber from Russia over here.'

'Which is why they're going to test a missile, of course! Because a missile leaves the atmosphere.'

'It's just to measure the extent of the phenomenon.'

'Oh, yes. Of course.'

Power transmission through the National Grid was down by some 8 per cent, due to loss over extra distances;

so consumers were being asked to be sparing in their use of power . . .

'I suppose we'd better do without toast, Silver. How about cornflakes?'

'For goodness' sake!'

'Well, we have to eat.'

'Don't you realize anything, Alan? What about fuel? Oil! Raw materials. Imported food. What price New Zealand lamb, coming from a million miles away? The ship would have to carry nothing but fuel. The crew would be old men by the time they docked.'

I worked it out in my head. 'No, actually it would take the ship about ten years. But I see what you mean.'

'I'm *glad* you do. Oh, we'll still be able to hear the news, from a hundred thousand miles away. As Japan grinds to a halt. As people die in famines that no one can reach with food aid. People *like us*, Alan dear.'

'God, we'll never see a banana again . . .' Curiously, it was this which popped into my head, rather than the wholesale demise of civilization. Or perhaps as an example of it.

'It'll be like living on Mars. And dying on Mars.'

The radio advised commuters with journeys of less than thirty miles to proceed to work normally, but allowing extra time and fuel.

'That's stupid,' said Silver. 'How long is there going to be any fuel in the filling stations?'

'Do you suggest we walk? I suppose it's possible. Twelve miles to Launchester? In the old days, some kids used to walk twelve miles to school.'

'Just what would you be going to Launchester for? Instead of, say, digging up the back lawn quickly – to plant vegetables *tout de suite?* And getting hold of some good egg-laying hens, before everyone realizes?'

'Well, for one thing Dan MacNamara's due at Geo-Graphics today.'

'What for?'

'The Mappamundi – what did you think?'

'And you're going to be able to export this TV toy a hundred thousand miles to the Land of the Free, in time for Christmas?'

'Look, we shouldn't assume this distance effect is going to continue. It sprang up in a few hours yesterday. It stabilized overnight. It could fade away just as fast. Still, I'd better phone Dave to check that Big Mac made it. Let's have orange juice rather than coffee, hmm? And it *isn't* a TV toy, Silver.'

Though, come to think of it, with my proposed extras it *could* come to resemble one . . . Maybe Maggie's taunt was on target.

Heading for the phone in my pyjamas, I lit a stick of my favourite Algerian camel dung, alias Disque Bleu; and I wondered how far away the factories of the Régie Française de Tabac were today.

Big Mac had indeed reached Dave's house – about three hours late – and Dave agreed with me about the sense of coming in to GeoGraphics. So after a rather fraught, cold breakfast I departed, Volvo-borne, towards Launchester, leaving Silver vowing that she was going to dig up the lawn all by herself and sow carrot or cabbage seed or something, if she could get hold of seed packets at the village shop in Hornton, down the road.

We had all got in to work, but it was a somewhat chastened team which met Big Mac in Dave's office. Redheaded Dan MacNamara was acting in a bluffly amiable way, though I couldn't help noticing a persistent

line of sweat along his upper lip, which he wiped away
frequently.

After a while, the sales conference ran out of steam.

'Oh, hell,' said Big Mac. 'Let's stop pretending. It's
okay for you guys. You live here.'

'And here we may very well starve, too,' said I. 'Britain
isn't self-sufficient. So my wife's busy digging up the lawn
right now, to plant cabbages . . . We've *got* to assume
that this business is going to reverse itself. And soon.'

Maggie drummed her fingers on a brochure.

'Or find some way out. Some way round the phenomenon. We're supposed to be the hotshot cartographers.
So how about *thinking* our way out of this, Alan, instead
of ignoring it?'

A challenge. Even with the whole world inflating expo-
nentially, she had managed to sharpen her teeth – as
other ladies might find time to powder their noses during
an earthquake.

'*Think* our way out of it? Maybe it *is* in the mind?
Maybe it's an illusion?' I was just talking off the top of
my head.

'If that's so,' objected Big Mac, 'and we're just imagining it, you'd get planes stalling in mid-air and cars in the
wrong gear, and all.'

'True. We've *got* to be covering extra space – but the
space has no content. It doesn't contain anything. Because
. . .' – and I searched around – 'because we can only see
the world that's here.'

We couldn't see the Wide World of childhood: the
world of El Dorado and King Solomon's Mines. Because
the map of the world was full up with roads and railways,
oil rigs and megalopoli. There was no room left for 'Here
Be Dragons' or sea serpents. So . . . what if the map of
the world had mysteriously expanded to include all of
these other things – at precisely the moment when every

last geographical detail had at last been calibrated and
computerized, including even prehistoric geography? But
no one saw anything new. People were just grossly
delayed in their travels. *Was* it possible to see something
extra, something new, in the interstices of the world?
Was it not space which had betrayed us – but vision?

No, it wasn't quite that . . .

The world was overfilled with people: people who all
shared a collective unconscious, a dream mind.

When a hive becomes too crowded with bees, the bees
know instinctively when to swarm; and away fly half of
them to find another hive. But we only had one single
hive, one world. So when the urge to swarm came, there
was no other space to fly off into . . .

'Penny for them,' demanded Maggie. 'Penny for your
thoughts.'

'Oh, I was just wondering how many disappearances
have been reported to the police. Missing persons. Dave,
you play golf with the chief constable, don't you?'

'Once in a blue moon, lad. What's that got to do with
anything?'

'Just a hunch. Would you do me a big favour, and
phone him to ask? Please. It'll only take a moment.'

In fact, it took many moments to get through, but that
was Dorothy's department. Shortly after Dave did finally
get to pose the question, he covered the mouthpiece,
giving me a peculiar look.

'There are quite a *lot* of people reported missing. He
wants to know how *we* knew. At first they thought it was
just a case of people not reaching their destinations.'

'Oh, they're reaching those, all right!'

'Getting delayed. Running out of petrol, that kind of
thing. But a lot of people have promised to phone home,

and haven't. There's no sign of them. Here, you'd better talk to him.'

I took the handset.

'One thing I *can* tell you,' I was saying to the chief constable a little later, 'is that you're going to be snowed under with missing person calls by tonight.'

'I'll bear this in mind, Mr – ?'

'Roxbury. Alan Roxbury.'

'I'll definitely bear you in mind.' He rang off unceremoniously, and I could see that Dave was embarrased by the episode.

'Would you mind going through that again, for us dummies?' asked Big Mac angrily.

'It's like this,' I said to him. 'Mind constructs reality. Our thoughts make the world – '

'Oh, in a sense!' protested Sally-Ann, with a toss of her brown curls. 'In a sort of philosophical sense. But' – and she thumped her hand down hard on Dave's desk – 'thus I refute you. Flesh and wood. Solid stuff.'

'But what if the mind really does construct reality? And the world has got too small for us. Breakfast in London, second breakfast in New York. We put a girdle round the earth in forty minutes. And every square inch is filled up solid with detail. The world has been shrinking for the last hundred years, faster and faster. Now here comes the bounce-back at last. Or rather, here's where we swarm. As soon as enough people have found the way out, distances should return to normal.'

'The way out?' echoed Maggie, incredulous.

'Into the extra spaces.'

'Obviously you're under a lot of strain, Alan. Why don't you go home and have a rest?'

'Why don't we *all* go – and look for the way out ourselves? And try to come back again? Of course, there'll be millions of exit points – and by tonight millions of people will have found these, of their own accord. The invisible boundaries. Well, we'll pinpoint one of these. We'll map it. That *was* your bright idea, wasn't it Maggie? Use our minds. Market the thing.'

I hadn't really expected that Dave would want to do anything other than feast Big Mac royally at Launchester's only *Good Food Guide* restaurant, the Sorrento, and sink a few bottles to take all our minds off the collapse (or, rather, the expansion) of the world which we had been so sure of yesterday. Well, he did – and he didn't. Or else he drank more than I noticed. For halfway through the *tagliatelle al prosciutto* he suddenly said, 'Okay, lad, we'll give it a try. Nothing ventured, eh?'

And outside, afterwards, he handed me the keys to his Jag.

'You drive, lad. Seeing as you know the way.'

'Which way?' demanded Maggie.

'Just let him drive. Spontaneously.' And Dave jammed his pipe into his mouth.

Pragmatic Sally-Ann would have nothing to do with this charade, and insisted on being dropped back at GeoGraphics; but Maggie was determined to enjoy this proof of my insanity, while Big Mac was filled with sudden wanderlust, since he was now effectively a prisoner in the Launchester area. (I suppose, similarly, one's immediate response to the threat of starvation could well be a bout of gluttony!) So off we went, and I took the most spontaneous, unconscious route I knew – which happened to be the road home to Ferrier Malvis. We kept our eyes peeled.

Some fifty minutes later I swung the Jaguar into our driveway. Silver's Renault was absent, so she must have driven the two miles (or four miles) to Hornton to buy cabbage seed. If indeed one does grow cabbages from seed . . .

And nothing at all happened. Except that the journey had taken twice as long as usual.

'You'd better all come in for a drink,' I said. 'I want to see what Sarah's done to the lawn.'

'Good job someone in the family's got their head screwed on.' Maggie couldn't resist it. 'Oh, by the way, Alan, you do realize that you'll have to drive all the way back with us?'

'Eh?'

'To pick up your own car.'

God help me . . .! 'So maybe something'll happen on the way back!' I snapped.

Maggie simply laughed.

We went inside, where I told them to help themselves to drinks, while I went through to the kitchen.

Out on the lawn a patch ten yards long by a yard wide had been stripped of its turf – the same turf which we had brought in so expensively a couple of years earlier. Sods were piled in a dirty mass on the patio. The spade was stuck in the uncovered soil, upright.

How long would this have taken her? Half an hour? Less than an hour, anyway. Whereupon Silver had decided that I could damn well finish the job. Alternatively, she had panicked about a possible rush on cabbage seed, and driven off to Hornton.

Hours ago. Well before lunch. Now it was three-thirty.

I hurried back to the lounge, where gin was glugging into glasses.

'Got any ice, Alan?'

'Fridge. I have to make a phone call.'

I found the number of the Hornton shop in Silver's own neat hand in the red book by the phone.

And Mrs What's-her-name told me that Silver had

indeed been in, buying packets of seed – about ten
o'clock in the morning. Then she had driven straight back
in the direction of Ferrier Malvis.

A distance of two miles. (Or four.) Five hours ago.

I turned to the others. 'My wife's gone missing. Sarah's
disappeared. She found one of the ways out.'

But, of course, as I realized when I returned the Jag
and passengers to Dave's personal parking space outside
GeoGraphics, the reason why *we* couldn't find any of
these exit points was that we were looking for them. We
were searching for one in full consciousness of what they
were. We *knew*. But it was the unconscious of the world
which was at work . . .

Recovering the Volvo, I drove homeward recklessly,
pushing my registered speed higher and higher so that (as
I imagined) I might take all the longer over the journey.
All too soon, it seemed to me, I arrived home.

Fixing myself a stiff shot of the bird – as a gesture
towards unconsciousness – I switched on the TV and
watched for an hour.

There were missing-persons reports galore by now. An
epidemic of them. A veritable Hamelin – with hundreds of
thousands of people in these British Isles alone somehow
following this Pied Piper of the extra spaces, away into
somewhere else. A lot of people had only needed to go
for a walk around the corner. Or potter down to the
bottom of the garden . . .

Drunk, I took the Volvo out several times that evening
to race towards Hornton and back again. But, drunk as I
was, I still knew exactly what I was doing.

Finally I slept alone, crying maudlin tears into the
pillow for a little while, before the bird put me soddenly
to sleep . . .

* * *

. . . to wake at dawn, sweaty with the alcohol, to the
bright carillon of other birds; finches, blackbirds,
thrushes; and to thumb the radio on.

'. . . clear signs that the distance effect has been growing steadily less during the past few hours,' was what I
heard.

'Silver!' I cried – though there was no one to hear me.

Hauling my clothes and shoes on, I raced downstairs
unwashed and uncombed. A couple of minutes later, and
I was on the road driving hell for leather towards the
sharp bends leading up on to the moors.

For the next three hours I drove back and forth
between Ferrier Malvis and Launchester, hearing the car
radio tell me with increasing optimism that the space
anomaly (for such it was being renamed) really was
receding as rapidly and inexplicably as it had first arisen.

Silver! Silver! *Where?*

I sped with all the mad possession of the last old rat
out of Hamelin – and it was I who was left behind while
the anomaly closed up seamlessly.

Eventually the Volvo ran out of fuel, by the same
tumbled drystone barn. I started to walk home. Then I
began to run as fast as I could, hoping that by exhausting
my body I might entrance myself, and so gain entrance
still. Soon, with a terrible stitch in my side, I had to drop
back to walking pace. The pain felt rather like a broken
heart.

We are decimated, at the very least. Perhaps one tenth of
the human race disappeared during the anomaly, overall.
The effect was more severe in highly populated areas.
Such as Britain.

Now, six months later, a sort of emotional anaesthesia
seems to affect our memories of that time – an inability,
in retrospect, to focus clearly on what happened, as great

as that of the Australian aborigines who reputedly paid no attention whatever to Captain Cook's proud sailing ship when it first anchored off their shores, for the simple reason that there was nothing in their previous experience as huge as it. Like animals we mourned our losses: lowing piteously for a few days, then walking on and forgetting. And at the same time, we're all rather glad to see each other – we who remain. We greet each other joyfully.

Not I, though. Because I failed – by knowing.

The jets fly from Heathrow to New York in exactly the same time as ever they did before. Yet when I drive back from Launchester over the moors, I know that Silver is somewhere out there – except that I can't see her or reach her. She's somewhere in the extra spaces.

Oh, Silver!

Maybe in another ten years' time – or twenty – when the population again reaches swarming density, the seams will open up again, and there'll be a second exodus . . .

Today I resigned from GeoGraphics. A foolish mistake, said Dave – just at the moment when Mappamundi is really taking off, worldwide, selling in the millions beyond our wildest hopes. It seems that something has triggered, deeply, people's interest in cartography . . . Hearing of my decision, Maggie brought her teeth together in a satisfied, crocodilian snap. I didn't care.

Tomorrow I shall burn all my old copies of *Wide World Magazine,* out on the strip of soil which Silver cleared. The stainless steel spade still stands upright there, just as she left it – a good test of the manufacturer's boast about weather resistance. I couldn't bear to touch the spade till now. But tomorrow I will, once all the tales of El Dorado and the poison darts of pygmies in the Belgian Congo have been burned. However hard the ground is this winter, I'll dig the ashes in.

I'm going to take over Silver's old job at the craft shop

in Forby. I'll forget about running a Volvo and smoking Disque Bleu and drinking the juice of the bird. In the evenings, come the spring, I'll dig up the rest of the lawn and turn the whole garden over to vegetables, to feed myself cheaply. The hens I'll buy should be good enough company for me.

And I'll wait, till the world widens out again. Then I'll be the first person to walk around the corner. Or to stroll down to the bottom of the garden.

White Socks

Harry and Helen Sharp had been married for a year; this African nation had been independent for two years. Back home Harry would have been an ordinary accountant, whereas here he was an expert, for the Ministry of Finance. Both he and Helen were liberal-minded, which was why they had come to work in black Africa; and Harry would have been the first to admit that their present conditions – house in the Oyster Bay area, interest-free loan for a Volkswagen beetle – were artificially exalted. No expert he, except by contrast with the locals.

One thing which they *were* expert on after twelve months, however, was marriage; which was why the Ismaili wedding reception they'd attended the other day had filled them with amusement and wry sympathy; and still did, as they drove up country.

The bride, Gulzar, had been a secretary at the Ministry; Harry had been kind to her, friendly, interested. The lives of these Asians in a black African country struck him as poignant, like those of an endangered species; and almost mysterious. So the invitation to the reception had given them both fascinating insights. Which they still mulled over, as Harry drove along.

'Did you see all that glitter on the bridal bed?' sighed Helen. (For all the guests had been invited upstairs to inspect the scene of the forthcoming defloration.) 'It was the same glassy grit they stick on Christmas cards to make them sparkle. Have you ever caught a speck under your fingernail? Imagine *that* sprinkled all over the sheets on *our* wedding night!'

'It all comes from weighing the Aga Khan in diamonds,' said Harry. 'Ismailis have a thing about glitter – and sweet stuff. What intrigued me was the bowl of chocolate and fudge by the bedside to give them strength.'

'The walls were only plywood, thin as can be. Gulzar was as white as a sheet, poor girl.'

'Except for her hands!'

True enough. Curly tattoo-like chocolate coloured patterns had been painted on the bride's hands for good luck, so that she had looked as though she was suffering from some skin disease. Etiquette forbade Gulzar to raise those decorated hands to her mouth. Consequently all the old women of her own family and her husband's in turn had forcefed her with chunks of wedding cake; crumbs had dribbled down Gulzar's white bridal dress. And as they passed by, one by one, the old fat women had each pressed a banknote into Gulzar's lucky hands till, by the end of it all, the bride had seemed to be clutching a huge crumpled napkin which she wasn't allowed to use to clear the crumbs away.

'Did you notice how silent the whole thing was?' asked Harry. 'No music or speeches. Blank faces, silence. I wonder how much Gulzar knew about sex?'

They both smiled with complicity.

The windows of the VW were wound down to ventilate the car, in the heat. Already they had covered a hundred miles of paved road, which was bound to end soon. The blacktop strip stretched ahead in an almost unwavering straight line through the bush, merely rising and falling with the lie of the land. Branching euphorbias rose as high as medium-sized trees. An occasional lone baobab was a giant white squid standing to attention. Other trees dangled long phallic gourds from their fingertips. Here and there narrow foot-tracks cross-hatched the wild bush, signs of hidden smallholdings – or a black-shrouded woman might be standing in shade balancing a great bundle of wood on her head; or else some baskets of charcoal might be placed by the roadside for collection. Otherwise at first glance who lived here; or could live here? By contrast with the tame green coastal wilderness, here was a vast barrenness. There seemed to be no human presence; though there was. It simply took a while to register it.

The road itself carried many oil trucks, some of which were old and rickety, stacked high with drums; others were new Italian models with fat rubber slugs of oil squatting on their backs. Already on their journey the VW had smoothly overhauled ten or twelve such, not to mention several wrecks, one completely upside-down and still leaking from burst drums. For the truckers of the oil-run continued driving all night long.

Presently mountains heaved into the sky, to the south-west.

'The Ulugurus,' said Helen.

A few weeks earlier they had gone to the cinema in town. In the bar over beers, with a fan clacking slowly overhead, they had talked to a Maltese prospector while they waited for the show to start. Helen had told him how she and Harry were planning a one-night safari to the Mikumi game reserve; every journey, no matter how slight or modest, was a 'safari'. He in turn had confided sourly that the mountains they would pass en route were full of lithium, solid walls of lithium; but since a South African company held the mining rights and no profits could be sent to South Africa, those mountains couldn't be mined.

'Uluguru: like the sound of the wind moaning through the peaks,' she added.

Foothills, sweeping gently down towards the road, were clad in sisal: an estate cutting a swathe through the bush. The monotonous rows of green spikes, in red earth, were serviced by a rusty narrow-gauge railway line.

Soon they passed a rest-halt for oil truckers: a lone mud hut, the thatch waterproofed with rusty drum lids. A few trucks were pulled up outside. The drivers stood around drinking beer out of old jam tins fitted with wooden handles.

A few miles further on, they overhauled a raggy man running along the road. He ran frantically, leaping and jerking, heading along the tarmac from nowhere to nowhere. He didn't appear to hear the car engine till the VW was passing him; then as they did pass he leapt into the ditch, and back out again, waving crazily after them, his arms semaphoring.

What did the man want? Was his child dying? Should they stop? They'd been advised not to stop, by the prospector. They had felt strong liberal qualms about such advice, but now that the situation presented itself, they heeded him. However, Harry and Helen said nothing to each other about the man; not at the time. Instead they carried on discussing the Ismaili wedding with a bitter humour. In any case, they couldn't have asked the man what he wanted; their Kiswahili wasn't adequate. And an oil truck would be along soon, driven by one of his own people.

Then the tarmac ended; quite suddenly, as though funds had run out unexpectedly. Or as though here was an invisible frontier, between dry wilderness with a few people dwelling in it, and the same with only wild animals present. Ahead the road ran straight as ever, but now it was red and rutted. Red dust was billowing up from an oil truck further on, blotting out the road in a sandstorm of grit.

Another oil truck barrelled through the clouds of dirt, going their way, its headlamps full on even in the middle of the afternoon. That vehicle also dragged a storm of sand and pebbles behind it. Harry slowed down. He couldn't see ahead now. Hastily they wound the windows up, and stifled.

'That fellow back there . . .' He spoke as though their loss of momentum had put them within reach of some form of retribution. 'What do you suppose he wanted?'

'Which fellow?'

'That strange fellow running along the road like a madman, kicking his legs in the air, waving his arms about . . .'

'He wanted a lift, I suppose.'

'I mean, was it something serious? People don't just run, not in this heat.'

'Well *he* was just running.'

'He did wave at us, didn't he?'

'No, I don't really think so. He was taken by surprise. Remember how he jumped off the road? He was waving his arms like that to keep his balance.'

'I watched him in the mirror. He carried on running.'

'Ooh this dust . . . Can't you get past?'

'Too risky.' Harry had to squirt and sweep the windshield with the wipers every minute or so; he wondered how long the water would hold out.

Dry grass by the road was red. Trees were dusted with red powder: the storm-drift from countless trucks. And a red giraffe flickered among the trees, twitching its hairy ears.

'Giraffe, see!'

'Where?'

'You've missed it.'

'You've imagined it.'

'No, it was there among those trees. It ran off.'

But not all wild animals were dismayed by the rattle
and stink of trucks. Soon the oil slug ahead pulled up.
Harry coasted the VW past, and there were elephants on
the road a hundred yards further on. He braked. In the
mirror he noticed the African truck driver high in his cab
sit back and light a cigarette. *He* didn't intend to bully
this elephant family with his heavy vehicle. Easy to see
why. Some other driver had done so in the past, and the
baby of the group was hobbling with one of its hind legs
bent double and the bare bone shafting through the hide.
Mindful of the cause, the bull lashed the road with his
trunk, scooping up spouts of dust and stones, squinting at
the vehicles malevolently. Harry engaged reverse and
backed up a few yards.

'Don't switch off.'

'No.'

On the far side of the group another oil slug halted and
doused its lights. And the road stretched off into the
distance, visibly at peace, with only a crippled baby
elephant and the moody bull and a dusty black slug on
wheels watching it silently . . .

'Still, I'd rather be an Ismaili than a Hindu when it
comes to dying,' said Harry, eyeing the bull elephant
nervously. 'That grisly barbecue of a crematorium by the
beach! The iron bars black with smoke, that greasy pile
of ashes underneath . . .'

'I like Ismailis. They're adaptable.'

'They're soft,' he said. 'Soft as marshmallows. It's too
easy to bully them.'

While they were waiting, they wound the windows
down. Hardly had they done so, than fierce flies were
clustering at their feet like a cloud of devils or Furies.
The flies bit right through their socks. They had to tear
them loose one by one. However, the bull soon moved
off the road and they were able to drive on, this time

ahead of the oil truck. Once the VW was in motion, with air whipping through, all the flies fled back to pester animals instead.

Mikumi camp was a half mile away from the main road, and once they were there the noise of the oil trucks using the route was reduced to an insect hum. Far from acting as an irritant to spoil the sense of peace, the occasional passage of trucks only seemed to exaggerate the stillness out in the real raw bush, where the camp was. Otherwise after a while this stillness might have gone unnoticed. By being punctuated, it became a rapt presence, of silence.

The camp's Land Rover was out in the park spotting game, which was easier to find at dusk and dawn, when the animals used the few waterholes. A couple of Peugeots, another VW and a Mercedes were parked beneath leafless barren trees outside of widely separated green tents – to which a white-aproned Boy, perhaps thirty years of age, was ferrying canvas buckets of water over the beaten brown earth.

There was no boundary line between camp and park. For that matter there was no sign of a 'park'. There was only a level plain of beaten earth with some tiny black dots moving about in the distance, and beyond those a long low belt of trees, and behind the trees, hills where sickles of fire were burning off dead straw. Smoke clouds hung over several areas, though from the look of the ground it was a wonder what there was to burn. Out of that barren emptiness flowed the silence, the everlasting lull, within which presumably secret little acts of violence occurred: the bites of flies, the breaking of gazelle necks by clawed paws . . .

The hunter's wife was German: an ample middle-aged Frau in a ballooning cotton dress. She was sitting in the largest marquee writing out a grocery list.

She offered Harry and Helen chilled imported German beer, though the white-aproned Boy had to be summoned to take the bottles from the paraffin refrigerator beside her, and uncap them.

For a few minutes the German woman talked about Lushoto, two hundred miles to the north, where it was just like the Austrian Tyrol with cows wearing clanking bells around their necks amid grassy meadows and cool fir-clad slopes, and where some of the old Africans only spoke Kiswahili and German, no English. She reminisced sadly about German East Africa, though she couldn't have known that time personally, and about cowbells in the misty mornings, gazing round her as she did so at the flat beaten plain, the desiccated trees, the burning hills. Then, having adequately hosted Harry and Helen in her opinion, she busied herself in her grocery list again.

'Maybe Gulzar went to Lushoto for her honeymoon,' speculated Helen.

'What on earth for?'

'And maybe they spent the whole time in that plywood cell amidst the glitter eating candy bars!'

A middle-aged Asian in shorts walked into the marquee and wanted a beer too; they had heard another car arrive a while before.

'Ech, back again, Mr Desai?' sighed the German Frau.

'As you say,' he replied affably, sitting himself in a canvas seat across from Harry. As he settled, a grey testicle bulged out of his shorts, lolling in shadow against the top of a brown leg. Somehow it looked a tired testicle.

'Every weekend I come here,' he told Harry and Helen, 'for photography.' His eyes gleamed and moved rapidly. He had large hands with prominent veins; a swollen vein also ran across his forehead, from which the hair was thinning away. 'Most of all I want to photograph leopard. I have all the others. Elephant and rhino and buffalo.

Lions: I have lions making love. I'd like to show you
those pictures. But leopard is what I want most. You see
leopard in your headlights at night but he runs away so
fast you don't have time to take a picture. Have a beer
with me, will you? It's a long time yet till your dinner.
Go on – go on! I come here so often, it's my second
home. Isn't that right, Mrs Boll?'

At the sound of her name the German woman looked
up from her list and stared vaguely at the Asian as though
she didn't recognize him in the fast-failing light.

'I said I come here so often it's my second home, Mrs
Boll.'

'Mr Desai is very enthusiastic about wild life,' said Mrs
Boll in a bored voice.

Since a half-litre bottle of German beer out here in the
bush cost five shillings fifty, Harry accepted the offer.

With the rapid onset of dusk, Desai's errant testicle
had retired into darkness. Paraffin lamps were lit by the
Boy, and hung up hissing. However, the world hadn't yet
closed in to the circle of light in the camp. The fires on
the hill slopes grew brighter. A half-moon hung hazily in
the smoke pall raised by the bush fires, cupped like a
crude yellow bowl, its flat rim parallel with the hilltops.

'I bring all my family with me,' said Desai. 'My wife
and my children, and this time my uncle and his wife too.
We bring our own food with us and heat it up in the tent.
I don't like German meals. Have you seen any game
yet?'

'Only a crippled baby elephant, and a bull,' said Helen.

'And a giraffe,' Harry added.

'A camouflaged giraffe. How many children have you,
Mr Desai?'

'Four children. Ages six, seven, eight and ten. One
boy and three girls,' he reeled off. 'You must see them.

They are pretty children. My wife would like you to see them.'

They chatted. Harry said that he worked for the Ministry of Finance, then joked – since Desai responded that he was an importer – that probably Mr Desai knew more about finance.

And how did Mr and Mrs Sharp like Africa? enquired the Asian. To this, the answer just had to be enthusiastic – though maybe Desai himself despised Africans, the wild life excluded . . .

When Desai invited Harry and Helen to share curry with him and family, Harry didn't refuse. Harry wanted to see those pictures of lions making love. Helen wanted to see Desai's pretty children, and to meet his wife. Besides, in the interests of economy they hadn't been planning to eat the Frau's dinner at ten shillings per head; they had brought sandwiches and boiled eggs.

What struck Harry immediately about Desai's tent was the smell. It wasn't a *smelly* smell, a stink, oh no. This was a heady, sense-assaulting odour compounded of curry and what Harry presumed must be recently burnt joss sticks.

'Do you burn incense?' Harry asked.

Desai flashed a quick smile. 'Later, I'll tell you later.'

The four children stared at their visitors with large round black eyes, and were silent. The girls were wearing thin cotton slips, which no doubt they would soon be going to bed in. Their mahogany legs were as thin as sticks; dingy ribbons tied their long black pigtails. The boy, who was the eldest, wore white shorts. He had the same thin brown legs and greasy black hair as the girls.

The two women in the tent greeted Harry and Helen with smiles, which soon faded away. Desai's wife looked surprisingly young, small and slender. Desai's aunt, on the other hand, was a fat severe-looking woman of about fifty. Her tall thin husband asked Harry a few questions, then simply sat looking. As soon as the women began dishing out the rice and curry, the children started to chatter to each other in Kutchi.

When Desai sat on the bed opposite Harry and Helen to eat his curry, his wayward testicle squeezed to the fore again.

After the meal the four children were packed off to bed unceremoniously in the rear portion of the tent. Desai fetched a box of colour slides, which he handed to Harry. The only way to view the slides was to hold them up to the paraffin lamp; thus the pictures were little more than confusing blotches. Harry felt light-headed, besides, and dropped several plastic images of what might have been copulating lions. Whilst he and Helen were doing their best to make these out, Desai and his Uncle popped large triangular folds of dull green leaf into their mouths, wads of leaf about as large as could be popped into a mouth and still leave space to chew.

'Pan,' explained Desai. 'You want some? Ha ha, very hot! Only we Indians can eat it.' But he didn't offer any, to test their courage. 'How do you like my exposures, eh? Yes, they're not bad, but I need leopard now. Tonight, I'll take the Peugeot out and look for him. I'll dazzle him in my headlights and take pictures of him with big frightful eyes . . . No, you can't eat Pan, my friends, but I'll tell you what: you can smoke some bhang with us.'

So it was Indian hemp, marijuana, not Indian incense which accounted for the smell pervading the tent . . .

Desai unscrewed a film cassette and offered round the dry home-made cigarettes packed inside.

* * *

After a while Desai switched on a portable radio. The nine o'clock news was just beginning, but Harry found the announcer's sentences hard to follow. Each separate word triggered a cartoon picture for him: an image caricaturing what the word suggested, with a speech bubble above containing the word itself written out. This parody vision was superimposed on the wall of the tent as on a screen. Cartoon images succeeded each other so swiftly that he couldn't seize hold of a single one of them.

So this, he thought, is the true quality of my imagination. It's a strip cartoon, a farcical helter skelter. For a while this seemed to be a profound and unsettling discovery.

It was as though he was hypnotized not to understand the whole message – yet in another part of his head he could follow the news perfectly well. A question of attention, therefore! He was finding it hard to pay attention. The paraffin lamp was hissing brightly. He had an erection from seeing Desai's daughters lying in their flimsy slips on top of those camp beds crowded at the rear; lying on, not in, because it was so hot. A forest of brown matchstick legs and arms teased his eyes, though he tried not to look.

The news seemed to be lasting an inordinately long time. What was happening in the world? The news must be vitally important to bother relaying it all the way to the middle of nowhere for their special benefit. Harry imagined the radio waves passing through a grazing rhino en route, printing cartoon pictures like X-rays on its huffer-puffer lungs . . .

If only he could just sit happily glazed like Desai, an idol among his incense, enjoying his own confusion! Harry was no more experiencing visions of the truth than Desai's slides of lions copulating were other than jumbled blurs . . .

'Leopard,' announced Desai, as though reading Harry's thoughts. 'Let's go and find leopard. It's time.' He rose.

'But you can't drive around in the dark when you've just been . . .' Helen tailed off, lost in the maze of her own words.

'You'll be safe with me, Madam. You said we would go out and look for leopard. That was the agreement. Are you trying to back out? You'll make me an angry man.'

'Don't go,' Helen whispered.

Harry could see the sense in her caution, but on the other hand there was a perfectly simple way out. It was night; their own tent was some way off.

'We'll go to our tent first,' Harry told Desai. He spoke in a manner which left no doubt. 'And when we're there,' he muttered to Helen, 'we'll see . . .'

Harry helped his wife up. 'Many thanks for the meal!' he called to the two Asian women. From the back of the tent, where they had both retired, Desai's wife and aunt smiled and nodded.

'Isn't your uncle coming?' asked Harry.

The gaunt man made a negative gesture, spreading his hands flat on the bed, two branches of grey veins.

Outside, it was pitch black. The moon had disappeared. The fires in the hills had either moved nearer, or else new fires had sprung up on the plain, though this didn't make the darkness any less dark. Drums were throbbing in the night, somewhere. Or perhaps this was the beat of Harry's own blood?

Helen was very reluctant to follow Harry into the black depths of the Peugeot.

'What's the matter with English Madam?' demanded Desai. 'Your gentleman's in the car!'

'We'd rather walk, thanks.'

'You're joking! What about the wild animals?'

'I'm sure they won't come into the camp.'

'Won't come into the camp! Last month a woman like you went to the toilet in the middle of the night and met a lion. My friend the German hunter had to chase him away with fireworks. So don't insult me.'

'We'd rather walk to clear our heads. It was so stuffy . . .'

'What's this *stuffy*?'

'Harry, please get out of the car and we'll walk.'

'Helen, *please*,' came her husband's voice. 'We're just going to our tent in his car, don't you understand?'

'Damn fool woman, she annoys me,' swore Desai. 'What's stuffy? You English come into our homes, then when you're bored with looking at us . . . But you aren't going to be bored. We're going on a leopard hunt!'

'Get in, will you!' Harry hissed from the front seat.

Helen did so, clambering into the back.

As soon as Desai had switched the engine on, he leaned over swiftly and locked Helen's door. While she was fumbling to try to unlock it and failing to find the catch in the dark, the Peugeot took off with a squeal of tyres. During the journey to their tent – where they were indeed heading, she was relieved to see – Desai alternately stamped on the accelerator and braked abruptly, shouting something over his shoulder about 'drifts'. Helen couldn't see any such thing and jarred her head against the window trying to. This bump on her brow, and the seesaw motion of her body as the car slowed and leapt ahead and slowed unpredictably, stopped her from solving the riddle of the lock.

'Have you ever slept with native girls, Mister Harry?' enquired Desai conversationally. 'No, of course you haven't. They're filth. We Asians like white skin. Stupid Europeans, lying on beaches burning yourselves black!'

By now their own VW was framed by the headlights; and there stood the tent next to it. This time Desai braked as though he had spotted a crevasse opening up in front of his Peugeot. Stretching over, he flipped the passenger door open and fairly bundled Harry out. Before Helen knew what was happening the Peugeot sped off again, throwing her back against the upholstery. The open door where Harry had sat swung wildly to and fro as Desai raced the car onwards through the scanty bush, swerving to avoid trees and termite mounds.

'Now you won't be bored, Madam!' The driver laughed. 'Desai's little joke, this.'

'I want to go back now,' she cried in anger. She tried to suppress the panic of her body, uncertain how far Desai intended to carry his joke; or whether he might not simply be driving her round in a big circle back to their tent, to frighten her into making a fool of herself.

'Take me back now,' she said sternly.

'Soon, soon, Madam. Don't panic yourself.'

The headlight beams bounced across termite heaps, thick pencils of hardest stone; across great bovine skulls with horns; across burnt treetrunks – none of which Desai hit, by a miracle. Perhaps he had driven like this many times, practising? If she did solve the door lock and leap out, she would probably break a leg.

'First we're going to find leopard. Then I'll take you back to your fine husband, Madam.'

Ahead there was fire. A licking wall of red flames. The flames weren't very high nor were they moving fast, though a sudden wind could whip them up. Then they would race away through the bush like a pack of athletes in red shirts. The fire wound through the bush in a snaking line, grazing on the straw, leaving a smoking black desert behind. Such a long line of fire! Desai steered deliberately close to the flames as if daring them to singe his tyres. The mad jaws of the flames crackled audibly as they ate the land.

Abruptly Helen clutched over Desai's shoulder for the steering wheel, though she couldn't say what use there would be in catching hold of it, or wrenching it to left or right. Desai imprisoned her wrists in one big brown hand. Steering seesaw with his free hand he pulled Helen forward across the seat where Harry had been sitting.

'Don't touch me!' she cried.

Desai laughed in her face. 'I know! I know what you're thinking.'

'I'm not thinking that! Take me back!'

'You're not thinking what, Madam? Er, *stuffy* means dirty, doesn't it, kind of dirty?'

'It doesn't. You're wrong.'

'So you say. But let's see a leopard, shall we?' He released her, and she drew back. 'That's all I want to show you, then back we go, deliver you safe to your husband, eh?'

During this exchange, Desai had let the car wander. All of a sudden the fire was directly ahead: a narrow flower border crowded with red roses curving to right and left. Instead of braking or trying to swerve, Desai gunned the engine.

'Now sit still, Madam Helen, or your goose'll be cooked!'

Desai raced the Peugeot straight through the fire and braked sharply, upwind of the flames. Now the route back to the camp was blocked by a low wall of fire which only a very foolhardy woman wearing a light cotton dress would dream of skipping over. Desai switched off, though he left the headlights on. Pocketing the keys he jumped out and walked once around the Peugeot to inspect it. He held his hand down to the still-smoking earth to see how hot it was. Satisfied, he stuck his head through the driver's window. Helen had huddled into the rear of the car.

'I'm not such a fool, Madam Helen. I don't think I will *touch* you. Even my friend the German would be upset if I did such a foolish thing. But we won't see leopard here with this fire about, so I shall just take your picture a few times before we head back to your husband. In the nude, eh? I'll take your photograph with no clothes on, then I'll take you back. But I'll not take you back until.'

'If that's your idea, we can sit here till dawn.'

'No, that isn't my idea, Madam. My idea is that if you don't pose for my picture you can walk back yourself. No harm in pictures, Madam Helen.'

'Stop calling me by that stupid name!'

'No one knows anything about these pictures except you and me, Madam Helen. And I can call you what I like. Why not slap my face? Ah, but you'd have to touch me then! And I might touch *you.*'

'I'll report this to the police. I will!'

'Have you tried reporting anything to the police? They have such odd ways of looking at things. They mightn't be able to see any crime here, but they might think it was a crime for a government servant like your husband to be smoking bhang when he should be drawing up the budget. That's the way their brains work. Twenty-four hours' notice! Pack your bags and get out! Take my word for it, they have simple minds.'

And Desai lit a cigarette. He puffed it through cupped hands. His lips didn't touch the cigarette; they only touched his brown stained hand. With the cigarette held thus at right angles to his mouth, he sucked smoke out of his fist like a conjuror . . .

Desai considered Helen, in the headlight beams. Though he had insisted she remove her white socks along with

everything else, he had let her step back into her sandals.
After all, the soles of her feet weren't those of an African
woman! They weren't horny pads impervious to thorns;
and he mustn't injure Helen, not physically.

He examined her, naked in the hot burnt night, through
his viewfinder. An auburn head of hair, cut short, haloed
an oval face with startled, shamed eyes. Mascara like
brown tears rimmed the lids. Her nose was small, her
chin childishly dimpled. She shaved her armpits, but not
her crotch. Her flesh was amber from visits to the beach,
though albino bands cut across her bosom and her loins
thanks to a bikini; this made her breasts seem larger and
rather shapeless as though they spread out around her
whole chest . . .

He frowned. 'Not there! Away from the car! Nearer to
the fire. I have flashbulbs.'

'Have you?'

He motioned her impatiently; and she trod awkwardly
towards the crackling line of flames. Odd, he thought,
how ungainly her stride became when she was reduced to
bare essentials.

'You don't walk very gracefully, Madam!'

'Don't I? What a pity.'

'You couldn't carry a bundle of firewood on your head.
But never mind! Stand there. Touch your toes then throw
your arms right up in the air, high and wide.'

'I didn't say I'd do tricks for you.'

'Oh come on, Madam. I want good photos!'

The first flashbulb popped off, blinding Helen with white
light. Then another, and a third. The radiance dazzled
her. Glowing after-images cavorted.

Suddenly, right in front of her, a scream tore the
silence. A crashing, a growling violence! Then another
piercing, deafening cry of agony, which bubbled away

like sea-foam into sand. She staggered, though nothing
had touched her except the noise.

Through the fading auras of exploding stars, picked
out faintly by the flames behind and the backwash from
the car's headlights, Helen saw Desai's body lying
crumpled and torn on the black soil – and a great spotted
cat astride him, shaking its head from side to side,
thrashing its tail like a rope. Impossible! Impossible! No
wild animal would ever rush in the direction of flames
and flashbulbs!

She froze. She blinked frantically, to see.

A man straightened up from the corpse: an African
man dressed in ragged trousers and a shirt so torn that it
had become a waistcoat. She thought that the man's feet
were thickly caked with soot and cinders till she realized
that he was wearing sandals cut from old tyre rubber.
The man's right arm hung down as though he was gripping
a panga in his hand, but in fact he was holding nothing;
certainly no long blood-soaked blade. Yet Desai's body
looked badly mauled.

The man approached her. She covered her crotch with
both hands, as nonchalantly as she could. He stepped
right up to her. She smelt sweet strong body odour. His
eyes had milky webs inside them like strings of burst
boiled egg in water.

'Who are you?' Her voice was feeble. '*U nani?*'

'We almost met earlier today, *Memsahib*. I am *chui*,
the leopard.'

'We almost met? What do you mean?'

'I was running along the road. Now I have caught up
with you.'

'What?' she gasped.

'*Hapo zamani palikuwa na mtu, Memsahib . . .*' It was
the traditional way a tale began. He continued in English.
'Long ago there was a man, who was knocked down on

that road by a driver who did not stop. So I lay there, hurt, and a leopard found me. And ate me. So I became the leopard. Now no one can catch me when I run. But I was always good at running. *Memsahib*. I won the rickshaw races quite often.'

'Rickshaw races?'

'Oh yes. In the old days, which are not so long ago, the white *Bwanas* used to get drunk, and when they got drunk they would spill out of the bar of the New Africa Hotel to organize the Great Rickshaw Race – from the New Africa all the way along the harbour front to the railway station then back again. The native who could pull the hardest and run the fastest would win five shillings – a little fortune!'

'Oh my God . . . This is madness.'

'Madness? Not so. Madness is having your soul caught in a cage. That man was catching your soul.'

'By taking my picture? No, that's nonsense. Why, even the Masai sell you the right to take their photo for a shilling or two. They don't mind.'

'Yes! With your nakedness pictured in his collection, he would always have owned you.'

'Maybe just a little bit . . . till I left the country.'

'Always! He would have been gloating over you constantly, showing you to his friends. You would have felt your soul touched in England or America.'

'What are you? Are you human?'

'I told you, I am *chui*.'

'And it was really you we passed running along the road? It must have been – or how else could you have known? But we didn't stop. So why did you . . .?'

'Why did I kill this man for you?'

'It's out of proportion. He has a family. It's horrible. Is he truly dead?'

'His veins and nerves are torn by my filthy claws. His

throat is bitten through. This way, *Memsahib,* I have caught your soul, not him. Wherever you go to in the world, I can always find you.'

'All because we didn't stop. That's out of proportion too.'

'It was a sign to me, of a million other things.'

'If we *had* stopped . . .'

'Ah, but you didn't! You would never wish to stop. But you wished that this man's heart would stop and he would fall down dead. All to save your shame. Your white spotless pride. White as the excreta of diseased dogs.'

'What do you want? What should I do?'

'Clean yourself. You're unclean. You have pissed yourself. Your urine has run down your legs.'

Helen realized that this was true. 'You're *worse* than him,' she shouted. 'Much much worse.'

He laughed. 'Why did you ever come to this country? That's what you're thinking now. And I say: why indeed?'

'To help. I came to help.'

'No. You came to *use.* You use so many things: cars, refrigerators, electricity, oil, roads, gin, whisky. You need them all. And you use so many people. By coming here, you use Africa. Then home you go again with the spoils: the pictures, the carvings, the zebra skin drums, the bonus and the happy memories of servants. And you bind us to you also, with your things: your used clothes, your used money, your trash.' He leaned even closer. 'One day, *Memsahib,* all your things will *burn*, just as the grass burns here. But nothing new will sprout. Your land and your air and your water will be poison. I see it! You will be burnt one day, along with England and America. But I have caught your soul. So you will come back here to the womb. I shall make you be born, as a little shy dik-dik or a zebra foal. Then I will hunt you. You will

remember nothing but that I will always hunt you till I
catch you – and eat you. Then your flesh will repay what
you have taken from us. Just wait for the fire that comes,
Memsahib!'

Helen fainted.

When she roused, the African had gone. Her body was
hot and sooty from lying where she had sprawled. Her
legs were sticky where she had wet them. She scrambled
up. The car headlights still glared. The line of fire hadn't
moved far. Desai's body lay brokenly, his camera nearby.

Nerving herself, she darted close to him and seized the
camera. The film inside! She tried to release it but the
camera was unfamiliar. Besides, she realized that she was
smearing ashen fingerprints all over. So she ran back to
the line of flames, braving the heat as closely as she
dared, and tossed the camera where it would burn, be
fused, disfigured. Then she walked back to the Peugeot,
fumbled for her underclothes and dress, put them on.

There was no key in the ignition. No: it would be in
the dead man's pocket. She hesitated. She couldn't bear
to go back and touch him. Anyway, she mustn't take his
car.

She walked away at random through the night. After a
while, off to her right, she heard a throaty growl. Hastily
she changed direction. But she mustn't run; she mustn't
run.

A softer growl came from her left . . . correcting her.

As she walked through the blackness, the faint pat of
padding paws accompanied her.

She couldn't understand why the camp was so dark and
silent when she reached it. Surely that German hunter
should be out searching? Surely the Asians' tent ought to
show a light? Surely *Harry* . . .?

She made her way to their tent, with the VW parked beside it.

The flap was unzipped.

'Harry? Harry?'

'Eh?' Sudden commotion in the darkness inside. A flashlight snapped on, dazzling her. Quickly this was redirected towards the paraffin lamp, which Harry lit fumblingly.

'Are you all right?' he asked. 'Helen, are you all right?'

'What are you doing?' she demanded. 'Why didn't you – ?'

'Me? I passed out . . . It was the bhang.' He spoke falteringly, and groaned faintly – as though to convince her that he was genuinely groggy.

'You mean you went to bed?'

He gestured. 'I'm still dressed. Look, aren't I?'

'So you went to bed dressed.'

'If I'd driven after you . . . well, I didn't know which way he'd gone. So I waited. And I passed out. You *are* all right, love?'

'Do I look all right? So you made no effort to tell the German, hmm!'

'I didn't know . . . I mean . . .'

'You don't mean anything. Not to me.'

'I thought you'd both be back in a few minutes. I didn't want to make a fuss too soon. I was *drugged*.'

She laughed bitterly. 'Then so was I. Did that send *me* to sleep?'

'What happened?' Harry stared at Helen's soiled legs and arms. 'He didn't – ? If he did, I'll – !'

'Desai's dead.'

'What?'

'A leopard killed him.'

'Oh God.'

Helen sat on her bed. Harry moved to put an arm

around her, but she thrust him away. 'Get off! Don't touch me.'

'Are you sure Desai didn't – ?'

'*He* didn't do anything, you fool! Nothing important. He just died.'

'You're upset about his death. The shock. That's natural.'

'*Natural*?' she snarled. 'What's natural?'

'Darling, you're safe. We've got to . . .' Got to what? Harry wasn't quite sure. 'We've got to pull ourselves together. Have you told anyone? Does anyone else know yet?'

'And if they don't, shall we pack our bags and drive away right now in the middle of the night? Drive, drive! Then no one will be any the wiser?'

At least, thought Harry, Helen was still speaking. It wasn't his fault that he'd succumbed.

'No, but we could say that Desai delivered us both back safely, then drove off on his own. That way, we aren't involved.'

Said Helen, 'I think that I left my socks in his car.'

'You did *what*? Why did you take your socks off?'

'I must have been hot, mustn't I?'

'You aren't serious!' Harry's tone was accusatory now.

'Well, it must have been the bhang, then. If you want us not to get involved, you'll have to go and fetch my socks, won't you?' Yes, she thought, the police would find her socks. Or maybe not. Maybe no one would wonder about a pair of socks.

'You mean, drive out there now, to his car? You'd have to show me where. Someone might notice us starting our car and going for a night drive.'

'So you'll have to walk – the same way I walked back. At least you'll have a flashlight with you.'

Harry swallowed. Was this a test of love? A way to redeem his failure, the fact that he'd slept?

'I don't know the way, damn it! I can't just wander round in the bush all night . . . How far is it?' It occurred to him then that Desai's car might be close by.

'I've no idea.'

'It's ridiculous. Impossible.'

'Nothing's impossible,' said Helen. 'If I know one thing. I know that!' She crossed to the water bucket and quickly washed the ash smuts from her arms and legs. 'I'm going to bed now. Make your own mind up.' Turning her back on Harry, she undressed, slid into the camp bed and turned her face to the wall.

Harry fretted for several minutes. He turned the paraffin lamp down lower.

'Are you asleep?' he whispered.

No response. Helen lay unmoving and silent.

'Shall I go?'

No answer.

Harry doused the lamp entirely. With flashlight in hand, he parted the flaps of the tent and stood out in the night, feeling sick. 'Oh damn it, damn it,' he swore softly. He could at least go as far as the toilet tent . . .

Urrrngg . . .

A low growl in the darkness! He flashed the light-beam around. The low-set eyes reflected the light momentarily. Beast eyes. He couldn't see the shape behind the eyes.

He backed into the tent and zipped the flaps, then lay down on his own bed, listening. He imagined claws ripping through the canvas wall beside him, and gripped the torch light. Strike the leopard on its nose, he thought. The noses are sensitive.

Something moved outside. Something brushed the tent. Harry lay rigid, sweating coldly. He lay for an

immeasurable time, wide-awake. Ultimately the torch
battery began to weaken. Eventually he fell asleep.

'It's light!' he cried, sitting upright in a rush. 'It's dawn!'
   'Uhh?' Helen turned over.
   He shook her shoulder. 'It's dawn, love.'
   She opened her eyes, but didn't focus. 'What?'
   'I said it's dawn.'
   'I'm tired. I'm going to stay in bed.'
   'But you can't . . . we told Frau Boll we'd be going out
in the Land Rover this morning. If we don't . . .'
   'I'm not going. Stop bothering me.'
   In despair, Harry went to unzip the flaps. How could
he persuade – no, *beg* – Helen to act normally?
   The African dawn assailed him: light, air, emptiness,
vastness, a faint drift of smoke, calls of nameless birds.
Barren hills, trees, clouds.
   At his feet just outside the tent lay a pair of white
socks side by side.
   He stooped and seized them. *She brought them back
with her after all! was his first thought. The bitch, oh the
bitch!*
   But this didn't figure. When he had stepped outside
with the flashlight the night before, no socks had lain
there. Maybe Desai wasn't dead at all. Maybe *he* had
returned her socks. Maybe what Harry feared, had indeed
happened!
   Then why should Helen have lied about a leopard
killing him? It didn't make sense – none of it. Only the
socks made a kind of sense. They at least were tangible.
They were right here in his hand, like a gift from
providence. He went inside, shook Helen brusquely,
dangled the socks before her eyes.
   'I have them,' he said. 'Here they are.'

She sat bolt upright, then gathered the sheet to her breasts. 'You fetched them? You did?'

'I have them,' he repeated cautiously. 'These are your socks.'

'Yes, they are.'

'So we're all right now.'

'Are we? Is that what you think?'

'Please get ready. We have to be at the Land Rover. Then back for breakfast afterwards. We must act normally.'

Helen considered. 'All right. Go to the toilet or something while I get dressed. Take a walk.'

He did. He went nowhere near the Asian's tent, which was still silent. The African Boy was about, though, doing his early morning jobs.

The German hunter, Herr Boll, looked like one of Rommel's desert captains, somewhat aged: and maybe he had been, too. He spoke English with a perfect exactness daunting to native English speakers, making their own normal use of the language seem slovenly by comparison. But he carried no gun in the Land Rover, since he was only a hunter on rare occasions.

Apart from Helen and Harry, a Canadian diplomat and his wife and two Italian men rode out to the reedy waterhole some miles away.

Warthogs were about, and giraffes; a few wildebeest, a solitary elephant, a small pride of lions.

On the return journey Helen spotted Desai's white Peugeot standing solitary on the plain in the distance.

As did Boll. 'I wonder what our Indian friend has found,' he said. 'We shall take a look.' He turned the Land Rover off the track and headed across country.

'*Gott*,' muttered the hunter, a few minutes later.

'Everyone will please stay here. Do not get out of the vehicle.' He walked the last fifty yards.

'There has been an accident,' he said when he returned.

'What is it?' twittered the Canadian woman, raising her camera.

'An accident. Please do not take photographs.'

'A man is lying there,' said one of the Italians.

'Yes, I know.' Boll engaged gear and drove off, dust pluming in their wake.

'An accident,' Harry said to Helen softly. 'An *accident*.' He stressed the word. It said plainly that they had nothing, and could not possibly have had anything, to do with it. He glanced down at Helen's feet. She was wearing those same socks, which didn't look too dirty. Harry tried to tell himself that they had always been on her feet, safely inside her sandals.

Later, since they had only booked into Mikumi Camp for one night, Helen and Harry drove off. A police Land Rover had arrived from Morogoro, but this had nothing to do with them. If Desai's family had mentioned the meal and the proposed leopard hunt, this mustn't have seemed to matter; and Harry had avoided going over to the Asians' tent. Desai, after all, had hardly even been an acquaintance.

They drove back in the direction of the coast in silence along the main road, through the dust-storms of oil trucks till they reached the hard-top stretch. Then they sped faster.

Just short of Morogoro, an African man tried to flag them down. He was old, wizened, rather neatly dressed.

Harry broke their long silence to suggest, 'Maybe we should – ?' He even slackened off the accelerator.

'Don't stop,' Helen said coldly. 'Don't ever stop. I hate this country. I want to leave.'

'What? But I have a three-year contract . . .' Harry's words sounded phoney, almost rehearsed.

'You do. I don't. I want to leave; I want to fly home.'

'Be reasonable.'

'Reason has gone away,' she said. 'There only seems to be reason. There's madness. And shame. And death. And ghosts.'

'I don't understand you.'

'No, you don't. That's true.'

Something was puttering inside the engine at the back of the car. To Helen's ears this sounded like the pad of feet pacing the car, pursuing it effortlessly. It was a sound she feared she would always hear.

'My socks smell like an animal's mouth,' she said. 'Do you know why?'

'No.'

'Because you didn't bring them back. The leopard brought them back for me last night.'

Harry couldn't answer. He knew that he would never be able to answer such a statement. Yet somehow he knew too, in this moment, that he had escaped – whereas Helen hadn't escaped. Even if she carried out her threat to leave him, to pack her bags and be gone on the next week's flight, she wouldn't escape from whatever possessed her now. But he would be free of it. Free of hate.

Of a sudden he felt bitterly glad. He tried to detach himself further, by squaring his shoulders and pressing down on the accelerator.

Already he suspected that after their divorce he might marry an African woman. Miss Nsibambi, yes. Why not? She was a graduate in economics but she had to work for the Ministry during her first three years after graduation at National Service pay rates, to help this poor country with its nation building. So her life was difficult; but she

was beautiful. And black. How dare Desai say that about
black girls! Desai was a racialist.

After Helen had gone, Harry would take Miss Nsibambi to the cinema and buy her dinners of Malayan
lobster curry on the roof restaurant of the Twiga Hotel.
He would identify more deeply with Africa. Then when
his contract was up, he would take the black Mrs Sharp
away with him and she would be happy to go – happier
than Helen had been to come, in the event.

With the experience of one marriage behind him, the
next one should work out much better. And whilst he
remained in this country, with Miss Nsibambi he would
be safe.

Beside him, Helen cocked her head attentive to some
sound he couldn't hear, yet.

He wondered what it would be like to make love to an
African woman. He would have to leave the light on, to
know. To lighten her ebony darkness.

He drove a little faster, to bring this future closer.

Twenty miles further on, he reached for Helen's hand,
knowing in advance that she would jerk it away. Which
she did.

'If *that's* how you feel,' he snapped.

Ahead, another African man danced right out on to
the road to wave for a lift. This man was raggy, his
sandals cut from old car tyres.

'Why, he's just like – !' Harry checked himself.

'Run him down,' said Helen. 'Run – him – down!'

'But I can't possibly – !' She was insane. Quite insane.
Run the man down? That would wreck everything. Miss
Nsibambi would never marry him then.

'It's the only thing you can ever do for me! Run him
down!'

The closer they approached, the more the man thrashed
his arms about and grinned and nodded. Harry angled

the car out to pass the man. He was only fifty yards ahead.

Suddenly, Helen grabbed the wheel and wrenched it over. The car slewed. Harry was aware of it striking the man. Then they were skidding off the road, turning right over. The world went black.

Voices, speaking Swahili. A stink of petrol. Harry's head ached fiercely as the hands pulled him up and out through the window. Blurred, he saw two oil trucks parked. Before the hands lifted him clear he looked down, saw Helen, the blood on her face, the angle of her neck.

As the two African drivers laid him down on the warm soil he shivered in the aftermath of shock. Then he calmed; relaxed. It was over – and all so soon. And he would be pitied. Miss Nsibambi especially would pity his loneliness, and admire the way he worked on despite bereavement.

Or was that only the angry fantasy born of a quarrel? Marry Miss Nsibambi: what sort of delusion was that?

Helen and I would have got over it, he thought. *We'd have made it up. Now we can't. Not ever.*

'Man on road,' he said in bad Swahili to one of his rescuers. 'How he?'

'*Hapana mtu,*' said the African. 'No man on road. Only you and *Memsahib* here.'

'*Hapana mtu,*' his rescuer repeated.

Harry began to feel afraid.

Away in the bush, a zebra foal was born. Licked by its mother, it staggered on to its legs, which were frail and rickety as yet. Unlike the other zebras, this foal's hooves and fetlocks were an unbroken snowy white, for all the world like ankle socks. Its nostrils sucked the amazing air. Its ears pricked up, when it heard a far-off growl – as though it had always known that noise.

Ghost Lecturer

As soon as Lucretius materialized, stark naked, at the focus of the Roseberry Field, one of the Institute technicians rushed to drape a bathrobe round him. Another technician furnished our ancient Roman with a pair of sandals.

It seems a genuine toga took at least half an hour to don; so a bathrobe was the next best thing.

Then Jim Roseberry advanced to greet our honoured guest and explain the set-up, in Latin. Jim really radiated benevolence – you felt you could trust him. With those twinkling blue eyes, that shambling gait, that wild halo of grizzling hair, he looked like a friendly bear whose only wish was to hug you.

'Magister,' he declared, 'welcome! We of the future salute you, who are about to die. With our science we have plucked you from your deathbed, to honour your wisdom . . .' And so on.

Titus Lucretius Carus stood listening, his head cocked. He was a short skinny fellow with a crimped, tiered hairstyle surmounting a large, lined forehead. His nose was long and thin; lively brown eyes were encased in lugubrious lids.

He didn't *look* on the point of death, but of course Jim had already explained to me the night before that in snatching a dying man from the continuum and prolonging his dying moment into seven days' life in the present, the Roseberry Effect revitalized its subject thoroughly, for as long as he remained with us.

Me, I'd originally suspected that the resurrectees

weren't real people at all but were more like a sort of ectoplasm, like ghosts at séances. No, Jim had assured me: real flesh and blood. And if I was a continuum topologist like him, I'd understand why.

Real flesh and blood: that gave me an idea or two for livening things up. Because of course the problem facing us at the Network was that Roseberry's Memorial Laureate Lectures were simply *not* prime TV material. Naturally the first announcement of the Roseberry Effect and the fantastic piece of science behind it had been a sensation. But following it up was the problem. Charles Darwin was simply *not entertaining*, and as for the second resurrectee, Galileo . . . well, computer translation in that monotonous synthesized machine-speech is a real bromide, and we couldn't expect millions of viewers to rent hypno-teach equipment to learn medieval Italian. It was only the rumour that Jim was thinking of resurrecting Jesus Christ which persuaded us to buy TV rights to Lucretius, in order to get an option on subsequent resurrections. I mean, who cared about Lucretius or what he had to tell the world?

So here was I burdened with directing the show. We just *had* to concentrate on the personal angle: the week this old Roman would spend after his lecture, *en famille* with the Roseberry family. And already I knew it would be up to me to personalize his visit.

Once the initial shock was over, Lucretius approached this whole business of his resurrection with admirable composure – though from my point of view it wouldn't be so admirable if he kept his cool all week long.

So presently we all adjourned from the resurrection room with its power cables, continuum-matrix-engine and other doodahs, next door for a buffet of canapés, cookies, and cola prior to the guest lecture itself . . .

. . . which Muhammed and Carl dutifully filmed and

recorded, while Lucretius held forth from the podium to an invited audience in Latin on atomic theory and the nature of the universe. Obviously we would have to edit 99 or 100 per cent of this out. My thoughts drifted to Tony, who was away at the Roseberry home elsewhere in the Institute grounds, fitting it up with auto-mini-cams and snoopy-mikes as per the check-list I'd handed him.

After a while I began watching Jim Roseberry; and noted how slyly he smiled from time to time during the lecture, how knowingly he nodded.

It occurred to me that something wasn't quite kosher about Jim . . .

Afterwards, when the audience of Nobel laureates and whatnot had departed, we walked back through the rhododendrons towards the Roseberry residence, leaving the mirror-glass and concrete of the Institute behind: Jim and Lucretius and me. With Carl and Muhammed pacing us assiduously, taping every golden moment.

Lucretius mustn't have been used to our modern toe-grip style of sandal – or else delayed shock caught up with him – since we hadn't gone far before he stumbled and collided with me. I took the opportunity to slip my arm through his.

'Is it true you were driven mad by a love-potion?' I whispered. (This was something my researcher Karen had turned up, cheering me considerably. Our Roman reportedly had died raving mad, crazed by aphrodisiacs. Too, he had always been a manic depressive, forever flipping from ectasy at the beauties of the world to gloomy horror at all the carnage in it. Though he had tried very hard to maintain a philosophical detachment.)

Jim overheard. 'For God's sake!'

Lucretius eyed Jim with a pained expression. 'Do you *still* believe in gods?'

Me, he continued to clutch. I guess my knee-boots, micro-shorts and halter must have turned him on. Goodness knows what he thought Muhammed was up to, bobbing about with his mini-cam. A black slave, fanning us?

Invited to dinner that first evening were two people from the afternoon audience: tubby Max Stein the astrophysicist, and particle physicist Ingrid Langholm wearing a full-length orange gown with organdy insets showing flesh discreetly. Our hostess Martha Roseberry was definitely a Rubens woman: portly and pink and powdered. Daughter Harmony Roseberry, an adolescent know-it-all, was plump too, and spotty, thanks to her addiction to greasy doughnuts. Mother and daughter both obviously regarded Jim as the next best thing to God.

Muhammed and Carl had gone off to the local motel; Tony was relegated to the kitchen, whence Machiko, the Japanese maid, served drinks and the products of the family's Filipino cook. Whenever Machiko came into the dining room, Lucretius inspected her oriental features in puzzlement. Finally, in the midst of the smoked salmon and asparagus, he enquired whether she was Egyptian – which sent Jim rushing off to his study, to return with a globe of the world: one more modern marvel to amaze our Roman with, to add to electric light, TV, and flush toilets.

And as I listened to Jim explain how we had explored and mapped every last inch of the Earth, and even gone to the Moon, I began to understand what wasn't quite kosher about him.

It was like this: Jim's great scientific breakthrough was to yank past geniuses out of time, supposedly to honour them so they would know their lives had been worthwhile in the eyes of the future. But then he would go on to tell them – oh so kindly – where they had gone wrong or fallen short of the mark. And how much more we knew nowadays. 'You almost got it right, boy! You were on the right track, and no mistake. Bravo! *But . . .*'

That was why he chose scientists to resurrect and host. An artist like Mozart or Shakespeare could never be upstaged; but a scientist could be – by superior knowledge. Thus Jim Roseberry became superior to Darwin, Galileo, and whoever else.

True, Lucretius was a poet, but he only wrote poetry in order to explain science. He was sort of the Carl Sagan of ancient Rome.

Beef Stroganoff with pilau rice was next. Max Stein devoured second and third helpings; but Lucretius only toyed with his food.

'How do you find your meal, Magister Lucretius?' Martha asked in Latin. (We had all spent a night with the hypno equipment, of course.)

'Bitter,' he replied. 'Sour.'

She passed the salt cellar. Harmony demonstrated its use. Lucretius tasted and grimaced.

'Do the rough atoms tear your tongue?' asked Jim with a twinkle in his eye.

The Burgundy was a success, though.

During the dessert (lemon mousse – and a doughnut for Harmony) conversation turned to electrons and quarks, and the Big Bang. Ingrid Langholm proved rather ingenious at coining Latin words to explain what happens when you split the unsplittable. Coffee and Cognac followed; and Lucretius began to frown and ask for more Cognac. He was still keeping his cool; but for how long? I was next to him; I rubbed my bare leg against his bathrobe, innocently. (Tonight was too soon. Perhaps the next night . . .)

That was when I heard thunder. Jim jumped up and

went to part the drapes. Outside the night was black and moonless, and no stars showed. A wind seemed to be rising. 'Dirty weather brewing,' he told Max and Ingrid.

Max consulted his watch and sprang up. 'I'd better be going!' He stuck his hand out at Lucretius. 'A real pleasure to talk with you, Magister!'

'Me too,' said Ingrid, also rising.

Lucretius stared at Max's offered hand. 'That's all right. I don't wish to go outside to vomit.'

'Goodness!' exclaimed Martha.

'Roman feasts were so gutsy, Mom,' said Harmony, 'the diners usually had to vomit between courses.'

'Was this a feast?' asked Lucretius. 'I admired its moderation, if not its flavour.'

'Well, I never!' Martha said.

And so the party broke up.

I spent a scary night in one of the guest rooms. That storm kept circling round and waking me. Every hour or so, fresh bouts of thunder erupted and lightning flashes squeezed through the drapes. Most of the time, a real banshee of a wind howled. Occasionally I thought I heard a cry or owl-screech. I felt *edgy,* and burrowed deep under the duvet, even if it overheated me.

When I got up the next morning, the wind was still wild. Enormous cloud galleons scudded through the sky, sail piled on sail high up to the stratosphere.

My bedroom window looked on to woodland which hid us from the highway. Amidst the general grey-green I noticed something brightly orange.

Suddenly it seemed as if the area of trees I was staring at, well, *threw* itself at me – shucking off veil after veil which flew towards me. I felt the impact of each thin copy of the scene like a physical blow upon my eyes. What I was looking at was *radiating* its surface at me. For a moment I thought I was having a flashback to an acid trip, years ago. But then I focused on that orange patch.

It was Ingrid Langholm, and she was half way up a tree!

Was this a hallucination? It didn't seem to be.

I dressed quickly, and went to rouse Tony and Jim Roseberry too. If Ingrid had spent the whole night up a tree in a storm, she must have had a damn good reason.

When we got back to the house, supporting a bedraggled, worn out particle physicist, Martha Roseberry was out-doors too, in her housecoat, ignoring the wild weather. Lucretius had also emerged, in his bathrobe.

'Whatever happened?' squawked Martha.

'Front wheel gave out,' gasped Ingrid. 'I had a flat.'

'Her chariot wheel gave out,' Jim said in Latin, mindful of his duties as host.

'No flashlight with me . . . so I started walking back . . . and a goddam *lion* – '

'A lion chased her up a tree. It kept prowling about.'

'Lions fear the cry of a cockerel,' remarked Lucretius, sagely.

'Eh?' from Martha.

'So it would flee at dawn. Pigs shun perfume and marjoram, lions fear a rooster.' Lucretius regarded poor Ingrid with dour satisfaction. Her gown was torn and sodden. Her make-up had all run. Her hair was in rats' tails. She looked a bleary ragbag.

Just then, Ingrid's face detached itself and flew at mine – time and again. It was as if she wore an infinity of masks, which each peeled off in turn and flew through the air, without in any way diminishing her. Martha, too, rubbed her eyes in disbelief.

But Jim was too busy staring up at the wild and roiling sky. He pointed shakily. A giant face was grinning down at us from the side of a cloud. It became a snarling lion's head, then dissolved, dripping like wax.

'Did you see *that*?'

'Flimsy films of vision sometimes generate themselves spontaneously in the sky,' Lucretius said helpfully.

As though this wasn't bad enough, at that moment two neighbouring Douglas firs suddenly burst into flames. Jim rounded on Lucretius.

'Oh, and what's the reason for *that*, then?'

'Why, wind rubs the trees together. Friction enflames them.'

By now the steady rain of blows from the wind was dislodging the atoms of my mind and body from their station so fast that I felt I hadn't slept at all the night before. I'd lost a lot of density and I needed food to fill the cracks. (And part of me asked another part, 'What the hell am I thinking? Blows? Dislodged atoms? Loss of density?') My limbs tottered. I didn't notice the snake sneaking through the grass till Tony shouted, 'Look out!'

Hastily I jogged my vital spirit, to get it to jog my body aside. (I did . . . *what*?) Lucretius spat casually at the snake. Instantly the serpent writhed around and bit its own tail, stinging itself to death.

Lucretius clucked in satisfaction. 'Luckily it's one of those which human spittle poisons.'

I was reeling. And in the furnace of colliding clouds, seeds of fire were being crammed together. A thunderbolt burst forth and smashed into the ground quite near us.

'What the hell's going on?' cried Tony.

'I need some breakfast urgently,' I told Martha. 'Please! I've lost too many atoms. My vital spirit will quit.'

'Are you into some new kind of therapy?' Martha asked, baffled.

'We'd better get inside fast,' advised Jim.

*   *   *

We breakfasted on waffles with maple syrup; the smoothly trickling particles of syrup seemed to please Lucretius's palate. Soon the storm was on the wane.

Jim gazed across the table at me balefully. 'What's happening? I'll tell you what's happening. Those "films" you see flying off surfaces and hitting your eyes – that's how our friend here thought vision worked. And now we're seeing it happen, as though it's true. All the crazy rest of it, too! His world-view is affecting us. Somehow it's . . . projecting itself. And I'll tell you why. It's because you sexed him up! On account of how you're dressed. Or undressed!'

'So what's wrong with shorts and a halter? I'm not exactly nude with body paint!'

'I watched you at dinner. You caused the onset of a love-frenzy.'

'A what?' asked Harmony.

Martha said mildly, 'Do you think we should be discussing this in front of our guest?'

'Aw, the hell with that.'

I spoke from the depths of me. I cut sounds into words with my tongue and moulded them with my lips. (At least that's what it felt like.) 'The hell with my costume and morals, too! *How* is this happening to us?'

'It's his world-view taken literally – and taken to extremes . . . This must be an aspect of the Roseberry Effect I hadn't taken into account. With Darwin and even Galileo we were on the same general wavelength. The modern scientific world-view,' Jim mumbled.

I just had to laugh. 'So instead of *you* wising Lucretius up, he's changing things to suit his own half-baked ancient notions? Oh, that's too rich!'

Jim went white. 'I'm going to make some phone calls. Excuse me.'

Harmony looked daggers at me, then rushed out of the

room after him. I hoped the mini-cams and snoopy-mikes were working okay, getting all this taped.

While Jim was away, Ingrid, wrapped in a spare bathrobe, drank a lot of hot coffee. After a while Lucretius coughed, to clear his throat of sticky atoms, I suppose.

'Indeed I must confess that I felt love-frenzy coming over me. Will we never reach a state of equanimity? Will we never heed the Master's word?'

'The Master?' asked Ingrid.

'Epicurus.'

'Oh.'

'And yet . . . if one concentrates on the defects of a woman, however fair at first she seems . . .' He looked steadfastly at Ingrid, who resembled a drowned rat after her night out; and I realized to my chagrin that Lucretius had been more excited by *her* than by me.

Maybe that was just as well! Otherwise I might have been the one who was trashed. Still, the snake had been heading for me . . . I could almost imagine myself swelling up and raving, and black flux pouring from my bowels . . . Where were such notions coming from? I *must not* think along those lines!

Presently Jim returned, followed by Harmony. 'The phone's okay. Those little atoms still rush along the wires. The effect's quite local.' He sat down, though he wouldn't meet my eyes at first – because I had seen through him. 'I've been thinking.'

'So have I,' said Ingrid. 'If Jesus Christ were here instead of Lucretius – if this were *His* Second Coming – then we could experience joy and peace and true love. For a while. In one little corner of the world.'

Oh beautiful! thought I. Bless you, Ingrid. Press that button again. I'd been trying to get on to the business of resurrecting Jesus, but whenever I broached the subject Jim had neatly evaded it – till I suspected that maybe he had begun the rumour himself, just to get hold of a fancy chunk of TV money for the Institute.

Ingrid blushed. 'I guess I was praying a bit last night. Old habit, long forgotten. It kept me company.'

And maybe it wouldn't be so beautiful, after all! Lucretius was an unreligious man. Would we want real archangels flying about . . . and Satan knocking on the door in person?

'As I say,' resumed Jim, 'this is a local problem. Reality has become a little unhinged in our friend's vicinity. And definitely more plastic. His imagination is moulding it – and he always had a strong imagination! As to *why* exactly, it's too soon to say. We'll have to put our heads together at the Institute. But for my money I'd say it's a function of how far we've gone into the past this time. Apparently the further back we pluck a fellow from, the more we loosen the continuum. Don't worry, it'll bounce back afterwards.'

'After he goes home,' said Harmony, rather grimly.

'Meanwhile we'll have to watch our step. Avoid exciting him too much.'

'Who,' asked Lucretius, 'is Jesus Christ?'

'Ah. Um. Long story, that,' said Jim. 'I guess you could call him a teacher. Like Epicurus.'

'He was the Son of God,' said Ingrid, with eyes downcast.

'A god?' cried Lucretius irritably. 'Then maybe *I'm* a god, if I can produce storms and thunderbolts? But I have already pointed out in persuasive verse that this is nonsense. Lightning strikes where it wills! Do you mock me?'

'No, no,' Jim hastily assured him. 'It's just that reality is a bit more complicated than you thought . . . Look,' he said, with an effort at bonhomie, 'it's brightening. Let's all go for a walk in the grounds. That'll clear our heads.' He switched to English briefly. 'I'll fetch my hunting rifle. Just in case. I'll pretend it's a walking stick.' And in Latin: 'We won't meet any more lions, will we, Magister?'

Lucretius was offended. '*I'm* not responsible for hallucinations. Wild beasts are sometimes seen when none are there, because the mind is constantly beset by images; and if a person happens to be afraid, and thinking of wild beasts – perhaps because her chariot has broken down at night – then from these images the mind selects . . .'

'Sure, sure,' said Jim. 'We won't think of lions, will we? Not any of us! We'll think of nice things: like flowers, and poetry. We'll walk down by the lake. Feed the geese. That's always soothing. Fetch some doughnuts for the birds,' he told Harmony.

Jim hustled us outdoors rapidly, so that I hadn't any time to summon Carl and Muhammed from the motel; though Tony came along, with a mini-cam hastily mounted on one shoulder and a snoopy-mike fixed to the other. Ingrid had flaked out by now and was being put to bed by Martha. So five of us set out: me, Tony, Lucretius, Jim, and his daughter.

The wind had dropped. Clouds were evaporating quickly. As we stepped out of the house, suddenly the sun shone forth. Unfortunately I glanced up at it – and a film of solar disc hit my face with force. Particles of fire scorched my eyeballs. 'The sun!' I yelped. 'Don't anyone look at it!' It was a whole minute before I regained my vision, and even then my eyes remained untrustworthy; they kept watering and unfocusing. Tony helped me along for a while, but I shook him off. I wanted him filming, not guiding me as once Antigone led blind Oedipus.

On our way to the lake we passed through woods,

which were moist and warm. The sunlight dappling down was genial, here.

What I took at first to be a giant puffball sprouting from the loam suddenly split open as we drew abreast of it – to disgorge a bleating baby goat. The young kid tottered to a nearby bump on the ground, from which white liquid began leaking. Splay-legged, the kid grabbed hold of this bump with its mouth and sucked greedily. Yes indeed, suckling milk from a breast of the earth!

The bump just had to be a nipple. Which meant that the puffball, now collapsed, must have been . . . not a fungus but a rooted womb!

We stared in amazement as the kid grew apace. Soon it was grazing contentedly on poisonous hellebore which had sprung up nearby.

Lucretius frowned, and tutted.

'How odd. In the late, decaying state of the world nowadays, only worms and animalcules should be generated spontaneously from the soil. This is exceptional.'

'Isn't it just?' snapped Jim.

'And if goats can get born from the soil,' broke in Harmony, 'why not lions as well? Gee, Daddy, *anything* could pop up. This is scary.' Oddly, though, the prospect didn't seem to scare her so much – how can I put it? – as encourage her.

Lucretius shook his head. 'I still maintain the lion must have been a hallucination. One must always select the most *reasonable* explanation of phenomena. Though in this case – '

'Oh, shut up,' Jim growled softly. Yet just then (when I thought back on it) he too looked oddly content.

And we carried on.

The lake was circled by lawns. Our group was still in tree shade, but all before us the sunlight was blazing down. (I took care not to look anywhere near the sun again, but one thing I remembered about it was that it had seemed to be only a few miles away – and no larger than it looked.) The rainfall of the night before was steaming off the grass. At that moment I could see quite clearly.

A flock of Canada geese came winging in towards the water. One moment they were flying blithely along; the next they were tumbling out of the sky. Falling like rocks on to the lawn. Thump, thump. Dead as ducks.

For one mad instant I thought Jim must have shouldered his gun and zapped the geese in an incredible – and silent – display of marksmanship. But no; he was still tapping the ground with the rifle butt, like the old man in the riddle of the Sphinx.

'And *what*, Magister,' Jim asked icily, 'is the cause of that? I *liked* those birds.'

'Ah . . .' Lucretius scratched his chin. 'A vacuum must have formed, you see. The ground has been rotted by unseasonable rain, and now it is pelted with sunbeams. Consequently a foul effluence rises, expelling all the air above.'

'Of course! How stupid of me! What other explanation could there be?'

Lucretius regarded the phenomenon equably. 'We must believe the evidence of our senses, as interpreted by Reason. I have a question, though.'

'Ask away.'

Thump, thump. A trio of mallards slapped on to the lawn.

'By use of Reason, I discovered the causes of pestilence: pestiferous clouds of atoms uncongenial to us, which fly about. Yet different air in different lands breeds characteristic diseases. Thus elephantiasis is only found in Egypt, while gout is native to Attica. Tell me, what is the characteristic disease of this land, America?'

'Cancer and heart disease mostly,' remarked Tony, who was otherwise occupied with the occasional tumbling bird.

'Jesus, what did you tell him that for? Magister, disease is *not* caused by atoms in the air. Well, usually is isn't . . .'

'Maybe it is, around this neck of the woods.' Tony pointed. 'Here come more kamikaze birdies.'

At this point my eyes blurred, as if they had just been attacked by cataract-causing atoms. I heard Harmony scream, 'A monster!' I heard the bang of the rifle. Then a thump.

'Holy Moses,' I heard Tony cry. 'You've shot him.'

My vision swam back to normal. Jim was standing with his rifle at the slope. Harmony had her hands over her mouth in a theatrical show of shock; she had dropped all the doughnuts. Lucretius lay sprawled on his back, looking very dead.

'Did you *see* that monster?' babbled Harmony. 'It was breathing *fire!* My Daddy saved us!'

'What do you mean, *saved*?' said Tony. 'That bullet hit Mr Lucretius.'

'What a terrible accident,' said Jim. 'Oh, this is awful, I hope you got it all on film.'

'Of course I didn't! I was looking over there. I didn't see any monster.'

'It was a lion,' said Harmony. 'But worse. It breathed fire. Now it's gone.'

'Did *you* see anything?' Tony asked me. I shook my head.

But I had the gravest suspicions that Jim Roseberry had just killed Titus Lucretius Carus deliberately. Out of almighty pique at how he, Jim, had been upstaged.

He must have thought this was the perfect murder,

too. For how can you be guilty of murder when your victim already died two thousand years ago?

Well, there was quite some fuss then. We rushed back to the house, where Jim monopolized the phone for a while. Soon as I could, I called Carl and Muhammed at the motel; and a bit later a police captain and a lieutenant arrived in a Buick, all lit up and screaming – just beating the Network minibus by a short head.

However, Jim must have already have been calling in a favour or two before he even called the police to report the fatality, since the two officers were so respectful and apologetic; and what's more, even as we were all heading back down to the lakeside, they were already deciding that the matter was right outside their jurisdiction.

And Jim was nodding so concernedly and saying that on scientific grounds the body *would* really have to be rushed back to the Institute of dematerialization; though he had felt it his duty as a citizen, et cetera.

When we got to the lake, Institute staff were already standing by with a stretcher. After asking the bare minimum of questions, the captain and lieutenant waved the body on its way; and departed.

Dead Lucretius departed too. To return to his own time. Back where he was already on the point of death. So nobody back in ancient times would notice any real difference; except maybe that Lucretius now had a hole in his chest. If he had indeed stabbed himself to death, crazed by a love-potion, this mightn't look too odd. Or maybe the murder, up in our present day, was what *caused* the tale of suicide? Even if nobody back in the past could locate a knife – since there wasn't one . . .

Very neat, Jim!

Except, it wasn't neat at all.

As I was the first to notice, while we headed for the

Institute in the wake of the corpse, when Jim's face
suddenly unpeeled and flew at my eyes several times.

'Hey!' cried Carl, staring at *my* face in alarm.

I tapped Jim on the arm. 'Notice something?'

'You mean, the effect still continuing. Hmm, I thought
it would fade as soon as he died – '

'Did you just?'

He flushed, 'So instead, it'll go away when we get rid
of the body. Be *very* careful what you imply.'

'Oh, I will be careful, don't you worry.'

And so we all saw Lucretius off, six days early, from
the resurrection room accompanied by crackling air and
sparks and a little sonic boom. And our show had gone
down the drain, thought I.

But on our way back through the rhododendrons afterwards, to the Roseberry house, I thought I heard the
distant roar of a lion.

'Just thunder,' Jim said dismissively, and scanned the
sky.

He froze, ashen. For up on the side of the nearest
cloud hung a familiar face. The cloud-mouth of Lucretius
opened and dripped red blood like a sunset, before
dissolving.

So the effect hadn't gone away, after all. It stayed. And I
could guess why. It was because Lucretius had died here
in the present. His vital spirit had already flavoured the
environment in a most exaggerated manner, courtesy of
the Roseberry Effect and its derangement of space-time.
Him being killed here, this feature was locked in. All
that Jim sent back to ancient times was a lump of meat.

The grounds of the Institute were haunted now.
Meteorologically, optically, psychologically *haunted*.

Storms broke out. Trees burst into flames. Birds

plunged from the sky from time to time. Phantom images flew about. Faces appeared on clouds. Love-frenzies possessed people.

One thing was for sure: the reputation of Lucretius endured in the modern world. Jim had seen to that. A couple of square miles were definitely Lucretian.

Ironically enough, Lucretius himself always poured scorn on the idea of life after death. As I discovered when I read *The Nature of the Universe* not long after.

I also discovered that our Roman never believed in fire-breathing monsters. 'If fire burns all known animals, even lions,' he urged, very rationally, 'then no animal can ever breathe fire.' Harmony went right over the top there. Which only proves how she conspired, hastily, with her Daddy. They must have loved it when they saw that kid goat born from the puffball womb.

At one point the Lucretius Zone overlapped the grounds a bit, and slopped over a stretch of state highway. Since nobody can drive safely when images might zap their eyes, this effectively rendered the highway unusable. Some real estate was hexed, too. So Jim was in trouble.

Not trouble as a murderer, of course. As I said, you can't murder a dead man. But soon he would be hit by suits for damages from neighbouring residents whose property values had crashed; not to mention the highway authority, who were going to have to build a very costly detour.

Those members of the Institute who hadn't fled were busy studying the new Roseberry Effect − of disordered reality. One thing they quickly found was that the old Roseberry Effect was blocked by the haunting. So there would be no more resurrections at the Institute.

One morning Jim phoned me at the Network. He sounded stressed.

'It occurs to me,' he said, 'that you could shoot a damn fine horror movie here in the Roseberry Zone.' (He didn't, of course, refer to it as the Lucretius Zone.) 'I mean, we have a genuine *phenomenon* here.'

'Do you really think anyone would want to act in *there*, when they could catch instant plague or be smeared by thunderbolts?'

'So do your location shooting here – build your script around the phenomena. Then find somewhere else that's similar looking, but safe, for the actors.' He was almost pleading.

'Do I hear the rattle of an almost empty money box?'

'Look, it'll stir up a lot more interest than laureate lectures. Or even a real live sermon by Jesus, and seeing how he uses the bathroom.'

'Ah, but we can't host Jesus now. Not any longer. And frankly I wouldn't want to. In fact, I'd personally whip up a real campaign to block any such proposal. *No,* Jim. But let me give you a bit of advice, out of the pure kindness of my heart. Get out of there fast.'

'*What?*'

'Take to your heels. I know that you murdered Lucretius – and his zone knows it, too. It's just biding its time.'

Oh yes. Pretty soon it would trap Jim Roseberry in a nasty doom. Worse than any law suits. Perhaps that doom would be such as overwhelmed the Athenians with loathsome ulcers and malignant fluxes of foul blood, descending to the groin, so that some men only saved their lives by self-castration, while other victims completely forgot who they were. As Lucretius reveals in the gory and psychotic climax to *The Nature of the Universe*.

'You're out of your mind,' said Jim.

'No, you're *into his* mind. Slap in the midst of all his cockeyed ideas, exaggerated and made real.'

Of course, Jim wouldn't listen. Was he not the custodian of a profound natural mystery?

Really, all that poor old Lucretius ever wanted out of life was peace and quiet. Resurrecting him had been a fairly unkind cut. But resurrecting him, then murdering him had been the unkindest cut of all. No wonder Lucretius died raving mad – mad at Jim.

A week after that, a snake bit Harmony – though she did recover, away from the Zone in intensive care.

A fortnight subsequent, the Roseberry house was struck by a thunderbolt and burned down. So Jim moved into the Institute, to camp out.

Just yesterday I heard how Jim has caught, yes, plague. A Lucretian plague isn't very pleasant. But you can't say I didn't warn him.

Mistress of Cold

Mistress Marguerite:

Perseverance is a beautiful word. I think of it variously as an obelisk of white salt, or as a pyramid of blue ice.

Contained within perseverance is the word 'severe'. This is the salt rubbed into wounds, the salt that preserves flesh all through the winter. Salt, too, was the fate of Lot's disobedient wife.

Also contained is the word 'ever'. This is the ice which endures.

Sometimes I wish I had been named Perseverance, in the way that other women are named Patience or Felicity or Grace. But my name is Marguerite, after the flower, now extinct as all the flowers are. At least marguerites were mostly white, as snow is white.

But no one dares to use my name. I am addressed as Mistress. And today I shall become mistress of the whole frozen world. Dr Sovrenian has promised me this, and Sovrenian has never let me down during all these years. His mind is crystal-perfect; he has never melted at the edges when it was time for some hard choice. I speak metaphorically, of course: he and I are as warm-blooded as anyone else in the Enclave. Yet I've noted a tendency for people to adopt the characteristics of their surround-ings. Our immediate surrounding, of course, is the Enclave made of metal. Thus the young guard who stands before my door is as stiff as a steel bar. He has been brought up amongst steel and imitates its rigidity and polish. That boy has never seen a field of grass waving in the wind, or the ripples of rivers. Possibly such chaotic motion would distress him.

There were marguerites once, growing in fields of grass. But if one is to win through in the end, one must be willing to make sacrifices of such things as fields and daisies.

Steel is our immediate surrounding. But beyond, all is ice; it is this ice which forms our character. So everything in my state room is either white or blue. Walls, desk, rugs, the eiderdown upon the bed. Even my hair is turning white with age. Our skins are white from never seeing the sun; but my eyes are a piercing blue. I wear a blue pleated skirt and a white blouse ruffed with lace. My shoes are white with blue bows.

And now it's time to meet my War Cabinet. After patting my hair twice or thrice before my mirror. I sit down at my desk. (Mirrors are like window-panes of ice, aren't they? Mirrors hang everywhere throughout the Enclave, doubling the size of rooms and corridors. These mirrors were my idea.) Presently I press the buzzer.

Dr Sovrenian:

And now I wish to wax poetic; for there is beauty in oblivion. Here is the last poem in the history of the world; if my poem is in prose, that's because I am that kind of person . . .

Oh, it was only a simple war of weather to begin with! A way to freeze the harvests of the Enemy, to cause snow and ice to lock their land in frozen chains. But they stole the technique from us or invented one of their own. They began to freeze our own hemisphere.

Do you remember the Diamond Dust Catastrophe? The glory of the ice crystals high in the upper atmosphere?

Do you remember the migrating birds falling frozen

from the heavens as though each had been shot by a bullet of ice?

Do you recall the glaciers growling forth? Like armies of Frost Giants fighting for the good and the true. Against evil. Or like evil giants fighting against truth and goodness – depending on whether we speak of our hemisphere, or theirs.

We had our own Enclave by then. But so did the Enemy.

I wonder where the last wild beast died; and the last exposed human being? I wonder where the last blade of grass perished?

But that was only the beginning of the Cold War – though little could we guess so, to begin with! Continually we refined our techniques; they, theirs. Do you recall when all the oceans froze solid, cracking the shores?

Do you remember when the atmosphere itself froze out and fell as snow, leaving the world as airless as Pluto?

How I wish I could sing this song to my Mistress of Cold. But I must only talk in scientific terms to her; she only in political terms to me. She is our inflexible leader, dipped in liquid oxygen. My song might shatter her.

General Harker:

5300 souls: that's how many of us there are in the Enclave. Several hundred have died of natural causes since the war began; a few dozen have been born, none recently.

5000 men, to 300 women. So naturally there's a tendency for men to become homo or mechanical or else to ignore the whole business of sex, as I have done. Our Mistress of Cold won't allow officers to pull rank regarding, uh, leisure activities. Without her discipline we might have fallen apart at the seams years ago. But we didn't: we're pure with purpose, pure as snow.

Homo or mechanical sex activity doesn't worry her. It's a safety valve. Some men need it. The flesh is weak. But actually I think that kind of thing's been dying out in recent years. One great sign of our mettle – one proud boast we can make – is that no rape of a woman has ever occurred down here in the Enclave. How could it, with our Mistress at the helm? Her leadership chills the groin; it certainly chilled mine. Long ago it transfigured me from animal into spirit, into Will. I think I could pray to her. But I have to discuss military matters instead.

She's keeping us waiting longer than usual, isn't she?

I think I've lost my sense of time. For example, it's hard to believe that the Cold War only began twenty-five years ago. Such leaps there have been since then, in the technology of heat control! In the course of my career I've seen as much progress on this front as during the entire million years previous, between the first taming of fire and the nuclear furnace. Yet what an effort it takes to gaze back through the lens of memory and recall how the world once was! It's as if my working life spans not decades but aeons, a whole geological era. From a warm world to an ice age. Yet from then to now has been a perfectly logical progression.

Ah, her buzzer summons us.

Mistress Marguerite:

'Gentlemen! Be seated, please.'

'Madam,' says General Harker.

'Mistress,' says Sovrenian.

The others don't matter much: Robinson of Home Affairs, Stanley of Materials, Food and Energy . . . But it's customary to have them here; they're a traditional part of my cabinet, and what are we fighting for, if not to preserve our traditions?

Even my General Harker doesn't matter much. It's Dr Sovrenian I depend on. I wonder if he guesses? Surely not. I must remain invulnerable for all our sakes. I have never let him glimpse this.

When it's time for his report, he permits himself the slightest smile of pride. 'The new modifiers have passed all the tests, Mistress. We may proceed.'

'Today?'

And he nods.

'Today let it be, then, Gentlemen. Today we will free the world of evil . . . at long last. I pray we do. I shall give the order personally.'

'But of course.' The others have an air of tiredness about them. I've gone through several Ministers of Home Affairs, several Generals during the past twenty-five years: but Dr Sovrenian always kept the faith.

'We shall meet in the War Room at 3.00 P.M. I thank you, Gentlemen.'

General Harker:

What a fine place this War Room is. There's so much open space. I shouldn't be surprised if some of the younger personnel couldn't tolerate it. They'd gasp and flop about like fish on land. Prostrated by agoraphobia.

Look around. Behold the ranks of thermo-consoles. Those are Dr Sovrenian's province, but the display screens on the walls are mine, and those contain the whole world in miniature. In one quick scan I take in the 'weather' across both hemispheres, then down through the various layers of the planetary onion, all the way to the still-warm core.

Up top, the world's surface is within a tenth of a degree

of absolute zero. The two buried hot spots in the east and west – our home Enclave and the Enemy's – show up as blazing specks of fire, spots of red blood amidst the other coded shades of blue. It gets colder further down, and even deeper blue; then a dull red glow marks the core itself.

A hundred people are on duty. As usual the War Room is quiet and composed – yet it's a hive of feverish activity compared with any other physical processes going on throughout the planet (except at the corresponding Enemy base in the east).

An absurd thought occurs to me: suppose the Enemy base actually went blue years ago, and we never knew this because of a systems malfunction?

There's no malfunction, of course. Perhaps I'm cracking up . . .

Sovrenian is eyeing me from his master console. On his face a grin – or even a leer. Have I betrayed myself? I feel impelled to go and talk to him, just to reassure myself.

It's a quarter to three.

Dr Sovrenian:

Harker looks as if he suspects something. Frankly I don't see how he could, unless he's taken a sudden quantum leap in intelligence. I've had to put up with the dull fool for years; I think I can safely taunt him. Actually, the end game is inevitable now. Our Mistress of Cold won't change her mind. If only she could appreciate the full grandeur of what is about to happen! Maybe she does, but I can hardly enquire. Intimacy would spoil our relationship.

The General looms over me. Asks, with stupid joviality. 'The last push, eh?'

'Maybe today,' I say recklessly, 'we will freeze time itself.'

'Eh? How's that?'

I *will* tell him. It can alter nothing.

'Well, it's like this, my dear General. Nobody ever really believes he'll die, right? It seems impossible that the world can carry on without him. Despite the evidence of a one hundred per cent mortality rate! True?'

He nods dubiously.

'Today, General, this changes. Today – perhaps – the whole history of life on our planet will be over forever. Finis, kaput. The whole universe will be dead too.'

'Eh?'

'Didn't our astronomers decide long ago that ours is the only intelligent species in the entire cosmos, existing on the only habitable world? What an enormous statistical accident we are, to be sure!

'So when we're all dead, there'll be no more minds left to observe physical reality. Philosophically, the universe will cease to exist. When *I* die, General, the cosmos dies with me.'

'Die? Are you mad, Sovrenian?'

'I've always felt that the question of why anything exists at all, is the doorway to real madness. Today we shut the door forever.'

Harker splutters. He looks apoplectic. 'But it's the Enemy who'll die! We're going to tap the last heat from the world's core. To store power for the Enclave. To crank up the neg-energy field even higher – to reduce the world to within an ace of zero absolute. And hold it there. The Enemy will freeze at last. They'll die, we'll have won. Right? Right? Right?'

I sigh condescendingly. 'So why haven't the Enemy jumped in ahead of us?'

'Because their theory's inferior. Their tech's inferior.

Always has been. Not much, but enough. The Enemy haven't got the new modifiers.'

'I think they may have.' Keying my console, I display the most recent neg-energy exchange of the war. I point out peaks and resonances. Harker stares stupidly at my screen.

'Put this through a Fourier analysis, General. Determine the harmonics of the wave. Hey presto.' He doesn't understand, but I do. 'They could take the core right down to Ab-Zee. They've held off.'

His eyes narrow. 'Right down, all the way? But I thought . . .' Perhaps he isn't as stupid after all.

'You thought it was physically impossible ever to reach Ab-Zee itself? Once you're on a downhill slope such as this, there's only one place to go: to the bottom.'

To absolute zero, to the lowest possible state of heat when everything ceases. When the molecules stop jostling. When the atoms stop vibrating.

'But . . .'

And because atoms are most certainly *not* little grains which you can freeze; because elementary particles only exist as dynamic vibrations in the fabric of space itself – when you reach Ab-Zee at last, the world must cease to exist. The vacuum flux of space, also. Into that total nothingness will be sucked all other space and matter in the universe.

Then there will be no more universe; no more thinking beings occurring by accident. No more space or time, ever again. There'll be peace. Nirvana, non-existence, oblivion. None of these words can quite sum up that non-state, of the absence of anything at all – even of vacuum. How beautiful it is. How Godlike. What a logical end to the Cold War.

General Harker is sweating, though the room is cool. He's trying to perceive whether I am insane. But of

course I am. And so is he. So he has no criterion to judge
by.

One minute left till she comes. How time flies, after
twenty-five years.

Mistress Marguerite:

So into the War Room I stride, flanked by guards. On
some strange whim I have put on a hat, in honour of the
occasion. My hat is blue, with white artificial flowers.

I make a brief but invigorating speech, then gaze
directly at Sovrenian. Piercingly.

'Increase the Cold!'

Suddenly General Harker bleats out, 'Don't!'

I'm utterly amazed. But I don't allow this to show. I
ought to have replaced Harker this morning; I *did* note
signs of weariness in him. Behold where sentimentality
has got me. However, I control my anger.

Harker looks embarrassed; and in any case his feeble
outburst makes no difference. Dr Sovrenian has already
thrown the switch to enact the final sequence. We all
watch the wall screens in silence.

Gradually the blue deepens. It invades the heart-core
of the world. I understand the theory fairly well. I myself
was scientifically inclined before I decided that my true
forte lay in government. The slight temperature differen-
tial should equalize out during the next few moments,
putting an unbearable strain on the resources of our
Enemy.

Ah! The red fire-dot representing them flickers momentarily – and such a cheer goes up in the War Room!

Now the temperature of their Enclave steadies again,
as they too are forced to pump heat from what remains
of the central embers to sustain themselves. Naturally,
the rate of temperature descent steepens as a result. They

won't be able to keep it up. The whole world (excepting the Enclaves) is now one hundredth of a degree absolute. Excellent!

Suddenly their red light oscillates through orange, yellow, green; touches blue.

One last flare of yellow. Then blue, perfect blue.

They're gone, frozen. They're dead.

Those present don't even cheer this time. What a quiet end to a war.

'Abort the field, Sovrenian.'

He grins at me.

Dr Sovrenian:

'The sequence, Mistress, is locked in,' I tell her politely.

We're one three-hundredth of a degree away from Ab-Zee. Still heading down. I knew it could be done. As soon as the world touches Ab-Zee we'll be sucked right in after it.

'Sovrenian!' she shrills. 'We're wasting power. This isn't an experiment.'

Abruptly Harker goes berserk. Snatching a hand-gun from a guard, he leaps back, levels it. He shouts something about taking command. The guard stands gawping, pawing at his empty holster idiotically. None of this matters. The General's intervention comes far too late. But how utterly delightful.

I whoop with joy.

'Ab-Zee,' I cry. 'Coming up *now*!'

General Harker:

A sickening lurch – in my heart and head, my belly and my vision. Lights vanish, come back on. The world flickers, returns. Something strange and awful has happened. I feel as if I've been turned inside out.

Oh yes. I know what it is! I've disobeyed our Mistress. I have blasphemed. For a moment I was cast into outer darkness.

Mistress Marguerite:

My guards shelter me faithfully. But General Harker has already dropped the gun. Abruptly he crouches down on the floor, hides like a little boy. Why, now he has curled up in a foetal position! He's rocking and mewing to himself.

I thrust my guards aside. 'Sovrenian: what has happened?'

'We . . . we appear to have pushed the world through into Neg-Heat, Mistress.' The man looks deeply shocked. So even he is a weak reed. I am disappointed in him. This is even worse than his misconduct a few moments ago.

'Neg-Heat? What does that mean?'

'The fall in temperature . . . has gone below Ab-Zee. The world ought to have vanished . . . It didn't. This is incredible: negative temperature! There's a temperature scale below absolute zero – running the other way! We're in the minus zone. Minus absolute.'

'But what's *that*?'

'I don't know, Mistress. I've no idea.'

My hat got bumped askew by one of the guards, in his haste to protect me. I resettle it on my head. There's nothing to be gained by panicking.

Dr Sovrenian:

Now that I've had time to review the data, it seems clear that the world didn't actually pass *through* absolute zero.

Rather, in that instant when everything lurched, the whole world jumped right past Ab-Zee – and on to the scale of absolute negative temperature: the minus-Kelvin scale.

No doubt it is just as impossible to attain true absolute zero as it is for any material object to reach the speed of light. (For if an object did so, it would attain infinite mass.) But we used to theorize that a starship could perhaps 'jump past' that barrier – and instantly be transformed into a mass of super-light particles.

Something similar has happened. The whole world has gone through a phase transition. We're familiar with the normal phase transitions: from plasma to gas, from gas to liquid, from liquid to solid. At absolute zero there is a further transition, hitherto unknown to us: a transition from solid to . . . what can I best call it? Negative existence? The immaterial? A wraith state?

And the phase shift of the world drew our Enclave along with it. From being at room temperature on the plus-Kelvin scale, suddenly we were at the corresponding temperature on the minus-Kelvin scale. And the outside world was catching up with us fast, rapidly 'warming up' on the negative scale . . .

We are wraiths. We still move around, we can still talk to each other. But most other bodily functions are suspended; we no longer need to eat, drink, breathe, excrete or sleep. I believe we have become immortal. (Certainly we have tried to kill each other, and ourselves. In vain.)

There's no hint of a universe beyond the world. The world is a hole in existence now; but it is a hole which endures, and evolves.

And inside this hole – within our Enclave too – the temperature is rising higher and higher on the negative scale.

Slow Birds

Talk not of minus degrees Kelvin. Talk rather of cold fire; of fire which burns most coldly, but consumes not.

Talk of degrees of pain; talk of the temperature of frozen agony. For nothing can destroy our wraith-flesh, but only hurt it inwardly. And every hour the frigid fire intensifies.

I've begun to wonder whether there is any absolute upper limit to temperature. Why has no one thought of this before? The concept of Absolute Heat!

Why, Absolute Heat can only be the temperature of the original cosmic fireball at the moment when the universe was born! And we know by calculation what the temperature was, just an instant after that: 10^{32} degrees Kelvin.

Shall I spell this out? Can you conceive a hundred thousand billion billion billion degrees – of pain?

At the present rate of increase we only have ten thousand years or so to endure.

Until what? Until we reach Absolute Heat on the negative scale? And another phase transition? When the world suddenly becomes a white hole gushing its light to the boundaries of the universe? When at last we die? I hope we can die then.

If only the Enemy hadn't given up! (Did their scientists guess the truth?) They could have been suffering as intensely as we are.

Mistress Marguerite:

'Let's be sensible, Gentlemen! When the going gets hot we need firm and confident leadership. I assure you that *I* can stay the course without flinching.'

'Mistress! Mistress!' they all acclaim me.

After all, I did win the Cold War. Now I must win the Hot War, if it takes ten thousand years.

What a beautiful word is perseverance.

In the Mirror of the Earth

Raoul was a Sleeper: the first Sleeper I had ever come close to (in either the proximal or the emotional sense!) during all my years of wandering across Thraea.

Not, I hasten to add, that I journeyed in order to meet Sleepers, whom personally I had always regarded as pathological half-persons.

Besides, their whereabouts are well enough known to every child. No diligent search is necessary; though perhaps a fair deal of patience, ardent persuasion and even greasing of palms is a requisite *sine qua non* for the actual admission into the presence of one of our pampered and protected treasures.

Who are to be found – all six of them currently, out of a world population nudging two billion souls – ensconced in their quaintly named Observatories in the capital cities of Atlantica, Pacifica, Indica, Mediterre and Baltica. (Oh yes, and there's one on the island of Caspia.)

Observatories, ah ha! I've sometimes wondered whether it is the Sleepers who are being observed there – or whether it is *they* who are doing the observing. Or both. Or both. Still, we Thraeans aren't an overwhelmingly superstitious people; so I suppose to describe those guarded palaces as 'Sleep Temples' or some such, and their attendants as 'priests' would hardly be deemed good form.

Though indeed, in so far as we do possess a secular religion – or maybe I should call it an 'imaginative mythology' – as anyone glancing at the place names on the map of the world must inevitably concur that we do,

this is entirely owing to the observations of all the random
generations of Sleepers; of whom sometimes as many as
nine have at any one time been alive, and sometimes as
few as one.

But never, as it happens, none. Would none be taken
as a dire omen? By some, no doubt; by some.

Never none, as I say; and very rarely in our history
only one. Imagine the feelings of that singleton! One
solitary sport of nature, one peerless lonely caprice! What
a fate.

But hush, I said that six Sleepers are alive today – in
our present well-endowed epoch. Yet a seventh is also
alive, far removed from any metropolitan Observatory,
unknown but to my good self. Quite a life of danger and
subterfuge is his: danger while he lies enslothed in what
the mystic poets call 'slumber', and which more scientifically inclined spirits prefer to describe as 'rapport with
the Submerged'; danger, also, from any of our dreams
which happen to encounter him during his waking hours,
against which he, unpractised and ill-equipped, obviously
has no defence.

Peril, yes, and subterfuge – for our seventh secret
Sleeper, Raoul.

Frankly, when I first found out his identity I was
astonished that he did not surrender himself forthwith to
the rich life: of servants, mistresses, excellent cuisine,
dream-guards and all the rest of the panoply – for the
simple *quid pro quo,* ego-flattering in itself, of having his
words hung on till the end of his days by a retinue of
scribes, sages, scholiasts and pilgrims.

Yet Raoul, it seemed, was in search of something of
his own. As was I myself! Besides, his parents having by
hook and by crook kept his sleeping sickness a dark
secret, perhaps he also felt that he owed it to their

memory to honour that unlucrative investment in his privacy.

Lucre . . . There. I've mentioned it; and I would rather that I hadn't. For this casts a tiny shadow of doubt on the altruism of my motives.

A handsome reward goes to the parents of a Sleeper as soon as they declare their child and hand him or her over into safe keeping. Which has even led in the course of our history to one or two attempted masquerades. Naturally, such deceit is bound to fail; for even if the miscreant mother and father pretend to have been completely out of touch with all civilization, stuck in some incredibly remote spot during the whole babyhood and infancy of their brat – till it reached an age when it could be trained to dissimulate – even so no child can possibly lie still with its eyes shut eight hours per day for a single week, let alone year in year out. Especially not for somebody else's benefit!

The question of lucre, though . . . To my knowledge the situation had never arisen before, yet it seemed a fair presumption that a generous reward might equally well accrue to anybody delivering news of a rogue *adult* Sleeper at large.

However, Raoul had no need to fear my betraying him. And I'm sure that the thought never really crossed his mind, except perhaps at the very outset.

But first things first . . .

I had been wandering for some years, as I say, paying my way where food wasn't free for the taking or impaling with my cross-bow, by selling my dreams for show – and on occasion pitting them against other waking dreams in contest or combat; since my own dreams are particularly powerful, coherent projections.

Powerful, indeed . . . But here I must emphasize that no Romantic am I. On the contrary! Dreams are a psychic superfluity; and my psyche happens to be particularly orderly. Thus my classic turn of mind produces strongly structured dreams which are, if I say it myself, a distinct cut above the slop that a lot of other people produce: outpourings of wobbling jelly, rather than creatures with real teeth, or objects with some design function to them.

Yes, I'm a classicist. Personally I've never felt inclined to warble song or revel in nature or cultivate ambiguous mysteries – unlike many other wanderers I have met with on my travels, not least of all those many perfervid pilgrims tramping their way from one Observatory to the next on the Grand Tour . . .

I'm sure that the main advantage of having as many as six Sleepers in residence all over the world is that it keeps such folk on the move! If there were only one known Sleeper extant – in the city of Seashells, for the sake of argument* – what a host of pilgrims would bunch up there like moths round a single lanthorn, like bees at the only available flower bed!

No, it wasn't in poetry, nature or metaphysics that I found true beauty and significance, but rather in the engineering and civil architectural masterpieces of Thraea; and it was to admire and assess these that I travelled the globe, taking in, to name but a few highlights, the Panama Bridge that links Pacifica with Atlantica; and the Gibraltar Ship Canal down the frontier between Atlantica and Mediterre allowing boats of deepest draught to pass directly from the Gulf of Algeciras into the Bay of Tangier; and by no means least the mighty Suez Bridge joining Mediterre with the Peninsula

---

* A curious misnomer, Seashells, for the main city of Indica! Set almost in the heart of a continent as it is, beside a few freshwater lakes; and at least fifteen hundred miles from the nearest part of the African Ocean. But there's the wisdom of the Sleepers for you . . .

of Suez, that long slim finger pointing from the crooked arm of Indica . . .

Why didn't I settle down sooner to design something equivalent? Well, you know what they say: one leaves home in order to return; one ranges the whole wide world in search of oneself. So if I had sometimes asked myself that very question in weary or frustrating moments during my wander-years, the answer had to be that during all this time I was still matching myself against what had already been accomplished. I was still in pursuit of a project grand enough: one which no one had yet dared, or even been *able*, to conceive.

Yet I realize that I have mentioned *Raoul's* name – but not my own!

Enough. If you haven't already guessed it, my name is Tomas d'Arque – from which you will have no difficulty in pinning down my birthplace to a certain fair town in Liguria Province of Mediterre, not too far from Lake Corsica.

And this is how I first discovered Raoul's secret, and became for a while his elder brother, protector, confidant . . .

It happened amid the seven hundred densely forested lakes of the Bahamas. Specifically it occurred some eight or nine miles north of the sporting resort of Providence, where the hunting is so well renowned, out in the woodland near North Bimini Pool.

I was on my way north to inspect the newly completed 150-mile-long dam built to drain the salty shallows of the Florida Polder, so that I could tick off one more engineering feat as not quite worthy of aspiring to. An admirable endeavour, to be sure! Make no mistake! Twenty long years it had taken. However, it was something which had already been dreamed, and done.

Here I must add an original insight of my own, stemming from my relationship with Raoul, concerning the surprise occasionally voiced by certain cultural historians that in our world where the tempo of life has ever remained demure, our people should nevertheless from quite early times constantly exhibit such devotion to mammoth, long-term feats of construction. I believe I know the real, *deep* reason why this is so.

Pray consider the way in which a Sleeper must view his life's span compared with all the rest of us. We are alive and conscious without ceasing; not even excluding the couple of hours every fortnight or so when we discharge our dreams (our psychic superfluity). Whereas he *dies* for eight hours out of every twenty-four, as regularly as clockwork.

For him the daily death of sleep – the robbery of time – may well breed a panic urgency, an inner allegiance to more short-term goals; to which I can juxtapose our own sense of continuity and connexion, which breeds in us the desire to connect: capes of land with other capes by means of very long bridges or causeways; and the bay of one sea to the nearest bay of a neighbouring sea by means of grand canals – so that everything will flow and join together continuously.

Yet there's more. From what Raoul told me, a Sleeper's fleeting visions of the Submerged are somewhat confused and not quite under the control of his own will. Of course it's otherwise with everyone else, particularly the more coherent spirits amongst us. So, being able to project in miniature a majestic bridge or other edifice, it is easy and logical to conceive of this project being carried through into actuality in brick and stone, somewhere appropriate upon the surface of Thraea; and a whole nation or city can easily be fired with a fine dreamer's vision, and act upon it. A powerful dream-projection readily becomes a building project.

Such was the case with the Swannee Project for damming and draining the Florida Polder, whither I was heading. Typically, the name seemed somewhat capricious, since neither the forests of Atlantica nor the grain-lands of Mexique to the west of the Polder were noted for any such bird-life as swans! Yet this was the name which had been chosen metaphysically, by the Sleeper of Atlantica, during one of his nightly sorties into the Submerged . . .

Raoul, however. Raoul, and what happened near North Bimini Pool . . .

I was riding my newly acquired bay gelding through dense woodland along a little-frequented bridle path. There was not *too* much danger of attack by angry boars or sore-headed bears; and by keeping to this byway I hoped to avoid any further encounters with brash sportsmen – who have even been known to try to pit their blundering dreams against savage prey, rather than use their crossbow bolts.

Ah, brash sportsmen: they have their uses, though! Only a few hours earlier in Providence I had obtained my fine mount and its full panniers as the result of a dream contest with one such . . .

Besides appealing to the hunting instinct, and to a modicum of gluttony upon the products of the chase, Providence also caters to gambling fever – which I suppose is a variant on the hunt, involving this time the bagging, or more often the escape, of money. A famous casino, there, occupies the wives and girlfriends of the addicts of the chase; and after a few days in Providence the women seem willing to wager upon anything and everything. Will the hotel chef dish up that newly bagged boar with an orange or an apple in its mouth? Ten gives you twenty it'll be an apple.

I had felt my dream-time coming on as I tramped into Providence earlier on foot, and decided to capitalize on this, as I was somewhat strapped for funds. Luckily for me the casino was fresh out of a main act to amuse the guests, due to a bout of tummy upsets amongst a newly arrived team of artistes, who were no doubt unused to the rich fare. So the casino compère was only too happy to comply with my request.

As usual with such dreamshows – lest they get out of hand – the venue was the open air rather than upon the indoor stage; though in this case the open air was graciously accoutred with a marquee awning stretched above a natural grassy amphitheatre, and lit by many lanthorns.

Deliberately I had held back my dreams for a few hours longer than need be, to build their power and organization; and as luck would have it none of the guests or staff were dreaming that evening – or else, if they were, they stayed discreetly indoors with their jejune projections.

All, that is, but for my sportsman; as I was to discover (to *his* cost) twenty minutes or so into my show.

First I projected before me a wondrous miniature city of considerable detail; and as soon as it was firm I invited selected members of the audience – the prettiest – down on to the floor of the amphitheatre to step along my city's boulevards and test the strength of its public buildings, before returning to their seats.

Allowing no fires to break our nor any tremors to escape into the audience, I then daringly destroyed my city in an earthquake.

For variety, next I dreamed a dancing, juggling bear. And it was at this point that the presumptuous oaf challenged me to a combat of dream-beasts, to the acclaim of his coterie of friends. I shan't expatiate upon his vivid but basically floppy projections. Suffice it to say that, having allowed him various vantages for the sake of his *amour-propre,* and to let wagers mount up, I trounced the fellow. The upshot for me: possession of that bay gelding, and full panniers.

So towards midnight I was about nine miles north of Providence, seated upon my spoils, occasionally checking that the bridle way ran true by reference to what stars I could spy through rifts in the foliage; when my keen sense of danger alerted me. That, and the snicker of the gelding.

Some way off the path in the dark underbrush I heard a grunt; then another. Reining in, as the rhythmic rasping noise continued, I reached for my crossbow, thinking: bear . . . or boar.

Another man might have ridden cautiously on; or, had his dreaming been upon him, as it was upon me earlier, he might have sent a dream-beast crashing through the dingy boskage; as it was, I was fresh out of dreams. And I must admit that my curiosity has led me into tight scrapes often enough in the past; this must go with being an inventive sort of fellow!

My steed pawed the turf, and whinnied; as I was hesitating a gibbous moon floated from behind some clouds, increasing the light. Recklessly I dismounted and tethered the gelding to a handy tree stump, soothing it, then I crept slowly into the underbrush, crossbow cocked, prepared to snatch back my foot should I feel a bending twig about to snap.

Ten steps, twenty; and a tiny clearing hove dimly in sight . . . where, wrapped in a blanket, lay what I took at first sight to be a severely injured man in his death agony.

A few paces more, and the amazing truth dawned on me: that the man was *sleeping* – the noise, as Raoul later

explained, in some embarrassment, was that of 'snoring'.
At his head, a knapsack.

What to do? I was consumed with curiosity, yet if I
broke his sleep I could shock or injure him. After thinking
this over, I sat down right there in the clearing and
remained so all night long, till dawn began to creep into
the east.

During my long hours of vigil – interrupted only by
two forays: once to the horse for a bite of pasty and a
swig of wine, and the second time into the bushes on a
call of nature – I noted how the man did not lie entirely
still in his comatose state. At times he shifted from one
side to the other, as if by some automatic instinct of his
muscles, to protect himself from cramp or gangrene. And
twice he cried out: once, the word, 'Everglades', and on
the second occasion as if in baby talk, 'Palm Beach, my
Mammy!' 'Everglades' no doubt referred to the extensive
woods we were in, in a submerged, mythistorical fashion;
though as to the latter I knew of no palm-fringed shores
closer than the equatorial strands of the South American
Ocean, down Cayenne way.

As the forest cover eventually brightened I discerned
that the Sleeper was only about twenty-one years old,
with an unruly mop of dark hair, and fine, almost feminine
features. When the bird chorus burst into song about us,
he opened his soft brown eyes; and so we first met –
much to his initial consternation.

Quickly I reassured him; though on awakening it
seemed that the Sleeper was still quite confused as to the
substantial reality of the world. So without further ado I
set to and cooked us both a tasty breakfast of venison
sausages. No doubt it was because I treated him thus in
comradely style as just another person like myself, not as
a wonder and a living miracle, that he soon began to
warm to me and to consider me as a potential friend and

ally after all his years of subterfuge and self-imposed isolation.

I did not just wag the ready ear of one who only listens in order to betray confidences and turn them to his own advantage; but I presented my own life's quest, and myself, to him, so that presently he began to trust me, and soon to see merits: such as a horse to ride in tandem with me, and best prospect of all, someone reliable to watch and ward him while he slept. That night, and the night after, and the night after that . . .

By the time we arrived at Jack's Ville on the eastern shore of the Swannee Project a couple of weeks later, Raoul had already told me much about his relationship with the Submerged – which he had actually used, rather cunningly, as protective colouration. For he had long since adopted the guise of a rather devout mythistorical pilgrim.

Thus whenever he was obliged to rent a room in a town, he could perfectly excuse his otherwise peculiar custom of locking himself away for hours at a stretch: such were his times of obligatory meditation upon the enigmas of the Submerged and our mythistory.

Hard times, quite often! In a room intended to shelter ordinary travellers, what could Raoul lie down on but the floor? In the absence of female companionship he could hardly rent an amour-chambre; alone in a cushioned love-nest he would have been regarded as very weird indeed – and I suspect, though he didn't answer this question directly, that Raoul had even denied himself the joys of intercourse entirely, lest with his seed spilt and passion spent he might fall *asleep* in someone's arms. Till he met me it had been a sad life for him.

So we reined in on a low hilltop above Jack's Ville: that once tiny hamlet which had grown into something of a mini-city with all the construction work; and we both dismounted to survey the long dam stretching out forever to the west, straight as a die. To the south, the beginnings of the Polder; to the north the white breakers of the North American Ocean (for it was a breezy day).

Raoul stared fixedly southwards as though the dam itself meant nothing to him.

'Florida is rising,' he said. 'Rising into view. Wouldn't it be rare if there were drowned cities to be found beneath the sea?'

'And who would have built them?' I asked, laughing. 'Mermen?'

I began to speculate, though, whether it might not be a grand enough project to build something noble _underwater_: with fishes swimming beyond the toughened windows, and air pipes leading to the surface? No one had ever constructed anything beneath the waves. How would one go about it? By means of massive caissons? Or using a circular dam, which one later demolished to let the briny deep flow back in? As you can see, already my intimacy with Raoul was beginning to stir strange and wonderful imaginings within me – amply repaying the care I was lavishing on our relationship.

Raoul cleared his throat. 'Some pilgrims say that when the universe was made, another universe had to be made too, for balance. Or maybe this was because the universe is made out of the void, say others; for a void isn't just emptiness. You can tear it apart, into two distinct but complementary things: the Real, and the Submerged, the Mythistorical. Yet there must be a place _somewhere_,' and he banged his fist into his palm, 'where the two join, if only as a thread, an umbilicus. A location. A door. Where land is sea, and sea is land, unseparated out.'

'Like a swamp, you mean? Ah, so that's why you were heading here now that we're pumping the Polder dry?'

From our vantage point we could clearly see the first of the great hydraulic stations two miles out along the dam; and less distinctly a second, and a third. I fancied that I could hear the thump and slosh of that first station like a distant heartbeat, powered by the spinning windmills on its roof. Bucket by bucket, at fifty such locations, Florida was being emptied out, reclaimed for Atlantica; and during a few moments of reverie I was overwhelmed by the certainty that here, for the first time in history, the actual geography of Thraea was being slightly modified; so that what had been coloured blue on maps hitherto, now would be painted green. Fortunately my sense of proportion soon reasserted itself.

Raoul gripped my arm. 'I wonder if that dam can really hold? There must be so much pressure of water against it!'

I assessed the structure with a practised eye.

'It looks well enough built. Yet perhaps it shouldn't be so utterly *straight*. That might encourage waves to build up abnormally high as they roll along it in the winter. Whereas if they'd built it with curving bays, giving it a scalloped edge, or if they'd thrust groynes out, which could have served as piers sometime in the future . . .'

His grip tightened. 'I wonder what other pressures are thrusting against it? Pressures, perhaps, from the Submerged itself . . . Imagine the inundation if the dam does break!'

'Oh, then you'd have land and sea mixed up all right, in one almighty pudding! But let's not carp at the work-manship, just because the design seems so linear and monotonous. It reflects, after all,' and I winked wickedly, 'our sense of continuity; whereas the periodic pump-stations, throbbing away – not unlike somebody *snoring* . . .' I nudged him in the ribs affectionately, just as he released my arm. 'Enough said!'

We remounted one behind the other, and rode on down together into Jack's Ville.

That same night Raoul cried out the one strange word in his sleep, several times: 'Okefenokee!' In the morning over a breakfast of muffins, bacon and cinnamon coffee, I questioned him.

He shrugged fretfully. 'Another of the place names of the Submerged, Tomas! Somewhere hereabouts . . .'

'But,' I asked him trenchantly, 'will it *still* be submerged, now that hereabouts is being drained? In a word, is "Okefenokee" the name of the door to your destiny?' (Several words, actually. But I thought I phrased it rather well.)

He stared blankly, hardly focusing. 'How would it be,' he muttered at last, 'to tread the Submerged lands? Would the denizens of the Submerged perceive us as ghostly wraiths? Spooks, or will o' the wisps? Vague blobs of light, occasionally solidifying into seemingly solid people? And what would they make of your projected dreams? Would these seem to be silver elves and hunking, dripping giants, and mothmen and such?'

'Do you *really* believe in the existence of these . . . counter people?'

'Counterfeit people?' He misunderstood me, or deliberately chose to do so. 'I must be one of those myself, born into the wrong universe!'

'Surely,' said I reasonably, 'the Submerged is simply our mythic dimension? It's like a sort of fifth dimension of our world, Raoul. The bulk of the people only notice four dimensions: length and breadth and time and height. But there's another one, as well, which *you* perceive – perhaps it's required as a kind of glue to join the other four together. Let its name be *depth*; depth is different in nature from height.'

'Height?' he retorted, as though I had offended him. 'Fat lot you know about height! Length and breadth and time, oh yes. But height? I'll give you height!'

'Now what would you mean by that?' I asked soothingly.

And he told me: and it came as a revelation.

Not, I hasten to add, because *he* intended it as such; but because then and there at once I was able to grasp that this was the missing piece in the puzzle of my life. With an instinctive sense of right structure I slotted that piece straight into place; and thrilled.

I did not tell Raoul that I had experienced revelation, due in small part to him. I feared that this might make him vain and swollen-headed with a sense of his own importance; which could in turn have made him reckless. So, while my brain buzzed inwardly with a grand conception, I simply nodded.

'There's something in that,' I allowed; and I ruffled his hair. 'Care for another muffin?'

That all took place four years ago.

I still can't believe that Raoul deliberately gave me the slip that day in Jack's Ville due to some paranoid suspicion that I might betray his identity. Still less could it have been caused by any disinclination for my company, since I was proving to him for the first time in his lonely life how valuable friendly human brotherhood can be. For a while I suspected that something ill had befallen him.

But now I realize why he went, and where he is to this very day.

Even now it will take several more years to drain the Florida Polder entirely since the water level only sinks slowly, even with fifty bucket-stations on the job. So the Polder is still betwixt and between: a queer region of salt

swamp, neither properly land nor water, full of dead
rotting seaweeds and the bones of fishes beached on
newly arisen cays.

I *know* that, haunted by inner necessity, Raoul will be
the wanderer of that half-land. He will be blowing into
empty conch shells to hearken for an answering echo
from somewhere in the murk, and to follow it, there to
fall asleep and listen to the whisper of metaphysical
names – some of which the Sleeper of Atlantica is already
enunciating publicly: Canaveral, Tampa, Orlando,
Lauderdale . . .

I take note of these announcements, even back home
here in Mediterre; though I must confess that I'm not
consumed with curiosity. These days I have my own work
cut out – ever since my own grand dream-projection,
and accompanying passionate explanations, convinced the
good folk of my native Liguria to undertake the work.

For what I realized during my moment of revelation in
Jack's Ville was that all the great engineering projects of
Thraea hitherto have been concerned exclusively, and
mundanely, with length and breadth and time – with
connecting land-mass to land-mass, and linking ocean to
ocean. Never have we dreamed of connecting the ground
to the sky in a purely gratuitous aesthetic way with no
strict linear purpose.

Already here in Liguria midway between Lake Corsica
and the Azure Coast the foundations and base of my
tower are complete, and the first stage will soon be rising.

To begin with, I thought of naming it the 'Eiffel
Tower', after a phrase that spilled from Raoul's lips once
while he was asleep – followed the next morning, on
enquiry, by a description of a most unusual erection.

Yet on second thoughts I have decided not to use any
Submerged name: for on the contrary *my* creation will
soar upward and upward. So instead, I may well call it

'Raoul's Tower' to honour a well-loved if briefly known friend; thus to tantalize all future visitors, without betraying any confidences.

Though somewhere in the structure – well concealed in a strong casket, yet so placed that a future generation will come upon it while refurbishing some part of the fabric, thus unlocking an enigma of years – I shall secrete this true account of the genesis of my masterpiece. Which will inevitably be a Wonder of the World.

On the other hand, though, if I *do* call it 'Raoul's Tower', future biographers may leap to the conclusion that Raoul was my lover during our brief sojourn together; or even that I may have taken advantage of him while he *slept*! That lays *too* much stress upon our relationship.

So on balance maybe the 'Tomas Tower' is the better name; and if I deliberately leave my work untitled – thus emphasizing its nonfunctional purity – so it will inevitably come to be known. People are impelled to give names to things; what other *raison d'être*, I sometimes wonder, is there for our precious Sleepers in their Observatories?

Tomas Tower: I think I like it. But let time and history decide.

And to time and the future I bequeath this little memoir: to a posterity when maybe – though I doubt it – the world will have changed out of recognition; for which reason, pardon me my explanations of items that will surely appear to you completely obvious and well-known.

Such as my own name:

(signed with a flourish)

Tomas d'A.

Cruising

From where I shelter, hidden underneath my concrete burster slab, I can feel the swallows flocking outside. Above my airfield they mill wildly in the sky. Their beaks click like tiny castanets as they gulp a stream of gnats to put a last gram of fat on their bodies before they undertake the great journey. The swallows are drunk with a sweet panic. They're a host of fairy children dancing streamers round a hidden maypole which holds up the sky; right now, they're busily unwinding the maypole of the year.

My mind goes out to them. 'The fogs are coming! We smell the fogs!' they cry.

'How fat the berries on the bushes!'

'Wind's from the south today. It calls!'

'Can you hear the dunes of the desert booming? Can you hear the screaming of the apes?'

'Can you hear the cough of the camel and the roar of the lion?'

'We'll be late!'

I understand them perfectly. My own brain is very like their brains. In common with the swallows I know in advance every rise and dip, every river and valley of my destined route. Their instincts are my instincts; but mine are held in check. How I envy their freedom to migrate, even if it spells death for them.

Am I the only one of my flight to overhear the swallows? Am I the only one to feel excitement, frustration, jealousy? Perhaps. In our mighty mobile metal nest my three companions (for want of a better word) sit silent and inert. No emotions leak from them. Any thoughts they think are masked and secret.

But not the thoughts of the swallows. Winding themselves up like stones swung round and round on strings, the swallows race through figure-eights.

'*Tswit! Sweet! Sweet!*' one of them cries out. This is the call to take wing and fly south, forever south, until they arrive in the sweet heat of southern Africa.

I decide to name this swallow Amy. I follow her with my mind. Amy, wonderful Amy, flier beyond compare.

She fans her tail. She turns in full flight to dart in a different direction, wild to flap her wings in another quarter of the sky. She snatches a tiny spider floating on a silken thread.

In her breast she feels a strange kind of hurt. This is a lovely hurt, teasing her wonderfully; it will draw her ever onwards.

'I can't bear to stay another day!' she tells her mate Nijinsky. (I name him for his nimbleness.) Amy's voice is the chattering of a mountain stream, the babbling rush of water over pebbles.

She and twenty others dart down to the line of telephone wires at the perimeter of the airfield. There they chatter about their preset route: the mountain passes of the Pyrenees, the dusty plains of New Castile, the apes screaming from the Rock of Gibraltar. Next, those desert forts and oases. Then the dry Sahara, with such stunning oven-heat reflecting from its sands that many swallows will die on the wing. Many will drop from the air like stones.

Naturally, Amy and Nijinsky are worried about the youngest of their brood, whom I call Pavlova.

'The desert may be wider this year,' Amy twitters. 'Last year it was wider than the year before. But we can't stay. Soon the cold will come here. When it comes, it'll kill all the insects.'

'But is Pavlova chubby enough yet?'

'Chubby or not, we all have to go.'

'Oh, it puzzles me, Amy, that we can never act in any other way! What we must do, we must do. Is it the same for every living creature?'

'But doing what you *must* do is what living is all about!' cries Amy in astonishment. 'That's the perfect joy of existence.' She preens quickly under her wing. 'If the world quit turning, then a swallow might stop flying! But only then. Don't worry: we'll all get there safely. It'll be the most wonderful flight ever flown. I know it in my heart.'

Swallows are spaced out on the wires as neatly as soldiers on parade. They all wear the same dark steel-blue uniforms with frock-tail coats, the same rust-red caps and chinstraps, the same soft snowy breastplates.

'I'm dying to see this desert of yours,' burbles little Pavlova. 'I mean, I can *already* see it in my mind's eye. I'm not scared. I'll skim it in a day.'

'No, nor two days, either,' says Nijinsky. 'Your mind's eye's out of date. Every year the Sahara desert grows greater.'

Momentarily I pity these swallows; my mind's eye is never out of date. But what do I care about the Sahara desert? Africa isn't mapped in *my* mind. *My* migration route lies eastward.

Something is happening! Down here in the bunker my soldiers are scrambling into their armoured jeeps, my maintenance men into their trucks. My metal nest awakens, engine roaring. The bunker doors descend over the empty debris pit.

And they drive me out, under the open sky!

* * *

Presently we're on a country road, crunching southward away from the airfield: me and my three mute siblings in one transporter, four more of us in another, together with a whole convoy of wagons, trucks, and jeeps.

It's been a good summer. The harvest is all safely in. Golden hay lies piled in great rolls in the barns. My swallows have seen the stubble burning off fiercely, reddening the sky by night, clouding it with smoke by day. Now I observe how most of the blackened fields have already been turned over by the plough.

I spy rams in a pasture, serving the grazing ewes, marking their woolly backs with blue and red wax. The rams wear tight harnesses which hold the coloured wax. The sheep glance at our convoy, then lose interest.

Reaching out with my mind, I sense that Amy has just forked her tail straight and true – and leapt into flight. After her leap all the other swallows. For the moment has come. Only Nijinsky glances back at the little village beyond my airfield where he and Amy nested this summer in the eaves of a farmhouse. He glances once, but already it seems as if the village has receded infinitely far away. As indeed it has. Already it's on the very far side of the map in his mind. Away beyond the whole of Africa. Even if Nijinsky wanted, he couldn't now turn back.

Let me not be turned back, either!

While my transporter navigates the byways, heading south by east, I follow Amy in her flight. And I begin to hope.

An hour later our convoy turns off the country lane, up a broad woodland ride to a clearing surrounded by fir trees.

The soldiers fan out through the woods. My launch officer tips me up in the steel nest, pointing east. And we wait. And wait. A few nearby soldiers pace

about, nervous as swallows themselves. They sweat.
Occasionally they joke. Or urinate.

Amy, Nijinsky, and Pavlova link up with a straggling line
of other migrants on the sky-road. Oh yes, there are
roads through the sky. Quite narrow roads: these are the
caravan trails of the blue. Such roads rise or sink at the
whim of the wind. My flock of swallows is flying high now
to catch a side breeze from due east.
    They fly quite straight, with little swerving or veering,
hardly any capricious jinking. Instead of chasing insects
as before, now they let the insects come to them. Bristling
out the tiny contour feathers at the sides of their mouths,
they funnel their fuel in to a scooping beak.
    Click: a fly.
    Click: a little moth borne aloft by some mood of the
wind.
    Click: a winged beetle.
    Lifting and thrusting, they overtake swifts and martins.
    Upstroking, they feather the blades of their wings to
lessen air resistance. I understand all this very well,
though I have never flown before. Below, the curves of
the rolling hills are a caress.

And suddenly I do burst free – with the power of a
million swallows. A second later, my nozzle controls start
to steer me on course. Five seconds later, my fins flip
out. A few seconds more, and my wings swing into place
to balance me. I'm the first to leave the nest. After three
years of waiting, at last I can migrate! My booster drops.
My jet commences. I gulp air hungrily.
    At last. I'm a bird.
    Swiftly I skim forest and water meadow, flat fields and
heathland. I swoop past a solitary windmill, its sails
pointing like a road-sign. Long before Amy and Pavlova

and Nijinsky are anywhere near the coast, I'm over a beach, then out across the blue chop and toss of the sea, exulting . . .

Whilst flying, Amy is dreaming of the reed beds of the Lualaba river down in Zambia. Survivors of the Sahara, replenished by the insects of Nigeria and the Congo, may roost a while along the Lualaba. They will cling to bending reeds, twittering at one another while in the dusk an elephant trumpets and the tick birds peck vermin from its hide. Amy will dart into the river for a quick dip to clean herself, ever wary of the snap of the crocodile.

But she isn't there yet. The wind threatens to veer. If a strong tail wind gets behind swallows they need to find a wire or reed to roost on till the wind shifts or drops. Otherwise they'll be pushed along too quickly for the map unrolling in their minds. They'll overfly it, get lost.

No such problem for me! I fly faster than any normal wind. My mind-map is impeccable. As soon as I've crossed the sea, I shall scan my map in mere fractions of time too small to be called seconds.

For her part, Amy rises higher where the wind is slower. I rise slightly too, since waves are swelling.

Within half an hour I'm over the polders of the Netherlands. Fifteen minutes later, and I'm across the German border, commencing my long sweep across the German plains. Here my map clicks into place. The terrain matches it perfectly. Farms flash by, bare fields, cows and churches . . .

In the City Park of Johannesburg there are reed beds. It is there that Amy will join up with fellow migrants arriving by way of the Nile valley from furthest Siberia. For in Joburg the two main streams of migration flow

together in the southern spring. In Joburg in the southern
autumn those two streams part again, like twin forks of a
swallow's tail. Last year in Joburg Amy and Nijinsky met
and roosted a while with Ivan Swallow, from Irkutsk
beside Lake Baikal. (I fantasize, of course.)

I dream along with Amy while I cruise over Germany,
comparing my mind-map with the territory from time to
time. Everything is as it should be. Of course. I'm a
specialized instrument – and why, so is Amy too! She and
I, we're both designed for cruising. For a life on the
wing. Only with peril and hardship can she ever alight on
terra firma. Earlier this year, when she was shuffling
clumsily about on the ground using her wings as crutches
whilst she scooped up wet mud for her nest, an evil tabby
cat nearly had her for breakfast.

Amy's making progress towards the seaside, but I'm
already over Poland. Flying fifteen metres low. I swing
around a pimple of a hill. A farmer stares at me in shock.
A policeman jumps from his car and empties his pistol
into the air; but I'm already past him and away.

Far behind me something flashes as brightly as the sun.
I'm soon buffeted by a fierce wind which presses me
down almost into the soil. But I recover my balance and
my proper height.

Something bright and burning has blinded Amy! I lose
touch with her; there's interference in the air and in my
mind . . .

Momentarily I feel a pang of grief that Amy won't
even reach the Channel crossing – let alone the breezy
Gavarnie valley with its pouncing hawks; let alone the
Rock lit by golden flames when the Levanter wind tethers
banners of sunset vapour to the Moroccan peaks. I fly

on, burning such emotions out. I'm stronger than she is. I consult my mind-map again. Cruising, cruising.

Where are you, Amy?

Amy, beautiful Amy!

Ach, beautiful me . . .

Russia!

Forests of oak, beech and fir . . .

I'm dimly aware of my destination already: a town called Vitebsk. That's where I'll roost.

Once more I'm faintly aware of Amy far away. She lies panting on a patch of mud. Her feathers are all burnt. She can't see. It's a wonder she's still alive. Soon she'll die of shock.

Oh, this is my cruise of a lifetime! Here's the West Dvina river. The little town of Beshenkovichi lies by a sharp bend where the stream alters course from south to north. Only sixty kilometres further to Vitebsk. Five minutes, slightly less.

And now Vitebsk lies ahead. So my mind-map is coming to an end. Nothing exists beyond it. Nowhere.

So soon! Yet as Amy said, 'Doing what you *must* do is what living is all about!' A mayfly only lives one day – a few hours of one day – and is complete.

One minute left.

Vitebsk is the town where the painter Marc Chagall was born. He imagined cows flying in the sky.

There'll be cows flying through the sky today, for sure.

Universe on the Turn

We parted softly, with a kiss. Jacques's face looked flushed in the misty, rosy light. Did I detect a hint of embarrassed excitement, a youthful coyness still, after so many visits? No, he was a young God! As he strode towards his woman, I could only helplessly admire the firm swing of his legs, the cleft apple of his buttocks, and the strong trapezius of muscles massaging his shoulder blades in a river of sinew that narrowed suddenly to hold high a jaunty head. He was an athlete of a swimmer, poised for the perfect plunge into the stream of woman's flesh.

His woman reclined enormously in her soft half-ovoid of a divan: three metres deep, twenty metres long. Her great parted rump-cheeks were as high as Jacques himself. The flipper protuberances of her one-time legs waggled gently on either side as she scented him. She could not close those stumps around him, of course, yet ancient nerve and muscle memories seemed to be still urging her to try.

Upon the brink of the divan Jacques turned, and grinned impishly. Oh, he knew that I would be admiring him! At a distance the purse of his lips looked harsher: his mouth a mauve, almost maroon gash. Yet the soft bud of his penis had shrunk to a tiny ivory knob – just as if, with so much blood engorging the erect musculature of the rest of his frame, none could be spared for his phallus and even the rosy light was drained away from there, eating a white moth-hole.

Oh yes, he was stiff: his whole body wore a velvet bloom.

Oddly, his woman seemed to wish to see him tonight. Squashed in the blank slab of her face, her little eyes squinted down the mountainous uplands of her thorax towards the fleecy hilltop of her tall mons. Of course she lost sight of him as soon as he stepped down from the lip of the divan.

Impulsively I hastened after him, to watch. As I arrived, he was still balanced on the fat triangular wedge of her perineum, the 'diving platform' bulging outward through the archway of her larger lips. Her fonts of Bartholin were releasing oily vapours, coating him with a lubricating veil and fogging her regrown hymen: that silk tissue curtain which hid the way within.

Abruptly Jacques launched himself through that damask, cleaving it into streamers. With a graceful twist of his hips he squirmed through the vestibule, between the lesser lips. His shanks flexed against the walls. His heels administered the final push.

And he was gone. Inside.

As the woman's uplands quivered with the motions of his body within her, a low resonant moan rose from the lips of her mouth; and this noise was taken up by women in the neighbouring divans as though their numb vocal chords had become tuning forks in sympathy.

A soft solitary cooing sound was usual – but not this hint of mutual lamentation. Which was curious; and which made my head buzz.

Choosing my own woman at random – two divan-pits further round the hall – I too climbed down on to her perineum, descending hastily below her line of sight since I noticed that she also was trying to squint at me.

As I stood there momentarily on the fatty ledge, her spray smelled less musky, more acrid than usual; it even stung my eyes a little. Half closing my eyes, I dived forward, rending the veil, and hauled and kicked my way within her. As I butted through the soft squeeze of her muscles, up the elastic canal, my excitement mounted deliriously. For now I was laved by lymph, experiencing a quickening ecstasy as my whole body was massaged to joy from the glans of my head right down the shaft of my trunk.

Up into that darkness I thrust myself, up to the great infolding bud of her womb entrance. My fingers tore fruit blindly from her *arbor vitae*. My teeth bit upon it.

And yet . . . I was gritting my teeth, too. I felt as though my whole body had already climaxed once in her, and now I was trying to force pleasure upon myself a second time. I was having to think about this, and compel it, instead of simply surrendering to the flow of feeling. It was as if my frame had already detumesced.

Yet at last my fists thrust through into her cervix. As her plug-bud burst open, her rich inner ichors drenched my head and breast and loins, and all my tense erect expectancy was finally fulfilled – in that moment outside of time when the orgasm of the whole organism sets time itself aside . . .

My woman also climaxed in her own way, in that 'no-instant'. Very soon her muscles were squeezing me back and down again, to pop out on to the fatty triangle from which I had first dived.

She squeezed me hard, though. She almost . . . *hurt* me.

And although, thus expelled, I glowed with fresh vitality, somehow I also felt seared and corroded. The first, reborn breath that I gasped should have tasted sweet; instead it smelled rank. The air in the divan pit seemed subtly poisonous.

A hand gripped mine. Jacques helped me to climb out.

He read the expression on my face. 'You too?' he whispered. 'It seemed fine, inside – but then *afterwards* . . .!'

I nodded, unwilling to speak. The strange air pervaded the whole hall: not a dizzying musk alone, but musk laced with acid gas.

Those leg flippers wagged at us almost mockingly as we walked away to collect our clothes.

We returned from the great basalt block of the harem, that night, Jacques and I, puzzled and hurt by the strange repulsion we had both felt in that palace of love.

To be sure, the women had accepted us as always, becalmed there in the dim rosy light like so many beached whales – massive, mysterious, truncated beings dazing us with their scent attractors; yet there had been that bitter, tetchy undertang . . .

True, we had swum into their womb-ducts deliciously enough, and been reborn; yet afterwards we had felt aborted, sloughed off like dead womb linings, soiled and cheated . . .

Once, would you believe it, man could only enter woman's body a very little way? Man had specialized his sexuality into one tiny flute. His whole body could not act as an organ. No grand chorales of all-body love could be played.

Was this the way it had tasted long ago: this dissatisfying, partial union of which Jacques and I had now experienced a hint?

Once, man had ejected little homunculi of himself towards a tiny womb-entry. The sheer delirious act of bursting through into the very womb was unknown. (A violent act to us males, perhaps – one of force and rupture! – yet to those comatose giantesses, our women, how gentle; so that they cooed with sweet delight. Invariably they cooed . . . until tonight.)

What a strange world it must have been before the Change! Man and woman were the same size then; the female as mobile and fleet as any male.

We still possess, as one of the ur-documents of our culture, fragments from the *Case Notes of Ephraim Johnson MD*, first man to witness and assess the Change. I thought a lot about that ancient man as Jacques and I walked home that night, our fingers interlaced comfortingly. Could we be the witnesses, I wondered, of some equally epochal Second Change? Hating this idea, I rejected it. Yet the suspicion still nagged at me. I felt as though I had been hurled back to that time tens of thousands of years ago, when man and woman needed to wrestle together frantically to achieve a mere fraction of our own rejuvenating, polymorphous plunge; back to that time when the numbers of the population soared abominably in pursuit of this fleeting fraction of pleasure, until nature itself took a hand, or else humanity would surely have suffocated itself and the whole world.

Yet was it really nature, or was it man, that took a hand? Ephraim Johnson's *Case Notes* are of two minds on this matter. Written in the earliest purdah days, the *Case Notes* place the responsibility for the Change now at the door of those chemicals with which the world's water supplies were liberally saturated for a number of years: chemicals favouring the success of Y-chromosome sperm, for male offspring – and next at the door of sheer stress due to population pressure which *at the very same time* was producing hormonal changes in woman so that for every fifty males conceived, only one female would be.

Perhaps the latter explanation is nearer the truth. Perhaps it was really a case of man thinking along the same lines as nature – inventively mimicking what nature was already doing of its own accord; for without any further dosage by chemicals from that day to this the same ratio of 50:1 has persisted.

But of course the Change involved far more than a mere shift in the balance of the sexes. Did it not bring us our present longevity, by physical rebirth in the body of woman? For which, I need hardly add, the body of woman was obliged to grow big enough for a grown man to re-enter her, entire.

No, a far more profound alteration had occurred than could be accounted for by an intervention by those early pharmacologists. Though at first it was not noticed. For the ratio-shift led inevitably to the start of the purdah phase of culture; since where woman are rare, they must be guarded, and all their former 'rights' of mobility or activity are as nothing, then. Which ensured that the *real* Change could take place easily within harem walls, and even pass unremarked for several generations.

Certain documents are so epochal that they become part of our very thought processes, transcending the demise of old languages, and passing over into the new speech. So it is with Ephraim Johnson's *Notes,* the vivid memoir he wrote some years after his lost and reputedly rather turgid treatise, *On the Health of Women in Harems.* His fragmentary words, imprinted on us as children via the datanet, cling to our hearts.

To capsule them from memory:

. . . a special study of the indolent, recumbent existence that all women were now living, was long overdue . . . I must confess that at first I was mainly concerned with the risks of varicosity, obesity and thrombosis. I had no reason to suspect the true state induced by harem life: the alteration in the human female form away from a mobile, petite configuration towards an ovoid, recumbent form *together with* a general enlargement in bodily size . . .

I was able to measure the slow but sure progression away from the male archetype: away from those ratios of distance between foot, solar plexus, head and upraised hand as extolled ever since Classical Times, and explained by modern mathematics as the Fibonacci Series.

This had not been noted earlier because progressive enlargement of the torso-thorax region coincided with decrease in leg and arm length, as ambulation and manipulation became increasingly irrelevant to harem females.

Statistically, though, the *mass* of the female body was on the increase. Women were growing steadily larger as their limbs diminished, their physiology tending towards a soft, fruity, pearlike state – which males continued to find deeply gratifying without perceiving the real extent or nature of the change; for visiting males were dazed by the increased output of pheromonal scent attractors, and deceived by the discreet lighting of the harems (something initially intended to help tranquillize the 'exiles within').

I saw that humanity was dividing into two distinct, sexually symbiotic species: the one, small, mobile and active; the other vast, flaccid, passive . . .

But it might be years before most men noticed that they were riding their partners ever higher off the couch, enmeshed in an increasing mass of flesh. Many men indeed remarked on the delicious aroma of the harems, yet there was always an element of amnesia about their reminiscences. Besides, with strict social-reward criteria being applied for entry to the harems, long gaps occurred between individual visits . . .

Of course, that wasn't all. Ephraim Johnson had no idea how large the women would become within mere centuries; nor of the vastly extended life-span which this would bring to man. Thus his words thrill us, but amuse us too.

So I was brooding about Johnson, that man of the interface between *then* and *now*, as much as I was trying to avoid thinking about that air of change in the harem, while I escorted my lovely Jacques home to our pod, to lie in one another's arms, reborn. Though for the first time in memory we had been reborn astringently . . .

Our city spread out its aerial diadem of curving spoke-ways, which dangled living-pods beneath like raindrops on branches. It was the diadem of a splash, to be exact, with the point of impact in the earth being the central harem block – from which all arcing veins radiated, bending through the sky in fan tracery vaulting down to their final tips hanging within a mere twenty metres of the ground. Our elastic, sprung city of overwhelming beauty, delicacy and quake resilience.

Far below the spoke we walked along, there purred the starfish arms of life-support machinery, clinging to the earth around the harem core, drawing their power from the geothermal spike plunging ten kilometres deep. The city's root thus bore the harem upon it like the ovary of a flower, from which in turn our three hundred and sixty slim, graceful living-zone petals spread out, abloom.

Each pod beyond Inner Zone was a home wherein from two to twenty loving individuals thrived, speculating about the universe in a thousand different ways; while away beyond the barrier of the mountains on the horizon sprouted our giant cybernated telescopes (photon, radio, neutrino, whatever), unseen and unvisited by us person-ally. All of their gleanings poured into our datanet, making the city itself one great receiving dish. As well as a living flower.

Overhead, the air-blanket held thick warm atmosphere around us, setting the stars a-twinkle far more impishly than ever out at the cyberscopes, in the thin cold beyond the hills.

But we were both still walking through Inner Zone: a calyx of sepals underslung with gaiety pods for gourmets, drugsters, liquorites, musicamors. And we might have stopped by one of these to celebrate our rebirth. Only a sudden inexplicable scream from one of the drugpods stirred our anxiety anew, so that we only wished to hasten on over the rainbow bridge and reach home.

And as we hurried, below our spoke the pods rocked gently like lanterns, and the spoke itself bobbed up and down a few centimetres. A mild quake was nudging the city's base. But this was nothing. The Earth's crust was simply slackening out as gravity declined – albeit faster, noticeably faster than it should have done.

Naturally, we all connected the increasing decline of gravity with the coming Turn of the Universe. Using daring new equations of his own devising, Jacques had arrived at a startlingly tiny figure for how long it would take the cosmos to collapse in on itself once expansion halted and contraction began. His ideas were still reverberating round scientific circles, establishing him as very much an up-and-coming cosmetician – or 'cosmological theoretician', to give him his full glory – making my heart throb with pride for my chosen pod partner. Jacques had such a fine mind.

He argued that if the half-time of collapse of any massive star into a singularity is approximately one-thousandth of a second (a reasonable figure), and if the collapse of the entire universe commences everywhere at once, then the half-time of universal collapse must be proportional on a logarithmic scale to that of any lesser stellar body.

He disregarded the speed of light as a constraint on events, since it is the whole space-time matrix which is due to contract. He boldly discarded the gravitational mass of the universe as a prime consideration – and declared that Time itself was the general binding force and root energy of all. It was in Time, proclaimed Jacques, that the 'missing mass' of the universe was tied up: in elapsed, accrued Time.

If the radius of the cosmos at its maximum is estimated

at 10^{28} centimetres, then the half-time of collapse ought to be a mere 10^{14} seconds: a puny 33 million years!

So billions of years of leisurely contemplation hardly lie in store for us, once the critical size is reached. The smearing back into Superspace will take place very rapidly indeed. Hence humanity's justifiable obsession with predicting the moment of the Turn. It isn't simply an abstract quest for knowledge. It seems that we are actually elected as direct witnesses of the greatest cosmic event (bar one: the primal fireball, and of course no one can possibly witness that) – and it's one which will arrive sooner than anyone in the olden days expected!

Whilst gravity weakens year by year, and the Earth spirals further from the Sun, the most distant galaxies are visibly starting to slow down in their headlong flight. Their red shifts lessen perceptibly. Or rather, they began slowing down a long time ago, and the light only reaches us now. But according to the standard models, not long enough ago to bring them anywhere near a standstill yet.

Not so, says Jacques: as gravity grows less for us, so it 'pools' out at the periphery, slowing the far galaxies much more rapidly – and here Jacques's subtlest equations come into play, explaining how an observer on Earth can experience diminishing gravity, even though an observer on the fringes of creation (which would seem, *to him*, to be the centre) would see *us* as slowing down due to a tightening of the bonds.

I confess that this concept of relativistic gravity is almost too subtle for me to grasp – but Time, says Jacques, is the key.

Anyway, the question of how soon, and in what manner, the universe will turn is inevitably the life's work of all the specialists in our science city: philosophers, theologians, physicists alike. What else can really be important in these late days, as Earth spirals untimely towards the cold?

To march across the metagalaxies, let alone visit nearby suns in our own galaxy, we cannot; that dream is long gone. For how could we ship even a single woman off our world? As soon hoist a whale into the sky! The acceleration would destroy the great body. Man's earliest space ambitions faltered utterly on the nub of the Change; for woman appears to belong with Planet Earth which wrought this transformation in her – as though the Earth itself lives and thinks and breathes (even while its corsets slacken), and intends to keep its daughter at home.

As for sending men on their own to the stars, well, male love is fine and beautiful: Jacques and I lie in each other's embrace by night, enchanted, trembling with the bliss of polymorphous touch – yet it is woman-love which enables us to live this way. Far from orgasm being the 'little death' it used to be back in the human dawn times, now by being bathed in woman's ichors our cells replicate themselves way past the Hayflick limit; and we rejuvenate. We can live ten thousand years, until we choose to die. And when we do so choose, we simply avoid visiting the harem; death follows peacefully within a year or so. So how could we go to the stars, womanless? And without woman how would we have time to reach the stars?

Thus our longevity is at once our anchor – and the solace which Earth offers us, to allow us to wait and watch for the Turn, invigorated over and over again by that other side of our species which has been subconscious, dreamlike, vast and torpid for so many millennia.

Glancing up at the distant Moon, half as far again from Earth as when man first trod its dusty seas, Jacques exclaimed fancifully:

'You might say that the only enduring constant is the mass of woman! Gravity certainly isn't. Just consider:

one half of our species is only one-fiftieth by numbers. Yet woman is fifty times larger than a man! What if a woman anticipated the slackening of gravity long before man knew of it through his instruments? What if she intuited that there would be less gravity to weigh her down?'

'Maybe,' I quipped, 'that "missing mass" isn't locked up in Time at all – but in our women?' I hoped that humour might soothe him, upset as he was by the inexplicable nastiness in the harem. 'Perhaps new matter was created suddenly and multiplicatively in all the women's bodies – to slow down the expansion!'

Unfortunately my joke had the opposite effect: it wound him up still further.

'I'll swear there's a link between *them*, and the cosmos!' he insisted. '*We* think that we do all the observing. But why shouldn't they too observe the cosmos – using vastly different senses from ours, however extended ours are by the cyberscopes? What else can they possibly fill their minds with?'

'Why, with the job of operating much larger bodies!' said I. 'Far more thought-space has to be taken up by simple body-monitoring. Their brains remain the same size as ours, so conscious thought is squeezed out. Didn't they give up consciousness for the sake of something more valuable: to rejuvenate us?'

'Yes – by annulling Time! But how do they tap Time? Time is the key. Did they change just to give us a longer lifespan? Or was it to build a body-field of their own, which might discover the truth we're seeking? By another route: a biological one! Are we men perhaps just their slaves: remaining mobile and "intelligent" only so that we can service the harem and inflame their bodies every now and then to make more worker ants, and a few more Queenly Watchers? Maybe they sensed the quest long before us – though only an eye-blink ago, in the lifetime of the universe!'

Ridiculous. I couldn't entertain the notion. Poor Jacques was more disturbed than I feared.

My hand fell from his. In mutual silence we walked on above supposedly gay music, which that night sounded plangent, elegiac and funereal to my ears – as though other men had been hurt recently, as well as recharged, by the harem experience. The music, composed from the musicians' brain-waves via a skull-web, betrayed this in a dirge.

From amongst the musicamors below we heard another cry of fear. Immediately the music itself magnified this into a banshee wail.

As I said, Jacques was a junior cosmetician; and I was a senior prammer, in line for being prime prammer: a chief cyberscope programmer. He had experienced around five hundred half-yearly reincarnations in woman since puberty. I, considerably more. Still, we weren't so far apart in terms of city status. Even a junior cosmetician draws on the services of many junior prammers, and can even tap a prime prammer in pursuit of a particularly daring hypothesis. Junior cosmeticians have to be given free rein for flashes of genius, or else the quest would have hardened into dogmatics millennia ago. So we make a good pod-duo, Jacques and I. Things balance out; disputes are flash-in-the-pan affairs – and we were again holding hands by the time we got back to our pod.

Palming the entry panel open, we stepped downstairs to the roomglobe – which was currently a blue bubble in a tropic sea where tall angel fish wafted by like the sails of yachts: data memories of a warmer Earth. I had dialled these marine visuals before we left for the harem, expecting that on our return we would wish to float in amniotic bliss. But now we felt more like cold cod, with morose hooks of doubt beneath our chins, than graceful angels.

So I dialled another scene: of pastureland, with extinct sheep cropping it, and fleecy clouds puffing overhead like bales of steam. A pastoral – with flute music to accompany, being tootled by some unseen shepherd. Jacques dialled a picnic supper for us to eat on the floor, which he softened from the day's logic-hardness, half way to the softness of bed. We had bread, a bottle of wine, lamb and cheese analogues.

The mood still jarred, though.

'Let's eat out under the damned stars, then!' he cried. 'They're what's uppermost in our minds.'

So the Milky Way glowed all around us in coiling banners of light; and we were happy at last, to be alone in space together, wrapping bread around cold lamb in starlit sandwiches. Our viewpoint was from the memory of some cyber-observatory, long defunct, far out at one of the Trojan points of Jupiter.

Jacques glanced in the direction of Andromeda, and beyond.

'Consider,' he said. 'The expanding universe slows to a halt. Then it actually *does* halt, briefly. Is that moment "a moment in time", if nothing is taking place? Can the cosmos ever become static as a whole, even for a microsecond? Yet how else can it ever begin to rebound? Time must reach zero out at the periphery, relativistically, as gravity grows huge. And here in the centre, time speeds up – or rather it grows denser. Life, the sensitive register, knows this subconsciously. The body field can feed on it – hence our rejuvenations!'

'But how can Time be different in different places?' I asked him. 'You always said that Time is the binding force because it is simultaneous, everywhere at once.'

'That's simple. Time is denser near an effect, than near a cause. Right now the periphery of the universe is becoming the cause: of the future implosion. This is what the body-field of woman soaks up: that huge increase in effective time pouring inwards. She's receiving gradients of density of time. And we can't measure such a thing. All out netting of neutrinos is useless. All the data we've piled up is in vain.'

'Jacques, *tomorrow*, please! That's tomorrow's work, not tonight's pleasure.' I stroked his cheek in the milky starlight.

But he ignored me.

'In a sense woman *does* draw the universe towards her – by soaking up the effect of the changing gradient of Time. As matter ceases to flow outward, so Time streams back into the centre. A big enough body-field can sense this instantly, whereas our cyberscopes only tell us ancient history. So how can we men ever know when we reach the Turn? But our women will know the moment. It's been creeping up on us all for thousands of years already, in the shift of time density.' He laughed emptily. 'Woman was chosen to witness the Turn, and we to serve her. All our cyberscopes are useless. We already had our receivers all along.'

He gestured madly towards the Greater Magellanic Cloud; or was it towards the harem unseen beyond the pod wall? Brusquely I cancelled the star view, hoping that this might shock Jacques back to his senses. I dialled clear walls so that he might see our true and beautiful city, and held him tight.

In my arms he still ranted.

'If only we could read their thoughts, then we would know the Answer! They don't sense the passage of time, as we do. They respond to its density – and they pass on the effects to us men, in the form of renewed life.

Density, yes, density! That's it! That's why woman's static way of life doesn't offend her. My other equations are all nonsense.'

But at last he yielded to me, and to the yielding floor, which I softened still further, to sponge, to eiderdown.

We woke to a quiet quake that was jiggling the city spokes and rocking our pod gently. The weak morning sunlight, sparse juice of a lemon which the hand of gravity did not squeeze quite tightly enough these days, nevertheless cast grey bars of shadow from the eastern arms of the diadem to slant against the harem – bars which seemed, to my keen eyes, to tremble. Or was it that the walls of the harem itself were throbbing?

But even if the epicentre of this quake lay directly down our energy-root into the crust, I wasn't worried; our base and taproot were strong enough to withstand such shocks.

However, the trembling went on and on remorselessly, far beyond the timespan of any normal quake; and instead of keying our pod walls to cosmomathematical equations for the morning's work, we left the pod and climbed up on to the roof-road, curious.

We weren't alone. Other men were hurrying up on the spoke ahead of us; and along other spokes to right and left. Crowds buzzed up at the zeniths. Some people pointed; others cried out.

As soon as we joined the group of spectators up on the high point of our own spoke, we could see that the basalt blocks of the harem were rupturing here and there, pushing outwards. Other parts of the walls were crumbling like cheese or cobwebs, as though the constant seismic shock was eroding the very bonds of matter there.

Finally the vibrations ceased, leaving two-thirds of the

harem relatively intact, while the other third gaped with holes.

'It doesn't matter,' I reassured Jacques. 'The robots can cut new blocks. Our women won't die from a little sunlight leaking in.'

'Are you blind? Don't you see what's happening?'

No, I hadn't been able to see! Because I couldn't conceive of seeing it. Because my mind erased it. But now suddenly I saw.

Women were emerging from the ruptured harem, on to the broad base-joints of the spokes. Women, in daylight! Vast blank oval slugs, wallowing forward. Enormous sloths moving out on to the separate spokes – and crushing any man who tried to drive them back by waving his arms and screaming into their fathomless uncommunicative faces.

As yet, no woman had shuffled out on to our own spoke. But already, up very many others crawled a white, bloated enormity, dislodging pods from their moorings so that they fell and smashed like eggs. Each gay, buoyant bridge withstood, withstood – till the woman reached about half way up to the zenith.

Then, one by one, each spoke abruptly reached its catastrophe point and snapped or buckled to the ground below. Part fell across the starfish base, but the further reaches churned up the land itself, rock and soil.

Yet however many men died in each collapse, the women themselves seemed hardly affected by the fall. They continued to wallow out along the now-fallen sky-bridges: crumpled roads leading them away from the city in all directions.

Overhead, the air blanket flickered with lightning as its energies surged and faltered; picked up and faltered again – while our own crowd stood bunched together on the crown of a single isolated spike like a rib sticking out of a carcass.

During the night, the universe had turned!

Unashamedly I wept for all the lost alien civilizations which had risen and fallen during the billions of years throughout the youth and middle age of the universe, without ever knowing of this moment; and I wept because they had been able to flower and to fade away in peace without knowing it.

Yet it had not been Man, either, who had marked the Turn. It had been our alien, life-giving, recumbent Queens – who had now moved out from the prison of their contemplations, *towards what rendezvous*?

Our own sky-spoke shuddered as a limbless giantess grovelled out upon it. Jacques and I clung to each other in the crowd, waiting.

The Flesh of her Hair

Then a spirit passed before my face:
the hair of my flesh stood up.

JOB 4:15

I had decided to travel back to Europe from Japan as a passenger on a cargo ship. This would be much cheaper than flying – anyway, I loathed flying – and would give me a chance, I imagined, to finish the first draft of my book on the Japanese puppet theatre.

I did toy, for a while, with the notion of sailing from Yokohama over to Nakhodka and catching the Trans-Siberian Railway to cross the alternative 'ocean of soil'; but though this would be even cheaper and considerably quicker than the sea journey, I feared that it would be uncomfortable and oppressive. Moreover, I was full of 'Japanese sentiment' – a mood the retention of which seemed essential to the success of my projected book. To be confronted suddenly by Siberia on a train crowded (I imagined) with samovars and babooshkas, military uniforms, and a motley of international travellers squeezed together like sardines, would have seemed quite inappropriate. I fancied that I could very well concentrate and crystallize into appropriate words my Japanese mood amidst the emptiness of the Pacific Ocean. I could meditate before my trusty portable Swiss typewriter, I could type a page or two, then take a turn about the deck. I would be completely detached from the world at large, able to return in spirit to the time of Chikamatsu. There would be few other passengers to bother me: ten at most.

Nor would they speak my language. For I would choose a
foreign ship – neither Italian nor Japanese. (I thought of
myself as partly Japanese, at least in soul.)

The next six weeks would be a period of gentle weaning
from the Japan I loved – and, to mix a metaphor, of
peaceful gestation of my book.

They would also prove, from the very first day, to be a
terrible mistake.

I booked passage on the *Lübeck*, a container vessel
outward bound from Yokohama twenty thousand kilometres non-stop by way of the Panama Canal. (When
one is on the other side of the world, Italy and Germany
do not seem very far apart, merely a rail journey. Besides,
I had friends at Lugano in Switzerland, whom I dearly
wished to visit before heading south to the stately decay
of our family home outside Palermo.)

Arriving from Kyoto aboard the bullet train, I allowed
myself the luxury of a taxi from Tokyo station all the way
to Yokohama docks, since I had a fair amount of luggage
with me. The taxi was the usual lurid affair, striped in red
and orange, with French *chansons* warbling from a stereo
cassette player. But there was a fine miniature flower
arrangement in a glazed pot clipped to the back of the
driver's seat, and I congratulated myself that this was the
real Japan bidding farewell to me. The driver may have
looked like a gangster, and driven his Toyota like one,
but each morning when he rose from his quilt mattress to
go on duty, he arranged flowers of the season tastefully
for his vehicle.

We arrived at the docks by mid-afternoon. I checked
my luggage through Customs, and my driver whisked me
along to the ship where he helped me haul my bags and
traps up the gang plank on board the *Lübeck*. The 'cabin
boy' – if this is the right term for a very tall blond Nordic

specimen – shooed my driver back ashore and took over,
showing me to my cabin, and informing me casually in
impeccable English that dinner was at nineteen-thirty.
We would sail with the tide at three A.M. Then he melted
away.

I surveyed the little cabin with satisfaction. It was very
neat and orderly, in light pastel colours. There was a
single bunk-bed, a little table for my typewriter, a chair,
and a picture on one wall, of – of course – a merchant
ship at sea. A porthole of satisfactory size looked out
from the cabin itself, and its twin from the tiled shower
cubicle and water closet adjacent. The whole was not
unlike a *gasthof* I had once spent a few nights in at
Innsbruck – if one transposed the foaming breakers I
visualized outside (though actually the dockside sea at
the moment was flat and oily) into the snowy peaks of
the Alps.

I hung up some clothes in the wardrobe unit, unpacked
my typewriter – as a gesture of intent – then decided, on
the spur of the moment, to go out and see Japan one last
time, ashore.

I found another taxi prowling the docks and had myself
driven to the Motomachi shopping street – I was, after
all, a *bona fide* tourist now. From there, as dusk gathered,
I wandered down to China Town, where I ended up
eventually at a raw fish restaurant; there I dined, for the
last time, on thin strips of my favourite oily underbelly of
tuna on pats of rice, washed down with a flask of *tokkyu*
saké, returning to the *Lübeck* at ten o'clock or so.

So far, I had met no one on the ship except for Klaus
the 'cabin boy'.

When I woke up next morning, to the sound of a
breakfast gong being dinned along the corridor past the
cabins, the ship was out at sea, leaning gently from port

to starboard and back again in the timeless rhythm of
voyage.

I showered quickly, scraped my face clean of bristles,
dressed and was in the dining room within seven or eight
minutes.

And the public humiliation began: the humiliation
which, in the first shocked moments, I believed was
directed at myself alone, but which I soon came to realize
was to be shared equally amongst all eight of us paying
passengers, or victims. For this was the game of the
Captain and officers.

My own baptism into the game commenced almost
immediately.

The Captain, a red-faced man with meaty fists, rose
from table briskly and introduced me, Gino Landolfi, to
the Second Officer Herr Jünger (who was travelling with
his daughter – she occupied one of the other passenger
cabins), the Chief Engineer Herr Hausman, and the
Steward Herr Grünewald, who was busy serving breakfast. And then to the other passengers: there were three
British couples, and a Japanese boy of about sixteen.
(And of course the fact that so many British people
happened to be travelling on a German ship had gone a
long way towards precipitating the 'game'. I blame the
British at least partly for the situation, since they had
done their best to turn these particular Germans into
caricatures of themselves. Yet at the same time, as I was
to discover . . . *Yet at the same time*!)

We all shared the same huge table, which possessed an
inconvenient lip like a billiard table's, to prevent plates
and glasses from sliding off on to the floor. The *Lübeck*
apparently had no stabilizers. Thus it could travel faster,
corkscrewing through the waves from side to side. Behind
my seat stretched a long window. On the wall opposite

me, behind the Captain's seat, was a serene mural of the
palace of San Souci, in Potsdam.

'I must make one thing quite plain, Mr Landolfi,' said
the Captain, his face suddenly beetroot-red. He actually
thumped the breakfast table with his fist, violently jarring
the cutlery. 'This is my ship, and on it you will obey me.
Last night you were invited to dinner at this table. *You
were not here.* On this ship, in future you do as *I say*. Is
that clear? I have always found Italians very unreliable
people. Did you not find them so, Herr Grünewald, in
the last war? Ah, but for Italy – the weak underbelly. Ah,
but for Italy!' And casually he instructed the patrolling
Steward to pile my plate with sausages.

Conversation around the table resumed, as though
nothing out of the ordinary had happened.

It was a conversation conducted entirely in English,
about the likely weather at sea. The Japanese boy
remained silent. (It transpired that he spoke hardly any
English, and very poor German. Speaking Japanese
myself, I had to take him under my wing, as it were. His
father, a fanatical militarist, was sending him to Germany
to qualify as a glider pilot, and presumed that he would
pick up fluent German *en route*. Unfortunately for the
eager youth, nobody was speaking German. This first
morning, seeing me rebuked – without understanding the
meaning of the words – he stared at me with blank
shining enmity, like a kamikaze pilot.)

To say that I was shocked to the core, would be an
understatement.

I shall not recount every such incident which so disturbed
my serenity and tormented my 'Japanese sentiment' that
within a few days – with an apparent eternity of time
before me, and an infinity of featureless blank water
before we were due to catch sight of Panama – I despaired

of being able to write a single page of my book, or concentrate effectively upon anything. So much in despair was I, that I even thought – almost seriously – of stepping overboard. *Anything*, to be able to drift away from this wretched prison-ship! (I should add that the cargo hatches were so loaded down with extra, chained containers – two deep – that from the crew deck one only needed to *step* down into the ocean.)

But I must recount a few incidents, simply as a setting for what happened later.

As I have hinted, the British passengers – two of whom had journeyed all the way around the world on the *Lübeck,* with the other four joining at Colombo – and the German officers were engaged in a masque, a mental drama re-enacting the national hostilities of the Second World War. These passengers were British officers (with their ladies) under the guard of a brutally polite Komm-andant, and were determined by various subtle little acts of sabotage – such as witticisms which the Captain could not quite understand – to undermine him.

For example, the frail-looking (yet tough spirited) Mrs Hetherington one day quite casually and innocently asked Herr Grünewald whether, since he had been in the Brown Shirts, he had learned how to goose-step; and was it difficult? She soon had the ageing Steward kicking out his legs in the Nazi march, parading right across the saloon – at precisely the moment that the Captain happened to put in an appearance.

But this 'innocent' British joke was to rebound; later, we all saw the Chief Engineer raise his right arm to the Captain in the Hitler salute – and the Captain responded in kind. For the Germans were subtle too, in their own way. And in the isolation of the Pacific, with not another ship in sight – except once – this game became immoder-ately real.

So much so, that when one ship did pass us by a couple of weeks later, heading in the opposite direction, all of the British passengers – and myself along with them – flooded to the rail, and waved and capered, and cried out, 'Help! Help! Rescue us!' Naturally, no one on the other ship heard our cries; but the Captain of the *Lübeck* heard us clearly enough, up on his bridge, and descended upon us in baffled fury.

It was during meals that the Captain and his officers usually had their revenge. For, though they could not starve us – since we had paid our fares, and it was a point of honour with them that we received full value – they could nevertheless see to it that we were *fed* . . . in the spirit of prison warders in charge of a group of hunger-striking suffragettes. The Captain would slam his fist on the table – his favourite gesture of emphasis.

'That was good flesh,' he would call out to Herr Grünewald. 'What flesh was that?' (Well might he ask, since all the meat we ate had been transported deep-frozen all the way from Germany. They did not believe in provisioning in alien foreign ports, such as Colombo or Yokohama. Whether the meat was swine flesh, or sheep flesh, or cow flesh, it all tasted exactly the same.) 'Bring more flesh for everyone!'

This was a particular torment for me, with my taste for the subtleties of Japanese cuisine; and it affected Mrs Hetherington too, with her weak stomach – though she soldiered on. But it was merely a preliminary to the more exquisitely sadistic rite which the Captain decreed for every Sunday morning, in lieu of worship. For then we passengers were all mustered on deck at eleven A.M., the crew was assembled on the lower deck, and a canvas seat was slung from a meat-hook attached to a balance. We were publicly weighed. This week's weight was called out loudly, and last week's for comparison, from the Captain's notebook. The crew either cheered or booed, depending on whether – or by how much – each passenger had put on weight. (In fact, we were soon all putting on weight steadily, with the sole staunch exception of Mrs Hetherington. I presume that she vomited up her meals when she returned to her cabin. Would that I had studied such Yoga.)

The Captain's imaginative excuse for this ritual, when I challenged it, was that he must declare the exact 'kerbside weight' of the *Lübeck* to the authorities at Panama before he could use their canal. So he was merely being methodical and obeying orders. How could one argue with such a – yes – stroke of genius?

Yet if he was 'obeying orders', of his own inspired invention, the ship itself was in relative disorder. That we passengers should be attempting to erode his authority was ironic, since his authority was already severely diminished in the eyes of the crew, who saw him as an inconsistent bully, a hypocritical martinet. *They* were not allowed to have women on board, but the Captain – on the way out to Japan – had bedded a woman passenger, a Japanese. He had made her his mistress of the voyage.

As though to express the crew's disgust at this miscegenation – or their envy of it – a Chinese cook, the only non-Aryan in the crew, had been 'lost overboard' somewhere in the Indian Ocean. The *Lübeck* dutifully returned and sailed a search pattern for the regulation six hours, but his body wasn't found. We suspected, of course, that the Chinese cook had been pushed into the sea by night.

Some fights had even broken out below decks; and one man was locked up now, for the duration, with his front teeth knocked out.

All of which leads me to the ship's attitude towards oriental people – an attitude which was agony to me, not least because I, an Italian (and worse, a Sicilian) was viewed by them as a kind of European oriental: swarthy, excitable and unreliable.

Herr Jünger's hobby was home movies; and second only to the torment of meals was the torment of watching his home movies, screened in the saloon after dinner to 'entertain' us.

There was no choice in this matter. One could not retire gracefully to one's cabin to curl up with a copy of Chikamatsu's *Drum of the Waves at Horikawa*. Mrs Granger, who was circumnavigating the world on board the *Lübeck* with her husband as a cheap form of cruise (and bitterly regretting it) attempted to escape one performance, protesting that she had already seen the movies twice over, and making various barbed comments about the quality of the film library in this floating prison camp. The Captain actually laid hands on her, twisted her arm behind her back, and – grinning jovially the while – marched her into the saloon and parked her in a seat.

Herr Jünger, the Second Officer, was a large grizzled man with wildly flying, electrified hair, who had been a midshipman on the pocket battleship *Graf Spee* during the Second World War. His wife, he always left at home; but for this trip alone his daughter was accompanying him, cruising around the world as a twenty-first birthday treat. A champagne reception would be held a day short of Panama, to mark the actual event – to which we were all, of course, invited. Fräulein Jünger was quite pretty, in a bourgeois way – and she had certain airs and graces, including a way of tossing her head in impatience. She had all the makings, I thought, of a highly *gemütliche Hausfrau*.

Herr Jünger was also travelling with another, inseparable companion: a grotesque red and blue plaster garden gnome named Friedolin – the Second Officer's mascot and familiar.

The home movies all devolved around the adventures of Friedolin. They were travelogues of the world seen from the viewpoint of a garden gnome – thus demonstrating, presumably, that Herr Jünger was at heart a sentimentalist. (But I shall make no rash generalizations about national characteristics. To me, the cliché is anathema.)

'Here,' Herr Jünger would proclaim, 'are the Pyramids. And here is Friedolin.' And because of the excellence of his movie camera, both were equally in focus. Friedolin appeared to be the same size as the Great Pyramid.

But worse was to come. For Friedolin, with his red nose and his big belly swollen with flesh and beer – this obscene Nibelung – was filled with a mixture of mischievous lust, cruel practical joking, and Aryan pride.

One film sequence showed peasant wherry-boats clustering around the *Lübeck* in some Asian port. The Second Officer ordered the decks sluiced and the bilges drained, at this moment. How Friedolin laughed from his safe perch on the rail to see the ragged oriental natives get a soaking. The fact that they had probably possessed a religion, palaces, philosophers and highly stylized dance-dramas three thousand years ago was of no consequence to Friedolin. His idea of art was far cruder.

Cut: to an Asian street, with lovely slender women in *cheongsams* walking away from the camera, ogled by Friedolin as their split skirts hinted at their legs, and their bottoms swayed. The camera zeroed in – telephoto – on one particular bottom, following it down the exotic street.

'Aha,' cried Herr Jünger, 'she was *not* Friedolin's! She is the one who got away!'

We were treated to many such images, of Asian women – most of whom were not to be Friedolin's; yet some of whom . . .

Well, it appeared that Friedolin sated his lusts in a number of Asian brothels; though, of course, since there were ladies present, this could be no more than hinted at.

This in some way explains our Captain's bedding of the Japanese woman passenger – so as not to be outdone by his Second Officer's gnome.

One of the worst of all the scenes was of rafts of starving Vietnamese refugees in some backwater, observed placidly by Friedolin.

'Too thin for Friedolin, that one!' commented Herr Jünger.

Friedolin was not, of course, being unfaithful; for these people were not quite human, after all.

The camera zoomed in, on a despairing face which had retained its beauty.

'Now *that* one, he could enjoy!'

Fräulein Jünger's interest in all these movies was quite different from Friedolin's, as I discovered one day when she talked to me freely on deck, in a moment of excitement.

She had her father's camera with her, having rushed to the rail to do some photography when Herr Jünger sent a crewman running to her cabin to tell her that the *Lübeck* had hit a baby whale.

Now, the *Lübeck* had a very bulbous bow, down at the water-line. Though it might seem that a sharper shape would cleave the water faster, in fact this was not the case. The 'bulb' dispersed more drag from the ship. Coupled with the lack of stabilizers, this saved perhaps a day overall in journey time – and profited the owners in proportion.

A little baby whale had indeed crashed on to the 'bulb' and lodged there, brokenly. Though the beast itself was invisible from where we stood at the rail, its blood was evident enough. Long thin streamers of red blood washed

past us through the blue Pacific water – to the delight of
the Fräulein, for this provided a beautiful colour contrast.

'Ooh!' she exclaimed, filming assiduously.

The only missing element was Friedolin, Fräulein
Jünger had neglected to bring him from her father's
cabin, to admire the blood-letting.

Alas. My elbow would dearly have loved to nudge
Friedolin accidentally into the sea, just as the Chinese
cook had been nudged. (Though I suspect that the conse-
quences of such an accident – to me – could have been
dire. One does not drown with impunity another man's
household Gods.)

'Ooh!'

'Ah,' she sighed in disappointment, as the blood-flow
slackened. She lowered the camera.

'You forgot Friedolin,' I observed, somewhat acidly.

She pouted.

'I think you do not like the movies which my father
makes!'

'Perhaps I take a little exception to Friedolin's viewpoint on the fair sex: namely, from the rear.'

'Oh, that is nothing! At home, many wives and husbands are very *intimate* with many other wives and
husbands. We think nothing of it. In fact, one is glad to
get away for a holiday with just one husband. I am
getting married when we return,' she added.

'So you're enjoying a rest cure, in advance?'

'Not at all!' She flushed, to think that I was accusing
her moralistically of intending to be a person who sleeps
around – when her future behaviour would be the height
of hygienic propriety.

'But I wonder why anyone would endure the monotony
of the oceans of the world – for how long: three months
in all? – when they are about to get married. It seems
odd.'

'Since you ask, Herr Landolfi, and since I will never see you again once we disembark, I shall tell you.' Fräulein Jünger patted her hair, which the breeze was playing with.

I should explain that her face, with its rosy cheeks and bright blue eyes and pert nose, was framed by a coiffure of short black curls. She was a chocolate box cover.

'I look like a little *Mädchen*, do I not? And I wish to be a woman. I do not look mature enough, to be my Carl's wife – with the company he keeps. His colleagues, their wives and mistresses . . . He has sent me away to become mature. When I return, I will look quite different.'

'But how?' I wondered.

'You will see, at my birthday party.'

'Tell me now, won't you? I'm intrigued.'

'That would not be interesting! It would spoil the fun.'

'And fun matters, doesn't it?' (*Like the bright blood in the sea*, I thought.) '*Please* tell me. I'll keep it secret.'

She relented.

'Oh very well. My father has a very special present for me: it is a long black wig. I will wear it when I return for my wedding. I will be a sophisticated woman.'

'But . . . anyone can buy a wig, surely? You could buy one in Germany, and wear it the next day.'

'No. You don't understand. I would be laughed at, in my circle. It would be too sudden: *die Verwandlung* . . . the metamorphosis. We have our little rules, of etiquette. My long hair must be won. It must be a trophy. An achievement. Anything of that sort must be. A suntan under ultraviolet lamps is *cheating*.'

'You mean, it's like a Red Indian head-dress?'

'Oh, I hardly think *that*!' She began to flounce away.

'Wait! Your friends will all conspire to pretend that

you grew your hair long on the voyage? ("For want of anything better to do . . .")'

'Have you noticed,' she asked dreamily, 'all the beautiful long hair in my father's films? Oh, it is wasted on those women – but only oriental hair grows so quickly and strongly. That's why they can sell it, and grow a new crop.'

'I think they probably sell their hair because they're starving!' I protested, incensed. 'They sell it to the wigmakers because it's the only way they can get a little money for a bag of rice. That's even worse than selling one's body: it's selling years of one's life – the years spent growing the hair. It's . . .'

'Oh, you think so, do you?'

'They aren't a flock of sheep, you know.'

Suddenly she looked as though she was about to burst into tears.

'I have told you my secret! And now you pour scorn. You are no gentleman at all.'

But I couldn't help recalling the hills of shaved hair inside the concentration camps, as captured on film by the Allies. Yet this thought provided a way out of my dilemma, since I did not dare quarrel with her – not on this ship, where she was the apple of her father's eye.

'Well, don't use all your film on the sea,' I suggested. 'Your father will want to make a movie of your birthday party.'

'He has many packs of film in his cabin,' she retorted. 'And many exposed films that you have not seen!'

This time she did flounce off, all the way to her cabin.

True to her implied promise – or threat – there was another session of home movies two days later after dinner, which had consisted of double helpings of calf flesh.

We were herded into the saloon, the curtains were pulled across the windows, the lights were doused. The screens flickered white numbers, then went into hand-held Technicolor.

A junk was floating in a becalmed blue empty sea, weighted down with people and their possessions. Eighty or ninety people were crowded on to that tiny boat. It was a miracle that it hadn't sunk already.

'This was six months ago,' commented Herr Jünger. 'These are some boat people. From Vietnam. The *Lübeck* happened upon them in the open sea. But alas, we were not able to take them in tow. Our ship tosses up too much wake. Their junk would have overturned.'

Friedolin was beaming down with cheeky benevolence at the refugees.

'And we could hardly take them as deck passengers. The decks were too crowded with containers, as usual.'

The camera zoomed in upon the upturned faces, searching. It lingered long upon an extraordinarily beautiful Chinese woman with long black hair, dressed in a dirty torn shirt and skirt. As the *Lübeck* responded to the swell of the sea, Friedolin – lodged in his safe vantage point – seemed to nod.

'Naturally, we gave food and water – and radioed their position. They had been stripped of all their gold by a Communist patrol, or pirates.'

The next few frames of the film were underexposed and of such brief duration that I wonder whether the camera had been operated accidentally – by Friedolin's plaster fingers? – or whether a whole section of film had been imperfectly edited out.

But I *know* that I saw a woman's semi-naked body lying on a bunk, black hair fanned out around her. And I know that at that very moment Fräulein Jünger glanced in my direction.

The next sequence showed the junk receding into the distance beyond the foaming wake of the *Lübeck*. It was late afternoon by now; the sun had moved on by several hours. Standing in the stern of the junk, in her rags, we could just make out a bald-headed figure (perhaps an old man, perhaps a younger woman) who was clutching a bundle of something or other to her, as though it was her life. Maybe it was a baby, maybe it was food.

'We hope they got towed into port. But who would want them?' sighed Herr Jünger. 'Anyway, they fed well from us – though I expect too much flesh would make their stomachs sick.'

'*Did* they get rescued?' enquired Mrs Hetherington.

'I do not know. We never heard. There are too many junks like that, adrift in the China seas. It is the fault of Communism. Anyway, we did our duty.'

'Poor souls – but what can one do?' asked Mrs Hetherington. 'There are too many immigrants in our own country already. One must be charitable, but they upset the economy.'

For a while, a conspiracy of mutual silence seemed to prevail between the German officers and the British passengers. And I wondered whether I, alone of all the passengers, guessed what had actually happened . . .

We had been at sea for an eternity, and had traversed as great an infinity as you can find on Earth – but the next day we should arrive in the roads outside Panama, where we would see ships again, queuing up to traverse the Canal.

And so Fräulein Jünger's birthday had arrived. And she was twenty-one.

The celebration was to commence as soon as it was evening, marked by the dipping of the sun below the horizon. The signal for the popping of the champagne

corks would be no launching of fireworks into the sky –
which, this close to the convergence of the shipping lanes,
might be misinterpreted as the firing of distress maroons.
Not fireworks, then, but a remarkable natural phenomenon, which we hoped would repeat itself this sundown.
(And if it didn't, never mind! It was hardly an omen . . .)
I refer to the 'green flash'. On cloudless, calm, hot days
such as this one in the Pacific, if you gaze at the horizon
just after the north pole of the sun has sunk, because of
some atmospheric characteristic a bright green light
flashes low along the sea horizon, for no more than a
second or two.

We all gathered to watch for it: passengers, officers,
and the Fräulein. We had seen the green flash faintly,
perhaps three times in the past few weeks – and the
search for it had taken on a kind of 'mystical' significance,
as though that flash of light was racing across the whole
of the Pacific from Asia, to catch up with us; as though,
could we film it and slow it down incredibly, we might
see in that flash images of pagodas and jungles, paddy
fields, Mount Fuji, Angkor Wat – as if this was the
oceanic equivalent of a desert mirage, of mountains
reflected from far away.

'There!' cried Mrs Hetherington, pointing unnecessarily
– since all our eyes were peeled.

It was the brightest that the green flash had ever been.
And already it was gone; the sea horizon was as ever.

The first champagne cork promptly popped; and a jet
of froth leaped the rail.

Soon all the glasses were full, and the Captain made a
little speech. We all toasted Fräulein Jünger, and she
laughed merrily, her chocolate box face wreathed in
smiles.

Herr Jünger produced a round box – like a hat box –
and presented it.

The Fräulein tore the ribbon off, letting it flutter away into the sea. It coiled on the water, like a red snake rushing sternwards.

From the box the Fräulein pulled out a long black wig. It dangled black and glossy, rich and full.

'Ooh!' she exclaimed, and rushed inside to try it on before a mirror, returning perhaps five minutes later, transformed. And then the party really got under way.

We all drank too much, even the British.

Fortunately – or unfortunately – it was then time to eat dinner. Some ballast.

'Oh wait,' called Fräulein Jünger, as we filed around the table. She caressed her long new hair. 'I think I do not wish to get flesh-juice on this.'

'Gravy,' the Captain corrected her. '*Fleischsaft* is translated into English as "gravy".'

'Of course,' agreed her father. For this special occasion he had brought Friedolin in and placed him in the centre of the tablecloth, to preside. 'Friedolin would be so unhappy. That is a very special wig, for a very special daughter. It is not a mongrel, made of many different people's hairs. It is all from the head of one woman, whom I paid well. I bought it specially, and had it made up specially for you, *liebchen*.'

The Fräulein rushed away to deposit her new hair in her cabin, while we took our seats.

Two minutes later she returned, frowning. She still wore the wig. The apples of her cheeks were blanched.

'But I can't get it off!' She surveyed the British passengers. 'What joke is this? Someone has poured glue inside it.'

'Nonsense,' said Herr Jünger. 'You felt the inside, before you put it on. It slips off easily.'

'But it *won't* come off.'

'Let me. Maybe it's a little tight.'

He tried, while Herr Grünewald hovered, impatient to serve the evening's flesh. The Fräulein's father wrestled with his daughter's head; and she cried out in pain.

'Stop!'

'Tugging your own hair, is it?' asked Mrs Hetherington, with a semblance of sympathy.

'No.' The Fräulein held her head. 'Not my hair. It's as if wires are in my head. Sticking in my brain. Like live nerves. I'm confused. My thoughts are crazy – they're not human words! I can't stand the pain when you pull.'

The wig wouldn't come off at all. It was as though the green flash, from Asia, had welded the wig to her head.

The Fräulein had to be given a sedative, and taken to lie down.

That evening, uniquely, there were no second helpings of flesh – though Friedolin watched over the soured feast with undiminished, tubby joviality.

Nor would the wig come off the next day, either. It clung like a black leech.

We had arrived at Panama, and we floated on a flat blue expanse behind several other merchant vessels, all pointing towards the cleft of the Americas.

The Fräulein sat out on deck in the sunshine, which was so much hotter now that we were close to land. An old sheet was wrapped round her. One of the crewmen, an electrician who doubled as ship's barber, had been ordered up with his shears to cut the alien hair from her head. Somehow it seemed very important to throw every last strand over the side into the ocean, to drift back towards Asia, before the *Lübeck* quitted the Pacific for a different sea.

As the barber made the first cut, Fräulein Jünger screamed out terribly.

'No!' She snatched the shears from him, then clutched

her head. 'The pain! It's alive. It's like cutting my flesh
with fire! Her hair is living. It's put down roots. She's
dead – I know she's dead. But she's alive in it! Her soul
flowed into her hair – like Samson, his strength!'

Then she babbled in tongues for a while, as though
talking to herself with two voices.

It couldn't be true, but . . . Appalled, there was nothing
that any of us could think of to do or say. Except,
perhaps, to beg forgiveness of something. Or of someone,
whose language we couldn't speak.

The ship tooted.

'We *have* to move, to sail through,' the Captain said.
'*Now*. The pilot's coming. Herr Jünger, please!'

Fräulein Jünger dragged the torn sheet around her like
the thinnest peasant robe. She still clasped the shears in
one hand – and I wondered whether the very same shears
were borrowed by Herr Jünger from the electrician, six
months ago. She stared ahead wildly towards the green
jungle fringe of Panama, the Asia of the Americas
haunted by natives in their rags. Her mind deranged, by
another dead mind.

And I was guilty too. As guilty as anyone. For I had
drunk champagne at the Fräulein's birthday. And I had
not stepped overboard, weeks ago, into the warm oblivion
of the Pacific.

How lush and rich the Fräulein's hair was. How it
thrived on her. She looked like a new woman. And she
would be alone with us all in the Sargasso Sea, then the
Atlantic, for another month, almost.

How would Friedolin survive that journey?

Or any of us. Or any of us.

The Mystic Marriage of Salome

How many times have I railed against the sterile depravity of this palace! And now that I am at last dragged inside, in chains, how true were all my words of condemnation!

Every surface glitters with enamel or gold leaf, with glazed polychrome brickwork or tiled arabesques, with onyx mosaics or mother-of-pearl marquetry, with lozenges of lapis lazuli. Gems encrust chests and other items of furniture as though these are coral reefs. If this palace were ever sacked, the besieging soldiery would hardly be able to stagger away under all the weight of prised-out treasure. Everything gleams and coruscates and shimmers prismatically.

Yet gloom pervades the whole – as if, from all these burning fires of jewelled beauty, soot is constantly rising into the air, drifting like black snow into the lee of any shadows.

Well I remember the tale about how the greatest of the pyramids was completed. Many years had passed by in the building of it since the court astrologers had first settled on the most propitious date for the future funeral rites of the pharaoh, who was already lying embalmed in his sarcophagus. The patterns of the planets and the constellations on that future day were already written into the twists and turns of the stone passages leading to the funeral chamber itself, which was piled higgledy-piggledy with rich ornaments and golden vessels. A granite maze mapped the shape of the sky on that future occasion into the entrails of this artificial mountain, and was fixed irrevocably by the weight of a million tons of stone. Yet the final decorations were still lacking when the chosen day arrived. Therefore the master craftsman was sealed up in the funeral chamber on the day, to complete the design. Granite plugs were hammered into place. The slaves who hammered these were put to the sword by the élite guard, so that they should not whisper any secrets, years hence, to the grandfathers of tomb robbers. When the élite guard emerged into the open air, they too would be waylaid and run through by yet other guards . . .

The master craftsman worked on, painting his frescoes of the Land of the Dead by the light of the oil lamps left to him, eating sparingly of the bread and water measured out for his sustenance. And when that was gone, he would starve or stifle. But this did not worry him. His only fear was that he would finish his work just at the moment that the last lamp gutted out, so that he would die beside his supreme completed masterpiece in darkness, without ever seeing it himself . . .

That's what this palace puts me in mind of: of that infinite weight of the pyramid pressing down, and of the smoke from the oil lamps, and of the stifling air – an air of death. It puts me in mind of this, even though here are vast chambers opening into chambers even vaster, and halls running on into other halls in a jewelled maze of interior space. Space, yes. Yet outside all this, beyond the walls which have no windows – for the palace is lit by lamps and jewels – may as well be a million miles of black stone: a solid void.

Perhaps I'm anticipating the dungeon underneath the palace. Perhaps I'm fearing that dark oubliette into which they will press me, and seal with a slab: that lowest drain hole, the run-off of piss and shit from the other prisoners?

No. It is the palace itself which is a necropolis, a dead place – despite all the iridescent peacock's pride of hues, despite all the garish filigree, the bijouterie and tinsel work.

My footsteps – the slappings of my sandals – echo against the vaults and cupolas as my guards hustle me along. Their own steps are silent, either from perfect training or because theirs are the steps of dead people, of ghosts of flesh. Their frequent blows hurt me, though. The blows, too, are silent.

Shall I preach to them about the pride of the peacock?

'Where is everybody?' I gasp out, instead.

One of the guards slaps me across the mouth. But the other tells me tersely, 'Throne Room, scum. It's his birthday. Or conception day. The old boss's. The virgin daughter's going to dance for him. Same every year. Inflame his loins, the old dried up prune. Ought to be a holiday for us. Except for you, you bugger. Preaching against lust. Raving on about purity of heart. Can't have that, today! Don't you hear the music?'

I do, faintly. Very faintly. Wild riffs on a guitar, far away.

The brass-bound dungeon door swings open. Whether from residual compassion, or simply as per regulations relating to equipment, the guard who addressed me unlocks my fetters and slings them over his shoulder before I am tossed inside, on to piles of straw with hard knobs of human dung in them.

I'm alone in the dungeon, after all. No other wretches are imprisoned here, not in this place.

Yet I'm not entirely alone. For this guitar music is much closer and wilder now. I realize that by some taunting trick of the architecture this dungeon is located *adjacent* to the Throne Room, though on a slightly lower level. A high slit of an embrasure is the only source of air or light. Or sound. I scramble up the rough wall to it and cling. At the vent, a balm of burning incense and perfumes, sprinkled or spilled extravagantly, masks the foul odour of this insanitary cell. Shinning up further, I behold the jewelled throne of the King.

Oh yes, the dungeon is deliberately positioned here. The vent allows prisoners whose limbs are still intact to spy on the opulence of the ruler who holds them so carelessly captive. In their starvation and their thirst it lets them be tormented by the sight of rich meats and wine. No wonder my fetters were removed . . .

The King wears a gold-laced white robe and a great turban with an emerald and ruby tiara set round it. He hunches, wizened and intent. His thin, lined, beard-streaked face is a waxen mask of impotence and lust.

Below him sits the Mother of the virgin, in red and gold and blue brocaded robes: a guest at the King's feast. She has brought her maiden daughter to perform the dance of the veils before him.

The guitarist squats at the other side of the throne. A woman as richly costumed as the Mother herself, she is performing arabesque cadenzas upon her inlaid instrument by means of finger plectrums on her nails. Each chord tears at my flesh – as I imagine it will be torn before this day is out, with my screams from the dungeon vent accompanying her music as the incoherent vocal line. That may happen, when the dance is over. When their capacity for pleasure is sated, when it can only be revived by another's pain.

The guards stationed in the Throne Room itself are an abomination, neither he nor she. Their faces half-hidden by cloths, they lean on the pommels of long sabres.

Posies, bouquets and nosegays are strewn about the floor, to be trodden into fragrance by the dancer's feet – and perhaps to stop her from slipping. As for the daughter herself, her I can hardly bear to look at. So beautiful she

is. So white as alabaster. So intoxicatingly veiled, over
her near-nudity – which I cannot help but visualize, as
though I have been tempted by this same dance many
times before in my haunted dreams, and here is – and
will be – at last merely the abominable confirmation of
them.

Jewelled gauze and brocade heap her body for the
moment, and upon her piled jet-black hair is set a bees'
hive of light-buzzing gems. Bangles clasp her arms. Yet
underneath, ah shamefully underneath, her breasts will
be plumped upwards by a begemmed corselet. And her
hips will be girdled as richly, though in scantier style,
with a thick pendant hanging down between her legs to
hide her mount of Venus. Oh yes, oh yes. Robes and
veils wrap her still, but I know that underneath is a body
which will drive men mad!

As though the King has been waiting for this precise
moment when I gain my precarious peephole, he claps
his hands feebly upon his lap. The Mother crooks a finger
at the virgin. The guitarist swings into a throbbing dance
routine.

At first the virgin dances slowly, but then ever more
frenetically – prancing, arching, dashing to and fro, undu-
lating like a feasting python, working up an acrid, lascivious sweat that gleams on her as musky oil. One heavy
garment after another tumbles from her; then one jewelled veil after another slides away, like so many snake
skins. Until she is clad only in hoops of wire crusted with
diamonds and sapphires – and one frail cloudy veil. It is
as I foresaw.

The King pants, gazing furtively. The Mother regards
the performance with a smug serenity.

And somehow as I cling here, staring through this
crack in the wall, it becomes obvious to me that this
dance of enticement is directed *at me*, as much as at the

King! The aged King may well lust for the virgin's body, yet only a youthful stallion could burst the hymen to impregnate her.

Can this be what the virgin anticipates? That a young prisoner should be dragged from the dungeon, to bed her on those crushed petals?

Ah no. She wills sterility. Therefore the flow of blood from her hymen will be transmuted into the flow of the prisoner's blood before her eyes . . .

Sterility, indeed! The sterility – of incest! And androgyny. For King and Mother and eunuch guards and the lolling, glaze-eyed guests alike all look remarkably like brothers and sisters. Worse, many of the male guests present resemble fey virgins as much as debauchees. And as for the virgin, in spite of the thrusting snow-apples of her breasts I fear that the heavy pendant might be lifted from her loins to disclose a lolling thin male organ between her thighs!

She bows at last. The King beckons: with a simple clutch of his fingers, burrowing deeper into his own robe-lapped loins. Maybe he has ejaculated at the climax of the virgin's dance? Since his expression is so furtively chill now. In which case: *consummatum est*. Except that the virgin remains unpenetrated. The blood of Hymen must be shed . . .

Briefly, she glances *directly at me*, hidden here in the gloom. Her glance is bold and taunting. Then she approaches the throne. She whispers.

I can maintain my grip no longer. I slide down the stones into the soiled straw. The guitar riffs again – and now there is discord in the music.

The dungeon door swings open as I lie here, unwilling to move. My arms are still aching from the effort of shinning up to see the dance. My vulnerable flesh, sworn to chastity, also aches from the sheer *taunt* of that sight.

The guards march in. From behind them comes the tallest of those eunuch throne guards. A long red skirt hides his nether regions. In his right hand he holds a sword almost as tall as he is himself. In his other hand he balances a golden salver.

'He' is a eunuch – or an androgyne. Sterility is everywhere. So how can offspring possibly be born in this place? How can there ever be an heir to the throne, except maybe by adoption?

The King, I realize, can only mate . . . by proxy. And it is with the Mother that he wishes, by proxy, so to mate . . .

As the eunuch approaches ever so slowly, pace by pace, I realize the significance of the virgin's parting glance at me. It is *I* who am the groom. That, and no other reason, is why I was hauled here from preaching in the infested gaudy bazaar. For my face is favourable, and has long been spied on from the ramparts of the palace while I inveighed against it; and I am young and wholesome; and my locks are long and golden.

They need to avail themselves of a *chaste* impregnator. Otherwise, half-brothers might abound in the land, disturbing the succession. But once the deed is done, the impregnator's chastity thereafter will be ensured, by a sword blow. The fact that I am the commonest of men, with whom no noble would dream of comparing himself, at once guarantees discretion and uniqueness, and also roots the succession of the dynasty in some potent ordinary seed. Strange are the customs of mad royal houses! But I have heard rumours, of course – hints that the sire of the heir is always secretly selected from the marketplace. Bazaar gossip is most untrustworthy, but perhaps true this time?

One of the escorting guards guffaws.

'She wants your' (I don't hear what) 'on a plate!'

And the sword dips towards my loins.

I was *wrong*. So wrong! So swayed by the dance!

They are going to emasculate me! They are going to bear my genitals to the Throne Room on that dish. The virgin will eat them cooked in sesame oil. She will swallow my manhood whole like an entertainer swallowing a toad. How can this possibly impregnate her? Unless she intends to bear the child quite literally in her belly, behind the jewel in her sea-shell navel? What sort of child would that be?

In a flash of vision I see her organs – her belly and womb, her tubes and entrails – as somehow writ large in the endless halls and chambers of this very palace. The palace is like a body itself – inside of which she is a mere homunculus, and I myself am a single sperm seeking for her. Or wilfully avoiding her! (Yet did I not climb up to that embrasure voluntarily, to gaze at her lascivious dance?)

Such visions are sometimes suspect. Yet this one does not seem entirely impossible. For in this palace everything seems to reflect everything else. All the plethora of decoration comments upon itself and mirrors itself excessively. While the motions of the virgin during the dance (abandoned though they seemed) were really all quite stylized – so that every disposition of her veils constituted the copulas of an obscene, wordless *language,* product of the place. The palace uttered the dance; the dance uttered the palace; voluptuous and sterile at the same time, each of them.

So what child might be uttered, out of that virgin? As the castrator advances closer, it seems to me fleetingly that another *palace* might be born, situated in some echo or shadow existence beyond this present world: another vast building of enamelled halls and bedizened corridors which would coast through time itself, sufficient unto itself, self-reflective, empty save when it wishes to summon up Kings and guards and servitors, and a virgin and a golden ram like me!

The castrator tosses the golden dish on to the straw. The other guards seize me and bow me over, dragging my head down by the locks – a crouch which I fall into willingly to protect my unused sex.

'She wants *your head* on a plate!'

That was what the guard said earlier. Now he repeats it gloatingly.

Is the virgin waiting just outside the dungeon door, to rush in and bestride my decapitated corpse? They ought to hang me if that's what she wants to do! I do not imagine that one ejaculates at the moment of beheading. But perhaps I'm wrong.

The sword whistles to and fro, slicing the air, as the executioner swings into his rhythm, building up momentum.

And I am tumbling, unable to halt myself. My arms and legs are stunned by shock – gone, useless. A stink of foul straw fills my nostrils. The executioner hoists me by the hair – and places me upon the golden dish! I squat on it, unable to move though nobody restrains me.

Like a superb banquet master, the eunuch lifts the dish, and I fly upward on it. He pirouettes it, no doubt upon the very tips of his agile fingers.

My body, that sleeve of flesh, lies tumbled in the straw. Blood pumps in ejaculatory spurts from my cleanly severed neck.

And I am *a living head*, upon a dish.

What kind of miracle is this?

No one eats a head. A head is too hard – though the brains are soft enough, if the skull is sawn open. A head is too bony, too lank with hair which would catch between the teeth. Nothing soft. Except for the eyeballs, cheeks and tongue. (And the brains within.)

I feel no emotion now. I'm free of the lascivious, hateful enchantment of the dance. The nerves and organs which responded earlier are quite separated from me. The body which her dance enticed is discarded on the floor. The head is far distant from the hot heart. I am . . . yes, detached.

The virgin ordered *this* as her prize – the fulfilment of the King's promise – yet the King never expected her to ask for this sort of prize. He expected her to ask for *my body*! But this is what she asked for, because she is a veritable Jezebel of sterility.

She must be revelling in my execution, awaiting the orgasm which will twist her loins as the eunuch bears me in to her upon this golden charger; the cold orgasm of unconsummation . . .

How she must have loathed the prospect of losing her virginity! How she must have hated the thought of conceiving a child, whose bones would be the walls and roofs of a second palace in the other world beyond this world – the world of similitudes, according to the philosophers of Arabia. A child, whose bloodstream would be ruby-studded corridors. Whose lungs would be mighty chambers capped with cupolas. Whose stomach, kitchens. The convolutions of whose brain would be written everywhere in arabesques. And outside of this child's body, too, the black granite of a void would reach as far as the remotest jewels of the stars themselves.

How could she possibly give birth to a palace, out of the little chamber of her womb – even in the world of similitudes? Are my thoughts totally disordered by the slicing of my spine?

Only I, in this dungeon, realize that I am still immortally alive . . . And all my feelings have been neutered by that sword stroke.

Yet something begins to glow in me. Something that will soon be incandescent.

So at last, not in iron chains but on a golden platter, I am borne in to that depraved, glittering, aromatic Throne Room.

The eunuch bows before the King, holding me to one side. The King merely nods. It is as much as he can do in his musk-maddened, frozen condition.

As I weave through the air towards the virgin, her kohl-shadowed eyes gleam bright with triumph. She smells enticingly of patchouli and other Eastern oils. Her waxen lips are slightly parted, disclosing delicate little ivory teeth like the milk teeth of a child. Rising up quickly on tiptoe, she kisses my dead lips. Her petal tongue flickers, lizard-like, between my lips. And she steps back. With a grand flourish the eunuch sets me down upon one of a flight of low steps leading to the preciously inlaid tabernacle.

And the incandescence bursts from me!

My head rises into the air of its own volition. Like an exploding sun, I illuminate the space around me. Blood, hitherto staunched by contact with the gold, oozes in a rope from my neck as though I am putting down bloody roots into the soil of the air.

'Why, damsel?' I demand. 'Tell me why!'

The virgin falters, aghast. With her left hand she tries to ward off this apparition, whom I am. With her right hand she claws at the banded necklace which laps her throat and shoulders, broad and sparkling as the rings of Saturn – as though that immaculate gewgaw is contracting around her windpipe to suffocate her.

If I cannot pierce those secret lips between her white

legs – now that my manhood lies flaccid and bloodless on
the dungeon floor together with the rest of my body –
and indeed the very thought of doing so appals my
chastity, at least I can pierce her soul. I can irradiate that
other secret part of her with spokes of sacred, reproachful
light. Thus she may become chaste forever too, her
organs of generation sterilized by my cold brightness.

No one else moves in the Throne Room. It's as though
people have turned to salt – as if the flash of this moment
has interrupted forever the sequence of time.

She moves, though.

She turns – and her last veil whirls away from her. She
flees from my presence, dressed only in tiara, necklace,
cuirass, anklets, bangles, girdle. Her buttocks are naked:
twin white-skinned melons. A spring of hair shows darkly
between them, unshaved.

Propelled by will, I drift after her at speed. Every so
often a gobbet of blood falls to mark my passage, from
high above the marble floors.

My preaching in the bazaar has by no means failed, I
see. For I have begun to understand that my fierce
speeches all along had been directed at the harlot-virgin.
They had been aimed at drawing me to her attention, so
that I could *win* her. Not in the carnal sense, but in the
spiritual. For if she succumbed, then King and Mother
and all the court must surely be converted in her wake.

As for sacred love (as opposed to profane), why, I am
guaranteed that now in perpetuity by the sloughing off of
my body with its shameful, involuntary erections and
emissions and all the teasing attendant dreams that trailed
the flag for these events. I am granted this at *her*
command.

So, as I chase her, it seems to me now that she was
wiser than me. She was well aware long ago that if we
should meet each other face to face in any ordinary way,

attired in our whole bodies, then she must inevitably
seduce me. I in turn must inevitably yield to her. Thus
would I lose that power of spirit which attracted her
perversely to me, and me to her, in the first place. I
would lose it as surely as Samson lost his strength to
Delilah.

Yet now instead, because of her choice, I am incan-
descently pure.

So why does she persist in eluding me?

Is it because she wishes to lead me to a private trysting
place, deep in this interminable palace of scintillating
brightness and soot-stained shade: a place where we can
be quite alone together?

The palace is a maze, indeed. I have little idea of the
layout of its majestic entrails. But soon I have no idea of
my direction either. She remains just ahead of me,
running on her white feet. Her footfalls are quiet, but I
can hear the panting of her breath. I can't *quite* catch up
with her. I'm attracted to her like a moon to a world, yet
I'm held off at a distance by the very speed of my pursuit.
Thus I follow her, falling through the air into the path of
her flight, unable to fall all the way.

Eventually she darts down a flight of marble steps.

To my astonishment – though naturally no quickening
of the heart accompanies this – the corridor at the bottom
of the steps is the very corridor of the dungeon! Close by,
the dungeon door still stands wide open.

She pauses to glance back, then she plunges inside that
rank, dark chamber. I drift after her inevitably, and in,
to illumine that stone room with my rays. These wash the
walls and floor as bright as the desert under full moonlight. The rumpled straw lies in ridgy dunes. Nutty
excrements mixed in with it are the droppings of desert
foxes and jerboas . . .

My headless body sprawls bloodless, as white as she herself. She reaches it and clasps it – like a child playing some game of Sanctuary. Some Hide-and-Seek – and here is the magical token of safety.

With a strength that I did not suspect in her, she hoists my corpse to its feet. She claps it in front of her like a shield – or as if she means to engage in intercourse with it in that position, an act of ultimate necrophilia which I must needs watch impotently!

Yet no. Now despite myself, I drift through the air. For my head heeds the attraction of my waiting neck. And so at last my lips meet her lips once again, at the very moment that my head rejoins my body. The saliva of her kiss is a rich gum coursing down my throat, sealing its wound.

She who took away, now gives.

And I am whole again.

Yet no blood flows in my veins. I feel the cells of my flesh unlock, to bleed lymph into my empty vessels in a strange transfusion.

Is this, then, my spiritual body which she holds in her white hands? A spiritual body, purged of rank hot blood?

Is this the dream which all along she secretly nursed: to empty out the wild blood from me, with all its throbbings and promptings, before she could bring herself to touch me? So that, when at last she did so, she would still remain at once both harlot *and* virgin?

The whitish liquid rises throughout me like sap. It is akin to spermatic fluid – the juice of the groin and glands! In all my veins flows cool white sperm like ass's milk. It engorges and stiffens me in an elastic rigidity quite unlike *rigor mortis*. Now I can stand without her aid.

I am as one of those saints from the exotic religions further East, in India: a saint to whom the sexual body and the spiritual body are one and the same. And she is a divine harlot from out of one of those religions. She is the temple whore who initiates the young novice within a temple of holy depravity, which is her body!

Without her ministrations, I fear that I will become a carnal monster like the old King himself, thrusting himself upon the limp bodies of slave boys and slave girls and eunuchs, of she-goats and shaven apes, his organ feebly inflamed by aphrodisiacs and peppery ointment!

She is the priestess now. And I am in her hands.

'Thou,' she intones. Her voice is both innocent and weary, as though she has been alive for a thousand years or more, yet is just newly born, too, newly awakened to celebrate another cycle of the stars and worlds.

She intends this soiled straw to be our bed; but her perfumes will drench and sweeten it. Transfigured by light, this dungeon will be our nuptial chamber . . .

She smiles, coyly. It is the first enticingly human expression I have seen in the whole of this monstrous palace; but it is fleeting.

And is her smile really directed at me at all?

I turn slowly, a statue of salt myself. The sea-tang of sperm-foam, oceanic spirit, teases my lips to thirst for her.

In the doorway of the dungeon I see the old King leaning, supported on the brawny arm of a massive eunuch. He licks his thin grey lips anticipatively with the tip of his tongue. Beside him loiters the Mother, nodding in appreciation.

And I feel the caress of a hand on my white shoulder, as the knowledgeable virgin reminds me why we are here.

The Bloomsday Revolution

'Why Bloomsday?' Teresa asked Dennis as he held her hand in the back of the bridal limousine: her black hand in his white hand, while St Anselm's peal of bells faded into the distance.

As ever, the sky was azure, with some puffy cotton clouds. White ribbons fluttered from the silver mascot of the Rolls. Massed daffodils trumpeted golden notes of spring. As ever, on this their perfect day.

'Oh, I see: because of all the flowers. I suppose you can't very well call today Saturday,' and her voice faltered, 'not when there isn't Friday or Sunday any more. But those aren't the flowers of my native land! They're all foreign flowers.' She seemed on the verge of tears.

Dennis squeezed her hand. He hoped to avoid any senseless bickering or heartache. This would be as beside the point as the question of whether they ought to make love tonight. (Of course they would make splendid, practised love, after the initial bother of defloration – with the experience of a thousand identical weddings behind them. Was this not their perfect day?)

'No, listen, Tess: that isn't why. I was chatting to Carla before the service yesterday, while we were waiting for you to arrive – '

'Carla?' his wife queried archly.

'Carla Rushworth, of course. What other Carla is there?'

'And you were simply . . . "chatting"?'

'Actually, Tess, we were having a fairly intense discussion. But don't feel jealous: that's all such a long time ago, me and her.' Casually he added, 'I invited Carla along to our reception today.'

'You *what*?'

'Goodness, I don't even know if she'll be able to *get* there! But if she can, it'll be . . . something new.'

'Oh, Dennis, Dennis, are you so tired of making love to me for the first time? You must be! The thrill of black flesh has faded. That's why you really married me isn't it? The novelty! Now it's worn thin . . . But not for me.'

'Damn it, we must break the pattern somehow.'

'Must we? Oh yes, Carla Rushworth would love to break *our* pattern, wouldn't she?'

'Don't let's argue, Tess. We haven't all that much time.' For already the Rolls was swinging past the War Memorial, with its draped flags sculpted in bronze; and more brazen daffodils.

Teresa sniffed. 'Time, indeed? We have all of time! And I'm your wife for ever and ever. That's what it's all about. Is that what you want to break up?'

'You know I don't.'

'And you're the reason why I'm exiled in an alien land, with all those wretched yellow blooms mocking me!'

Dennis Monsarrat sensed his point of vantage. 'Obviously you aren't entirely happy, Tess – those wretched blooms, eh? But getting back to the subject of Bloomsday: that's the name of the day when Joyce's *Ulysses* is set – June 16th, 1904. You see, his book immortalized that one particular ordinary Dublin day for evermore: the pubs, streets, people, horse races, newspaper stories, all preserved as if on a scroll of eternity. And the real Bloomsday is where James Joyce is likely to be, now that he's dead. Just as we're here, you and I, getting married for the umpteenth time. That's his Great Day; and this is ours. The day of our life, transfigured forever.'

'So?'

'Well, all these *other* people are here too, repeating a perfectly ordinary day in their lives, like the characters in *Ulysses*. This is what Carla has been getting at for ages, every time she can catch me alone.'

'Oh, has she?'

'Yes! Do listen. Carla believes that we two – that's you and I, Tess – hold the key to this particular slice of time. Or at least we're two of the people who hold the key. Just as Joyce must hold the key to that day in 1904. Today is *our* Bloomsday; and everyone else is locked up in it. All those who are here.'

And now they were passing the Alexandra Hospital; more beds of yellow daffodils outside, beds of white linen within – in one of which Teresa would give birth two years after this wedding, to the twins, one of whom, Kwame (readopting his mother's name, as Kwame Openibo), would become President of Panafrica West one day. Those twins, whom Dennis and Teresa would never see again, for this perfect day preceded their conception . . .

'All those who are here,' Teresa Monsarrat echoed bitterly. 'But your parents are never at our wedding now. They were at our very first wedding, when we were alive.'

'We've gone over that. I've told you: either they belong elsewhere because they're older . . . or just possibly I, uh, underestimated their feelings about mixed marriages.'

'Which makes this your mother and father's Hateful Day. So they're in a different slice of time, a better one for them . . . What sort of afterlife is this, that separates kin?'

'Maybe this is the only possible way to organize a Hereafter: slice by slice. You can't crowd all the generations of Humanity who ever lived into the same region. It would be, well, over-populated. That's what Carla – '

'Carla! Always Carla! The great TV pundit of other people's books! Hasn't it occurred to you, Dennis, that

all these other people,' and she waved from the car
window in a queenly manner, 'may simply be extras –
and only we two are real? Maybe this is our own personal
Heaven, which you'll soon turn into Hell.'

'Carla says – '

Teresa moaned.

'Carla insists that she's real, and all the others are real.
They're all subject to the same compulsion as we are to
re-enact this one day, in full awareness. With a kind of
intellectual free will, if you like. Although by now it's
become a very special day for them, it wasn't when they
were alive. It was just a day like any other. So she
concludes that each time-slice has to be built around one
person – or a few – for whom the day was extraordinary.
These souls are a sort of seed crystal – a focus for the
day.'

Yet already the conifer-guarded drive of the Monkton
House Hotel was upon them . . .

'That's us: partly because of what Kwame later became,
but mainly because of the strength of our love, Tess. I'd
never have made High Commissioner without you. I'd
never have stuck it.'

Relentlessly the chauffeur turned in through the
gateway.

Compulsion, thought Dennis, fingering the red rose in his
buttonhole, Teresa by his side before the still uncut tiers
of wedding cake.

Or a blessing for evermore?

Rising, he rested his hand upon Teresa's hand as she
stood to cut the cake; and the waitress bore it away to
dismember it. Champagne popped off and fizzed into
glasses.

The wedding guests, as ever, were Jenny and Laurie
and Kay, Colin and Barbara Seaford, Zsuzsanna Gilby

who spelled her name pretentiously with a 'z', Melanie
Alden with her Max, and Daniel Adebonojo, who possessed the only other black countenance. A small party,
smaller than at the original wedding during their lifetimes,
but these were the contemporary guests.

And day by identical day these same familiar faces
came first to St Anselm's for the service, then to the
reception – which was sometimes rowdy, sometimes
almost silent.

For necessity existed: the gentle urge to carry out the
selfsame actions, by and large, *ad infinitum*. Gentle,
unless resisted. And there was freedom, too: the licence
to think and feel and speak one's mind. Rather as actors
in the thousandth performance of a play might think
about other things, acting out a sub-drama of their own,
and even – such being the nature of this drama – ad-
libbing, improvising, and commenting on it, toward the
same general outcome.

The outcome, for Dennis and Teresa, being half a
night of passion . . . until they woke up apart elsewhere
in town, unmarried, back at the beginning of yet another
rerun of their great day.

But also here today, looking strained and tense –
fighting to be *here*, rather than where her own inner
imperative preferred her to be – sat Carla Rushworth,
accepting a glass from the waiter and promptly draining it
without waiting for Colin Seaford to propose the health
of bride and groom.

Duly Colin popped up to recite his piece.

And Dennis rose to reply.

'I . . .' He swallowed; it was an effort not to comply.
'Teresa's a long way from home,' he managed to say. 'It
hurts a bit, being exiled for ever . . . I'm afraid it'll hurt
even more today. Because today is different.' He tried to
ignore the expression on Teresa's face, as she guessed the

drift of his little speech. Laurie and Kay, at least, were nodding encouragement.

'As you see, Carla's here. I've spoken to her several times before the service, I . . . we . . . she was in love with me once.'

'Please!' protested Zsuzsanna. 'Have some pity! Try to think of Tess.'

'I do. That's the trouble: thinking. We have to think *harder*, about what we're doing every day.'

'But we all do, Dennis. Surely I'm not the only one. Every little action is becoming perfect, sacred. So is each blade of grass, and sip of champagne, and crumb of cake. It's all as bright as an acid trip by now. Etched, luminous, radiant.'

'Ah, but *où sont les neiges d'antan*?' quoted Kay, in a brittle tone. 'We see daffodils, but never snow. Nor chrysanthemums and autumn leaves. Nor rainbows and summer showers. Isn't that all a little sad? And isn't it sad never to see a lover again? Why can't I be there by the sea with Alan, clambering over boulders, with the salt spray in our hair?'

'I can remember perfectly well what a disaster *that* relationship was,' said Zsuzsanna. 'It simply didn't work out for you two.'

'But why can't I have a day during the first year, when it was wonderful?'

'Because, deep down, it was false – unlike Tess's and Dennis's marriage. How can you live a lie, for eternity?'

All this while, the waiter and waitress had been refilling glasses discreetly and circulating with little plates of wedding cake; this done, they toasted each other and started to flirt, as though Dennis's disruption of the proceedings had let them off the leash of their duties.

Dennis glanced at his watch. Thirty minutes till Teresa must retire upstairs to change into her casual clothes; less

than an hour till they would drive away together, to
Harmouth by the sea, to spend their eternal first night in
the Marine Parade Hotel. Until they fell asleep.

'I want you all to listen to Carla,' he said. 'You too,
Tess.' Pityingly he touched her shoulder: white lace upon
black skin. She shrugged his touch away.

Carla looked sick. Not from champagne or cake –
which she hadn't touched – or from the Chicken Kiev
preceding, which she had only nibbled at. She was sick
with determination.

'We're all prisoners,' she said, as firmly as she could.
'Prisoners of a Bloomsday Situation. Let me tell you
what that is . . .'

Dennis's head buzzed as he forced himself to listen
clearly. By now the waiter and waitress were kissing and
touching each other as if no one else were present to
observe them. It seemed quite indecent to Dennis.

'We're all dead,' he heard Carla say. 'And don't we
remember it! Dennis and Teresa, heroic victims of that
squalid little coup. Me, dead of a mere overdose. And
every day we repeat the same slice of time – even though
there must be thousands of other such slices, all separated
out. One with Marco Polo in it, and another with Napoleon, and others with the dead from Ancient Rome and
Egypt and human prehistory. Think of all the richness
we're robbed of! Think of all the days we'll never know!'

'And the horrors, too!' broke in Zsuzsanna. 'Do you
really wish to be everywhere and everywhen? Would you
really want to relive the whole of your own life? Suppose
you'd been tortured, would you want that over again? Or
been in a car crash or a war – or dying slowly of cancer? I
should know. I spent two years doing that, and I didn't
take the easy way out, either. Not that there was anything
wrong with *you*, Carla, but jaded boredom. I don't,
incidentally, remember the moment of my death. I was

too drained and drugged, hardly a person any longer. As far as I'm concerned, this is an innocuous day. And maybe that's why things are as they are. Maybe this is the greater compassion.'

'No! All time should be ours. Surely that's what eternity is. Not this . . . this endless celebration of one little day.'

Teresa looked up sharply. 'Oh, of course you wouldn't wish to celebrate today!'

Colin Seaford stuck his hand up. 'You'd imagine it would get to be an awful bore, over and over again. But really, as Zsuzsanna says, it isn't. There's such a, well, sense of security; and of striving, yes, striving for a fine perfection.' He coughed apologetically. 'All this fuss you're making, Miss Rushworth: it's spoiling things. If this is eternity, I'm content. Eh, Barbara?' However, his wife, fiddling with her glass, looked less sure. 'We ought to get on with things. It's . . . nasty, not getting on with things.'

'I'm in exile, too,' Daniel Adebonojo declared. 'I'm homesick every day. You're nice people, but you aren't my people. Where are they all? There's only Miss Openibo; and every day she's taken away from me by Mr Monsarrat. If you see what I mean.'

'"*If* this is eternity"?' Carla echoed Colin Seaford's words contemptuously. 'But it isn't. Eternity means the infinite. Yet everything about this afterlife of ours is so utterly finite. That's why I say that this is a Bloomsday Situation. Joyce's *Ulysses* is crammed with finite lists of every damn thing that existed on that single day. It's full of loops of events: closed paths leading back to their own beginnings. It's a time-prison. And I'm sure that Joyce is stuck in the original of his Bloomsday right now, because he conceived it so strongly and obsessively! Just as we're stuck here.'

Laurie laughed. 'So God, or whatever, read *Ulysses* and said to Himself, "Wow, there's my afterlife"?'

'No, no . . . it's such a strain fighting this damn compulsion. I don't mean the fictional Bloomsday. I mean the real one, the original. Joyce is almost sure to be the seed crystal for 1904 because of all the psychic energy he poured into that concept, of a slice of frozen living time. Dennis and Teresa may very well be the seed crystals of our own particular Bloomsday. Or, at least, two of the crystals. We all know how important Kwame Openibo will be.'

'True,' said Daniel. 'So what are you proposing?'

Teresa shifted nervously. 'I have to get changed. Soon! I must. Or we'll be late setting out. We mustn't be late.'

'I'll tell you what I'm proposing: none other than the Bloomsday Revolution.'

A strangled *'What?'* from Zsuzsanna.

'If this is the afterlife, I want a richer, bigger one. I want something evolving and changing and growing. We have to break out somehow. We have to cut our way through. And I'll bet you that James Aloysius Joyce is saying the same thing right now, after his thousandth or millionth Bloomsday.'

But at that moment Teresa rose and fled.

'We'd better talk about this tomorrow,' Dennis said. 'We really do have to get on the move. Will you come to the reception again, Carla?'

'Oh yes,' she promised fiercely. 'I'll come.'

So Dennis relaxed and let himself simply be a bridegroom once again. As though at a signal, the waiter and waitress disengaged from each other and began to collect the empty glasses.

Thus once more Dennis and Teresa were wedded at St Anselm's and chauffeured to their reception – following

upon another first night of hymeneal rites in Harmouth
where, to the lick and suck of waves on the sands, they
had made desperate love to heal the breach of faith
troubling her.

At the reception Carla spoke up. From the corner of his
eye Dennis noticed waiter and waitress begin, discreetly at
first, to misbehave . . .

And Zsuzsanna challenged Carla. 'It's all very well to
want something bigger, and evolving. But what if all the
evolving gets done while you're alive? What if that's the
lot? Finis, finito!'

'Maybe,' suggested Laurie, 'God, or whatever it is,
records everything you are and stores it in Himself? Yes:
on lots of floppy discs in His mind. And there's only so
much storage space on each disc – even though the
storeroom extends forever. There are only so many pages
in each book, though the library itself is infinite. Who's
to say that we're able to break fresh ground, once we're
dead?

'Though on the other hand,' he went on, 'if that's so,
then we couldn't very well be holding this discussion,
could we? We wouldn't be aware of anything unusual.
We'd just be repeating everything, word- and action-
perfect.'

'Ah, but people possess free will,' Jenny pointed out.
'If we lost that, we wouldn't be the same people we were
when we were alive.'

'Do you call *this* freedom?' Carla asked her bitterly.
'Our acts are programmed.'

'Now wait,' said Colin Seaford, 'That's true most of
the time during life, isn't it? A lot of the time we aren't
actually really conscious. We're just acting automatically,
routinely. So we can't be exercising all that much freedom. It seems to me that right now we're being thrust
towards a kind of perfect consciousness of every single

second of one day. Eventually we'll be truly aware, as we never were before. We'll notice everything. Maybe, once we've mastered one day, another day will become available; then another.'

'*I* notice that bird.' Daniel Adebonojo gestured out of the French windows, to where a solitary, very early swallow swerved and banked above the lawns. Sadly he regarded it, as it jinked in figure-eight flight, for its eyes had recently beheld Nigeria; or so it seemed to Daniel. 'I don't suppose *it* minds doing the same thing over and over, day by day. That must be pure bliss for a bird. Oh to be a swallow! It's birds' Heaven. Angelic.'

Yet they were distracted from the vista outside by the conduct of waiter and waitress: the man unbuttoned the young woman's blouse and fondled her breasts.

'Is that what you mean by revolution?' Colin Seaford demanded of Carla. 'Disorderly conduct? Impishness?'

'Maybe we ought to ask them!' Carla strode from the table and confronted the pair. 'Just what are you two playing at?'

The waitress flushed. 'I . . . you see, Miss, it's the only time we have to ourselves. All the work we have to do, then we have to go our own ways: it isn't right. We aren't being wicked, Tony and me. It's just the bloody frustration of it all! Oh yes, it's nice doing all the right things at the right time, neatly. But only to snatch one kiss in the kitchen, when Tony and me had ever such a good time once . . . I've forgiven him for running off and leaving me with the kid.'

Carla swung round. 'This needn't be how it is. It needn't be!'

And Teresa rose.

'Wait,' said Dennis. 'How can we do anything, Carla? What can we do?'

'I have to go,' said his wife. 'The urge, the urge is in me.'

'Just as a swallow has to migrate? And nest? And mate?' Perhaps Carla did not intend to reduce Teresa's status to that of a bird. Or perhaps she did.

'We'll talk about it tomorrow. Will you come to the reception again, Carla?' Dennis hoped to ease his wife's departure from the room, but his words had the opposite effect upon her, and she consequently left in tears.

'We could try to stay awake all night long,' proposed Daniel, soon after the obligatory champagne toast the next day. 'That way we might break through into the next slice.'

'And maybe,' Colin said, 'the next slice isn't tomorrow at all, but a year away. Maybe the afterlife is only a sampling taken every now and then: a set of cross sections. Maybe tomorrow's just an empty fog, and yesterday too; and it's that emptiness that seals us off from other slices. A *cordon sanitaire*.'

'If we're going to escape the pattern,' said Carla, 'I suggest that Dennis and Teresa break the mould of their own actions.'

'I knew it!' Teresa slammed her hand down upon her plate and then stared numbly at the broken china.

'For all our sakes,' begged Carla.

'Yes, but how?' asked Dennis. His tone was cold; yet this coldness was perhaps only a mask for a restless excitement: a cramping suffocating excitement. Heart-attack territory, almost. Carla Rushworth was wild and beautiful today; and suffering anguish, besides.

'*Why* is it your Bloomsday? Because you and Teresa got married. So next time – '

'No!' With a wounded cry, Teresa launched herself

from her seat; but Dennis held her – and the lace sleeve of her bridal gown tore.

' – do something else.'

Struggling free of her husband, Teresa ripped the whole sleeve away, then balled it up and threw it at Carla. She wrenched the bodice of the gown, exposing her shoulders and the cleft of her breasts.

'Here, take my wedding dress! Never fear: it'll all be back in one piece by tomorrow. Since I have to get changed anyway, why not here? Why don't I perform a striptease to complete my humiliation?' She tore the fabric open to her waist. 'There's just one thing, Miss Carla Rushworth: you'll need to collect tomorrow's dress from *my* flat. It won't appear by any miracle in *your* wardrobe.'

'Oh God,' cried Dennis. He gripped Teresa's wrists to stop her going any further. 'Carla didn't say that she and I should – '

'But she meant it, you fool! Don't you understand anything? I have to get changed. Let me go!'

'You've married him hundreds of times already, love,' called the waitress. 'Can't the other woman have a go? You could take it turn by turn. It might make it more fun for the rest of us.'

Zsuzsanna Gilby held her own head as though it ached. 'The beauty's gone away; it's all being torn to shreds. I can't stand it.'

'Well, something's got to give,' declared Carla. 'Eh, Dennis?'

He stared helplessly about, still clutching his shuddering half-stripped wife.

'Do it,' urged Daniel suddenly.

'Yes,' agreed Barbara Seaford, to the consternation of Colin.

'Do what? Marry Carla instead?'

'Think of it as an experiment in freedom, man,' said Daniel, encouragingly. 'A blow, to bring the walls down.' He smiled protectively at the betrayed bride.

'What a fine experiment it'll be, indeed!' shouted Teresa. 'Why should they even bother driving to Harmouth? Don't they have bedrooms in *this* hotel? We could all troop upstairs and watch. Just in case something interesting happens.'

'If you desperately don't want it to happen,' said Barbara, 'maybe that *will* be a fierce enough wedge? Passion, jealousy: what powerhouses those are. Can't you be brave, Tess? Dennis isn't really betraying you. It's for all of us: for all your friends.'

'It's monstrous,' said her husband. 'Though on the other hand . . . Are you sure, Babs?'

His wife nodded. 'Tomorrow Carla will stand in for Teresa. They can swap their clothes in one of the cars, before the service.'

'But won't our dear vicar wonder how the bride has happened to change the colour of her skin?'

'Not if no one else complains. Him? He'll think he has bats in his belfry. Or maybe he'll believe it's a miracle.'

'I wasn't exactly – ' began Carla tentatively.

'Come on, love,' Barbara egged her on, 'you've made your bed now, and you're bloody well going to lie in it. Tomorrow's *your* Bloomsday. So let's see you do any better!'

As the peal of bells faded behind the Rolls Royce on another azure, cloud-puff, daffodil day, Carla Monsarrat (*née* Rushworth) laughed with joy.

'We did it. What an awful strain it was at first: didn't you think so, Dennis dear? But what a weight lifted as soon as that old dodderer said the magic words. "Whom God hath joined," eh? Irrevocable!'

Dennis acknowledged that he had felt the same; though amidst such a welter of other emotions as well – which would have been even more tumultuous had Teresa been sitting in the tiny congregation. But Jenny had stayed outside with her; and had so well soothed her by the time the newlyweds emerged into sunlight that she had even thrown, lamely, some confetti.

'So we've crossed our Rubicon.' He breathed deeply. 'Or is it the River Liffey?' (Now they were passing the Alexandra Hospital, where shamelessly as usual the daffodil beds bloomed . . .)

Carla patted his hand. 'Husband mine,' she murmured. 'Sufficient unto the day?' Mockingly, it seemed, she patted the lace lap of her pristine wedding gown. The reception today was a muted affair, with Zsuzsanna and Jenny comforting Teresa in a suffocating way.

And in their bedroom, later:

'Should we, Carla?'

'We're married, aren't we? Oh, my bashful bridegroom, didn't you yearn to, achingly, about two years ago?'

'Ah, two years . . .'

'And many marriages ago. We must act married, Dennis dear, you know. We have to heap that one last straw upon the camel's back. Do you need me to seduce you, so that you can feel absolved of guilt?' And Carla began to undress.

'At least,' he joked feebly, as he watched her, 'I suppose I won't have to deflower you.'

She flushed. 'That's quite uncalled for. And you know it. Still, if you'd prefer a little preliminary quarrel, for us to make up, to add some spice and pepper and sincerity? Is that how you use sex: to make amends? Amends to Teresa, for instance, because she's black . . . Do you really need a sanctimonious excuse for passion?' Carla, tossing her curly auburn hair, crooked her finger. 'Come here, Dennis. Be mine.'

He obeyed.

A herring gull screaming against the window woke them raucously to morning light, in a bedroom spartan and antique.

An aspidistra commanded jadedly the windowsill: a pot of weed in an aquarium tank. For washing the sleep from one's eyes there was a china ewer and bowl upon a chest of drawers. From beneath the bed peeped a chamber pot. A print hung over the bed: an engraved crucifixion, nails and thorns and kneeling Mary. *Ora Pro Nobis*. Above a small firegrate, crucible of chilly ashes, the mantel shelf bore by way of ornament a heavy green glass paperweight or door stop – crocus blossoms of blown air within, amidst tiny stray bubbles – and also a china windmill egg-timer; in the test tube of the lower sail the sands of time were slumped to everlasting six o'clock.

However, Dennis's digital watch, lying on top of his casually piled clothes, recorded 0750. Stumbling out of bed and clutching a shirt to his nakedness, he hurried to the window and saw, first of all, the sea. With, half to one mile away, the crooked arm of a pier from bandstand to distant lighthouse sheltering a steamer, smoke pluming softly upward, slipping slowly forward.

But no such harbour, in spite of its name, existed at Harmouth. Nor had they gone to bed in such a room as this, beneath the image of the virgin Mary, mocking her passion by consummating theirs.

A moment more, and he glanced around the fronds of aspidistra. A few hundred yards away, past a detached dwelling house or so, a hump of bare cliffy land abutted on a slack green ocean: thalassic canvas painted darker by stray cloud shadows.

'Tess, come and see!'

'Do try to remember who I am.' Gathering up her skirt, Carla slipped tan-bodied, white-breasted, to his side.

They dressed quickly and crept quietly downstairs, avoiding a brush with the mistress of the house or any of her tribe, pausing only briefly by a calendar hanging in the hallway: some tea merchant's gift, the sheets torn off up to September, 1904.

Minutes later, they were both hurrying down the stony pathway towards the point with its stout granite Martello Tower. Upon the parapet a shaving bowl glinted, and a hand mirror semaphored the morning sunshine, from the hand of a fellow who was bantering with another young man – tall, attired in cloth cap, stiff white collar and waistcoat – who was squinting morosely out over the bay as the mailboat cleared the piers.

'You said June 16th,' panted Dennis. 'But that calendar – '

'He wasn't really here in June. He was here later on in the year, for just a few days.'

'It is him, isn't it?'

'By the looks of it.'

'Remember how the Count of Monte Cristo burrowed through the walls of his prison, only to break through into another cell? Is that all we've done?'

'At least it's a first step! A change of scene.'

'But how do I get back to my wife?'

'*I'm* your wife, Dennis darling. We got married yesterday. Till death . . .'

'But death can't part us.'

'Not when we're beastly dead already.'

They halted under the walls of the tower. Carla called up, 'Joyce! James Joyce! Is that you?'

And a face peered over, to inspect them casually. 'What do you want, then?'

'We're exiles,' shouted Carla. 'Dead exiles, in eternity. Like you.'

'Oh, *I'm* not exiled, evermore.' Joyce grimaced. 'Damn it!' And he gripped the jagged solidity of the masonry.

'Could we discuss something, Mr Joyce?'

'And what would that be?'

Carla patted her skirt, which fell barely to her knees. 'From the cut of our clothes, I think you can guess.'

'Why don't you come up? Eggs are frying. We can always crack another couple. There's a loaf and honey. Though the milkwoman's late. As always. And as always she arrives in time, with her Sandycove milk to save us. For ever and ever.'

He vanished from the parapet; soon a key scraped in the iron door below. This opened heavily, releasing a haze of coalsmoke and fried grease fumes. At the head of the ladder, legs apart, trousers baggy, stood Joyce; frowning, he beckoned them up.

'So: you're welcome to the *omphalos,* the navel of dead time.'

'Oh, there are other navels besides this one,' Carla assured him, mounting the rungs.

Joyce nodded, handing her up. 'As I see. One other, anyhow. It's something to know I'm not alone here, in some unbelievable condescending hell.'

'I'm sure there are thousands of other such days. Single-day slices. Dennis, show Mr Joyce your watch.'

'My watch? Why? Oh, yes . . .' Gaining the top, Dennis displayed his microchip timepiece to Joyce, who peered at it intently, with the scrutiny of a lapidary, and touched the tiny control buttons.

'It appears,' Joyce said wryly, 'to be time for breakfast.'
And led them inside into a large domed gloomy room,
where one young man in a tennis shirt loitered elegantly,
while the one who had been shaving wrestled with fry in
a pan, and glowered at the newcomers.

'O jay, what's this?' he protested. 'Am I running a
restaurant?' He transferred his attention to admiring
Carla's bare shanks.

'Don't mind Gogarty,' said Joyce. 'He never quite
forgave me – '

'For being Buck Mulligan in *Ulysses*!' exclaimed Carla
in delight, advancing.

Gogarty restored his scrutiny to the pan. 'I'll want a
few pints in me, before we can go into all that. Immor-
tality's one thing – but this gets a bit steep. Eating
the same bloody egg every morning: it's worse than
Communion. Or the Miracle of the Loaves. Oh, cyclical
theory of mystery! And speaking of loaves,' he addressed
the man in the tennis shirt, 'hack us a few more slices,
will you, Trench?'

Breakfast was soon devoured – with the milkwoman
arriving at their iron door with ewer and measure, and
words of praise to the glory of God and for the goodness
flowing from the udders, in the very nick to rescue them
from the rigours of Gogarty's wine-dark tea; after which
Gogarty and the English Erinophile, Trench, departed
with towels for the bathing place down at the cliff base –
Joyce, with inner struggle, steeling himself not to quit the
tower in their company, a refusal in which he was ably
assisted by Gogarty pausing on the threshold to deliver
an impromptu wicked limerick:

> 'There was a dead writer called Joyce
> Of all time and space he made choice;

A Martello Tower
Became his true bower,
So with his own petard was hoist.'

'Even so,' said Joyce, after the two men had gone on
their way, 'I shall have to be setting out soon.'

'On your Odyssey, yes. But with *us*,' said Carla.

'If you like to. And I don't suppose you have any
pounds, shillings and pence of this particular realm with
you, do you now?' In his great loose trouser Joyce jingled
change.

'You can break this pattern, you know. *We* did.' Carla
had already explained how, over egg, bread and tea.
'You can slip through into another slice of time.'

'And leave my Nora here all alone, while I run off with
another man and woman?'

'It's for the sake of the Bloomsday Revolution,' said
Carla hotly, 'as named in your honour.'

'An infamous honour, maybe, just like the fame of the
Wandering Jew? I don't mean Bloom, but Ahasuerus
. . .' Having pulled his chained watch from its fob, Joyce
consulted it. 'It seems to me that the pair of you only
arrived *here*, rather than anywhere else, because you
yourselves chose such a name.'

'That's true!' exclaimed Dennis. 'Carla, you chose the
name because you were brooding on Joyce. So here
we came. But *what* if you'd called this the Madeleine
Revolution instead? Wouldn't we then both be calling on
Marcel Proust and reliving one day of the *recherche du
temps perdu* – back in that slice of his youth to which the
taste of Madeleine cake had led him? Because Proust's
probably another "crystallizer" of a different slice of
time: some time in the 1880s or so.'

'And maybe Gogarty wasn't so far out with his little
jingle, after all . . .' Restlessly, Joyce paced.

Noting this sign of imminent departure – to be about his daily business – Carla pressed Joyce. 'What would be on *your* mind, then? *Who* would be?'

'Why, Nora. And Italy.'

'Do you remember how you wrote, in *The Dead*, "They escaped from their lives and duties, escaped from homes and friends, and ran away with wild and radiant hearts to a new adventure"? That was surely written about yourself and Nora Barnacle – who stuck to you like a limpet . . . But equally: what other people, in other times, are on your mind?'

Brooding, Joyce paused. 'Oh, Vico. Giordano Bruno . . .'

'Hang on a bit,' said Dennis. 'Wasn't Giordano Bruno burnt at the stake by the Inquisition?'

'By the scrupulous Holy Office, yes. In 1600, a fine round number.' And Joyce recited:

'Chi le catene ruppe e quelle porte,
onde rari son sciolti ed escon fore?

Who'll burst those gates and break the chains?
For rare's the man, who freedom gains.'

'Yes, but we don't speak Italian,' Dennis said.

'*I* do.' Carla held thumb and index finger a little apart. '*Così. Poco.*'

'But think of the Inquisition! Just imagine a slice of time with inquisitors rampant, still burning out heresy. That's a dangerous place to think of.'

'Dennis dear, these slices are perfect days, not nasty ones. Or at least they're innocuous. As Zsuzsanna said, maybe there's a compasison in all this.'

'So today is perfect, is that what it is?' Biliously Joyce eyed the door left ajar by departing, limerick-dispensing Gogarty. With its massive iron key protruding, it now

more resembled a dungeon door in some devout Domini-
can's stronghold. He shrugged. 'Well, if I can't go to
Pola, then maybe Nola?'

'Eh?' said Dennis.

'He was going,' Carla explained, 'to teach in the Berlitz
School in Pola on the Adriatic. And Nola is where
Giambattista Vico, his favourite philosopher, hailed
from.'

'But *how* do I go there? By abandoning Nora? Or by
running to a priest to kneel and profess faith, at last, and
confess my sins? That, I fear, would take all day . . .

'Still,' and he brightened, 'we do have all day to find
out, don't we? All day again and again. All moanday,
tearsday, wailsday in one. A paring from the fingernail of
time. And isn't history the nightmare from which we're
all dying to awake? Though to what else? So yes I say,
yes I will. Yes.'

And out of the domed stronghold, pushing the door,
he stepped into the brightness of the sun.

They all descended the ladder. Diminished, a seal's
head already was bobbing sleekly in green water:
Gogarty's, to which Joyce raised a hand in farewell,
unseen.

Soon Carla and Dennis Monsarrat and James Joyce
were walking swiftly up the path on the first course of
that day's ever returning Odyssey, to cover the half mile
to Sandycove Station; thus into Dublin itself, to search
out some portal of discovery: upon places beyond and
times before. Or at the very least to find a pint of porter
in a pub.